PRAISE F(

'Norse fans, or ju

characters, you need this epic book!' LOUIE STOWELL

'Seamlessly weaving Norse mythology into a contemporary tale, this fast-paced, fantasy adventure, with a cast of Black characters, is a compelling read.' BOOKTRUST

'A cracking quest with writing that crackles, fizzes and dances off the page . . . *The Unmorrow Curse* presents a world that's rich in Norse myth and magic, with a cast of larger-than-life characters whose sparkling dialogue adds to the pace and suspense.' *LOVEREADING4KIDS*

'Richards excels at weaving stories that mesh the real, modern world and classic mythologies. Readers will clamor for more, especially those who loved Rick Riordan's Norse-themed *The Sword of Summer*.' *BOOKLIST*

'An epic, action-packed adventure, sizzling with myth and magic.'
SOPHIE ANDERSON

'The combination of adventure, appealing characters, and high stakes should satisfy middle-grade fantasy fans.'
KIRKUS REVIEWS

HAVE YOU EVER WONDERED HOW BOOKS ARE MADE?

UCLan Publishing is an award-winning independent publisher specialising in Children's and Young Adult books. Based at The University of Central Lancashire, this Preston-based publisher teaches MA Publishing students how to become industry professionals using the content and resources from its business; students are included at every stage of the publishing process and credited for the work that they contribute.

The business doesn't just help publishing students though. UCLan Publishing has supported the employability and real-life work skills for the University's Illustration, Acting, Translation, Animation, Photography, Film & TV students and many more. This is the beauty of books and stories; they fuel many other creative industries! The MA Publishing students are able to get involved from day one with the business and they acquire a behind the scenes experience of what it is like to work for a such a reputable independent.

The MA course was awarded a Times Higher Award (2018) for Innovation in the Arts and the business, UCLan Publishing, was awarded Best Newcomer at the Independent Publishing Guild (2019) for the ethos of teaching publishing using a commercial publishing house. As the business continues to grow, so too does the student experience upon entering this dynamic Masters course.

Also available by Jasmine Richards

The Unmorrow Curse

Writing as Lola Morayo

Aziza's Secret Fairy Door

Aziza's Secret Fairy Door and the Ice Cat Mystery

Aziza's Secret Fairy Door and the Birthday Present Disaster

Aziza's Secret Fairy Door and the Mermaid's Treasure

Aziza's Secret Fairy Door and the Magic Puppy

Writing as Remi Blackwood

Future Hero: Escape to Fire Mountain

Future Hero: Mission to the Shadow Sea

Future Hero: Escape from the Clay City

JASMINE RICHARDS

Cover illustrations by Pypah Santos

With interior illustrations by Jill Tytherleigh

uclanpublishing

The Myth Keeper is a uclanpublishing book

First published in Great Britain in 2023 by
uclanpublishing
University of Central Lancashire
Preston, PR1 2HE, UK

978-1-915235-62-6

1 3 5 7 9 10 8 6 4 2

Set in 10/17pt Kingfisher by Becky Chilcott.

A CIP catalogue record for this book is available from the British Library.

Printed and bound in Great Britain by Clays Ltd, Elcograf S.p.A.

To my children, Zach and Tamsin. You are the authors of your own story. Every chapter will be different. There will be twists and turns. Ups and downs. Even rug-pulling moments. Always remember though that you are both the heroes of the piece. I am so excited about the adventures ahead of you.

PROLOGUE

The slender trees of the rainforest shook.

A breeze, at least, Natasha thought. But she quickly realised she was not going to be that lucky – there would be no wind to cut through the suffocating blanket of humidity, no gust of air to cool the sweat that trickled down her face and stung her eyes. She was grateful she had managed to cane-row her hair up into a bun so air could get to her neck. Nothing even resembling a breeze existed in this place. Even when the storm had taken place, all those months ago, the wind had found it hard to pierce the dense canopy of trees.

If not the wind, what?

Natasha paused, her fingers still on the plump papaya she was about to pluck from the tree. It was a dull thudding making the trees shake. Maybe one of her team was trying to cut down a tree.

Someone nearby began to whistle. It was a sharp and high-pitched noise in the rainforest. A jumble of discordant notes that matched no melody she knew.

Natasha mimicked the whistling for a moment in greeting. "Is that you, Arianna?" she called out. "I'm almost done."

There was no response except more whistling and the slow, steady thud. The sounds were getting closer, and the rest of rainforest seemed to go silent in anticipation.

Natasha shrugged. *Maybe she didn't hear me.* Her fellow botanist had a way of disappearing into her own thoughts, which wasn't surprising considering the situation in which they had all found themselves. Sometimes, it was easier to disappear into one's memories than to think about the fact that you might never get home.

Natasha plucked another papaya from the tree. There were two more on the stem, but she didn't want to strip the tree completely. She carefully placed the fruit into the satchel that was open by her feet. She smiled. It wasn't exactly a feast, but she knew the rest of her expedition party would be pleased. Papaya was always a treat.

"What gives you the right?" a low voice hissed from behind her.

Natasha whipped around. She faced a small man leaning on a walking stick. His skin was so wrinkled it almost looked like tree bark, and it had a strange greenish hue. His clothes hung in rags off his body, and his hair was white and matted, with vines and twigs knotted in the strands.

"The right? I'm sorry, I don't understand—" Natasha began.

"This forest is not yours to pillage." The man hobbled forwards, his walking stick thudding on the ground. He glared up at her. "You are a stranger. You don't belong here."

"You're right." Natasha held up her hands. "I don't belong here." From nowhere, she could feel the threat of tears, and she blinked hard. "We have been lost in this rainforest for more weeks than I can bear to count. My expedition party all want to get home, but we have no way of contacting the outside world."

The old man peered up at her with eyes as green as leaves from the *Pithecellobium dulce.*

"Home," he murmured. "Tell me about your home."

The old man's voice was wistful, hungry almost.

Natasha took a step backwards. She suddenly realised she should be scared. She had seen no one other than those in her expedition party for almost six months. None of the isolated groups that lived deep in the Amazon, no other sign of human life, but now this old man had just emerged from the trees and spoken perfect English.

"Who are you?" she whispered. "Where have you come from?"

"You first," the old man insisted. "Tell me about your life. The one away from here."

Natasha swallowed hard. Something about this man felt mythical. Mystical. She found herself telling him about home. It felt good, and once she started, she couldn't stop. Her longing to see her family again was like a tap she couldn't turn off, and the words poured from her. She told him about her home in the small town of Crowmarsh, so different to the London borough where she had grown up. She told him how everyone knew one another and not much happened. She spoke about her house on the edge of Tangley Woods. She explained that her husband was a professor of mythology at the university in the nearby city of dreaming spires, but didn't say how far away he had seemed before she left for the expedition. She explained that her daughter, Tia, was fierce and clever, and would toss her curls in the most flippant way when they had an argument but most importantly, she was loving.

"Then there's my son, Zach," Natasha said. "But we all call him Buzz." Her throat was burning now, her longing for her family almost overwhelming her. "He is as kind as he is stubborn. He's just like his dad, although he'd deny it. He is loyal and brave, and I miss him so much that sometimes I can't breathe. He's my best friend."

"Your home sounds like a very special place." The old man's voice was full of yearning. "It's important to have people to take care of."

Natasha nodded. "So, what about you?"

"I cannot remember my home," the old man said. "I have lived alone in this rainforest for a long time. The rainforest is my home. The rainforest is my family."

"But there must be someone missing you," Natasha persisted.

"Missing me?" the old man questioned. "Now, that would be quite something. To have someone who cared for me. To have a friend. A companion. To have a purpose." He leant heavily on his stick. "Tell me, Natasha, what would you do to go home?"

"Well, I'd–" She broke off. "Wait. How'd you know my name? I didn't tell you."

"I know lots of things," the old man said. "I know the way through this rainforest. I know the way to safety and the way to those who can help you get home."

"You do?" Natasha curled her hands into fists to stop them from shaking. "Tell me, please. We've been lost for so long. We'd almost given up hope." She looked over her shoulder to peer through the undergrowth. "My camp's not far from here. You can come and tell the others. They'll be so grateful for any help you can give us."

"No." The word exploded from the old man's mouth and ricocheted around the rainforest. "This deal is between the two of us. I do not wish to meet the others."

"Okay." Natasha held up her hands again. "But I cannot leave them behind. She lifted her chin. "I will not leave them behind."

"I am not asking you to." The old man tapped his walking stick on the ground with another *thud, thud, thud.* "Just know that the deal is between the two of us. If you want to leave the rainforest, you must understand that."

Natasha nodded. "Yes, I understand."

"So tell me, Natasha. What would you give to go home?"

"Anything," she whispered. "I would give anything."

The old man's eyes gleamed with delight. "That's the right

answer." He lifted up his gnarled walking stick so that it lay flat across his palms.

Natasha could see that it had a carving of a compass etched into the wood. She felt dizzy looking at the swirl of lines. It was like the points of the compass were moving, slowly turning until they were a blur.

"Tsk, tsk." The old man whipped the stick away and held it behind his back. "It is rude to stare, Natasha."

"Sorry," Natasha said.

He held out the walking stick once more. "Take this. It will guide you to a settlement many days from here. There, you will be able to contact those you love. You will be able to get home." He nodded his head. "Take it and the deal is done."

Natasha hesitated, but only for a second. Her hand closed around the walking stick. It was warm and rough in her hand. "Am I really supposed to believe this thing is going to work?" she asked. "How will it show me anything?"

The old man laughed. "This is not a test of belief, Natasha. I have never been the type that needs the faith of your kind to survive. Just know that I am El Tunchi, and this walking stick will get you home. It is yours, for now. Your eyes will show you what your heart already knows soon enough."

Natasha nodded. She did not really understand all that El Tunchi said, but she could tell that this strange man was not lying. And he was right. She did know that he could show her a way home.

"How will I ever be able to thank you?" she asked. Her voice caught on the last word as tears stung her eyes once more.

"No thank-you is necessary. We have a deal, Natasha," El Tunchi said. "And when the time comes, you will pay the debt. You'll give me that which is most precious."

The old man smiled, and for the first time, Natasha noticed how small and sharp his teeth looked.

"Debt?" Natasha's stomach twisted at the word. "What do you mean?"

"You'll find out," El Tunchi said. "Now go." He shooed her away with hands that were long and skeletal. "Your family are waiting for you in this place called Crowmarsh. Enjoy them, Natasha. We'll meet again."

El Tunchi turned and walked back into the depths of the forest. But whereas before the old man had shuffled, Natasha noticed that he now bounded through the undergrowth. Like a man who had never needed his walking stick. He walked as if he were full of joy.

"What have I done?" Natasha whispered into the rainforest. The sound of wildlife had now come back. The eerie silence was leaving with El Tunchi. The crickets chirruped their furious reply, and the stick hummed with a power that made Natasha's hand sting.

PART I

STRANGERS

CHAPTER ONE

SERIAL LOSER

Six months later . . .

"Sam, are you sure this is a good idea?" Buzz set his bike on the ground and sat down on the park bench. He scooted right over to the edge so he didn't squash the massive duffle bag that rested between him and his friend. "I mean, this whole thing sounds really dodgy."

"Mate, trust me, it's fine," Sam replied. "This is how things are done once you get to this stage of the game." He patted his bag. "I don't expect you to understand. This is a very different world for you."

I wish. Buzz had to work hard to swallow down a sigh. *But it's the same old world. That's the problem.* The thought wormed itself into Buzz's head, bringing with it a familiar sense of emptiness. The memories of his time in the underworld and the other magical realms he'd seen while searching for the mythical Runes of Valhalla refused to let him go. They seemed to be getting sharper rather than duller with every month that passed, and they mocked the ordinariness of his life every time he got ready for school or went to football practice or even thought about the Easter holidays, which loomed.

"The thing is, it's about having the right priorities. Making the right choices. Don't you think?" Sam's question reached Buzz as if it were travelling across a vast ocean.

"Um?" Buzz blinked at his friend, trying to work out how much he'd missed.

"You weren't listening, were you?" Sam shook his head. "It's like you're not here any more, Buzz. Or do I just bore you?"

"Samraj, don't be like that. I just didn't catch what you said. It's not a big deal."

"You're lying, Buzz. You're a stranger and have been for the last six months." There was a bitter tone to Sam's voice. "Something happened, and I can always tell when you're thinking about it." His slim fingers picked at the strap of the duffle bag. "If I'm really your best friend, tell me what happened to you."

Buzz opened his mouth. The words were there. They could explain how six months ago he'd bumped into an American girl called Mari who was on her way to her grandmother's house. They'd explain how he and Mari had witnessed the goddess of Sunday being kidnapped by Loki's dragon. How after that, the world had got stuck on a twenty-four-hour loop called the Unmorrow Curse and that people had become more cruel because of it. His words would describe the quest for the Runes of Valhalla and how Buzz, Mari, and a boy named Theo had travelled to the underworld to free the Norse gods and reunite them with the runes. How they'd saved the world.

Buzz could tell Sam all these things, but almost everyone had forgotten the Unmorrow Curse in a strange case of collective amnesia, so what damage might he do if he made Sam remember?

Oh, who am I kidding? Buzz thought. He didn't want to tell Sam what had happened because it hurt. All those terrifying, breathtaking, amazing experiences were behind him now. No gods, no mythical beasts, no adventure. Just a talking squirrel who he saw once in a while and a very normal, boring life. Talking about what had happened just made him feel worse.

Buzz crossed his arms. "Just drop it," he said. "Nothing happened, okay?"

Sam's lips were a thin line. "Fine. Have your secrets and I guess I'll have mine."

Something about Sam's tone made Buzz pause. His friend was angry with him – he could hear that – but there was something else in his voice as well. *Sam almost sounds scared.*

Buzz grabbed his friend's shoulder. "Hey, Sam, listen, you know you can tell me anything."

Sam shrugged him off. "You mean like the way you tell me?

It's okay – it's probably nothing." His voice had almost become a whisper. "It'll go away if I ignore it and—"

"Are you Samraj Matharu?" A young man of about eighteen was looking down at them as they sat on the park bench.

Buzz frowned. The guy was wearing shades. Big ones. It was warm for the end of March, but the oversized sunglasses were definitely unnecessary.

"That's me," Sam said. "And you're Jack Pretorial?"

The older boy nodded. "You got the goods?"

Sam stood up and unzipped his bag with a flourish. He then brought out a slightly faded cereal box, followed by a small action figure in a see-through plastic case. "One limited edition Dortmeld the Barbarian from the 1984 Cheerios' campaign, with original cereal box. I think your client is going to be very happy." Sam's cheeks were flushed with pride.

The older boy's shoulders shook for a moment as he looked at the small figure with its bejewelled sword. "Amazing," he finally managed to say.

A prickle of unease crawled up Buzz's neck. Jack Pretorial was either overcome with emotion by what he'd seen, or he was laughing at Sam. Buzz wasn't sure. *Not yet.*

"And did you take a photo of the rest of your cereal-box toy collection and email it to me as requested?" Jack's shoulders began to shake again, and he covered his mouth. "It's important to my client that I can prove the providence of the collectible and show it has been well looked after by an expert."

Sam frowned. "Don't you mean 'provenance' rather than providence?"

The older boy waved a hand. "Whatever. If my client is going to accept the merchandise, he needs to know where it's come from and that it's been looked after."

"You'll have no worries on that front." Sam carefully placed the cereal box back in the bag. He then held up Dortmeld so Jack could take a closer look. "I've taken photos of my whole collection but also made a video of my upkeep regimen for the toys and what protective casings I prefer to use. I thought it might be of interest to the third party you'll be giving Dortmeld to." Sam gazed down at the little action figure, his finger running along the case. "I'll be sad to see him go, but it'll be worth it."

"Of course, I understand. It must be so difficult to say goodbye to Dorkmeld." The older boy smirked.

Dorkmeld. Buzz felt his unease bloom even further. *This whole thing stinks.* And it wasn't just the smirking expression that was putting him on edge. Jack also looked really familiar.

"Dortmeld," Sam corrected in an aggrieved voice.

The older boy laughed until he almost couldn't catch his breath. "Yeah, right, my mistake."

Now, Buzz didn't exactly get Sam's hobby of collecting fantasy action figures, but Sam's dad was a big collector also, and Buzz wasn't going to have others laughing at his friend. "Something funny, Jack?"

"Don't start, Buzz," Sam begged. "Just ignore him, Jack."

"Don't start?" Buzz leapt to his feet. "This guy's laughing at you. Can't you see that?"

"Stop it," Sam demanded. "You do realise it doesn't always have to be about you? And you can't pick and choose when you're going to take an interest in me."

Buzz knew he was gaping like a goldfish and so he forced some words out instead. "What's that supposed to mean?"

"I mean you like the drama, you like it when you get to swoop in and save the day, but unless you get to be the hero you're not interested in me." Sam's hand clenched on the plastic casing around the action figure with a crunch. "I don't need your help. I don't even know why I invited you."

"And I don't even know why I came." Buzz eyed his bike. *I'll just go. Leave Sam to it.* But his feet didn't move.

Sam was looking at Jack. "Let's see it then. And we can make the swap."

"Ah yes, Brightblader from the 1964 box of Chocoflakes." Jack pointed at the bag by his feet. "Please help yourself."

Sam knelt down. His hands trembled.

Buzz held his breath as Sam unzipped the bag. He didn't know what his friend was going to find in there, but he was pretty sure it wasn't going to be Brightblader.

Sam's brow crinkled. "There's nothing in here except an iPad."

"Pick it up and press the big white button on the screen," the older boy said. "It's all set up." He pushed his sunglasses to the top of his head and stared down eagerly at the tablet.

Buzz realised now why his face looked so familiar. It was Liam Simms' older brother, Dylan.

"Hey, I know you," Sam said at the same time. "Dylan, right? I didn't know you were into collectibles." Sam's frown became even deeper. "Wait, why did you lie about your name?"

"Into collectibles?" Dylan snorted. "Do I look like a serial loser? Just press call."

Sam's hands were still trembling, but Buzz knew it wasn't from excitement any more. His friend touched the screen.

Liam Simms' grinning face suddenly appeared.

"All right there, Sam," he said. "Happy birthday!"

"It's not my birthday," Sam said.

"It isn't?" Liam's face fell. "When's your birthday, then?"

"April first," Sam replied.

"What? Actually on April Fool's Day?" Liam began to laugh. "Oh man, that would have been too perfect. How did I not know that?"

"What do you want, Liam?" Buzz demanded, peering over Sam's shoulder.

"Hey, Buzz, you're there as well. Ace. Thought you'd be sulking in a corner somewhere."

"I don't sulk," Buzz said.

"Whatever," Liam replied. "Tell Theo to call me if you see him, please."

"What do you want?" Buzz asked again.

"Well, I want to give Sam his birthday present." Liam wrinkled his nose. "Okay, early birthday present." He tapped his chin thoughtfully. "And not exactly present. More like prank." He leaned in so his whole head filled the screen. "That's right, Sam. There's no Brightblader, and there's definitely no client who wants to swap him for your dorky Dortmeld." Liam grinned again. "But thanks for that video about how to look after action figures. It's really fascinating. I wonder if anyone else at school will find it as interesting as I do. Laters, loser!" Liam ended the call and Sam dropped the tablet as if it were red hot.

"Hey! Careful." Dylan scooped up the tablet and gently placed it in his bag. "I just got that." He gave a sniggering laugh. "Ah, come on, guys, don't look so glum. You've got to give it to my little brother—it's a good prank. I taught him well. He even gave me an anagram for my alias. Thought that was a nice touch."

Buzz swiftly tried to sort the letters of Jack Pretorial in his head, but Sam was quicker.

"Practical Joker," Sam whispered. He shook his head. "I don't understand. How did Liam know I collected vintage action figures?"

Dylan zipped his bag and slung it over his shoulder. "I think that boy Theo told him. Doesn't matter, does it?"

Sam whirled around to face Buzz. "Yeah, it matters. Because

there's only one person in the whole wide world who knew about my collection."

The sinking feeling that had been growing in Buzz's stomach was taking on *Titanic*-like proportions.

"I, er, um—"

"I can't believe you told him."

"It was only because I was trying to think of a birthday present for you. I thought Theo might have an idea."

"Wow, Buzz, you really have changed if you think Theo is capable of having a good idea. He's a moron."

"That's not true," Buzz said. "It was once, but not any more." He knew defending Theo was not going to help things with Sam, but Theo had changed over the last six months. And the fact was, they had faced down a rampaging, power-hungry god together. Buzz couldn't help that Theo was his friend now.

"You're a fool, you know that? The only reason Theo is even hanging out with you is because he's got a crush on Tia."

No way, Buzz thought. His sister was two years older than Theo, and whenever their paths crossed she treated him like something she had accidentally stepped in.

"Listen, I'm sure it was an accident that he told Liam. He really was interested in helping me find a present for your birthday."

"Buzz, there's only one gift I want from you, and that's for you to leave me alone. Permanently."

"Sam, please—"

"Okay, guys, as entertaining as this little domestic is, I've got to be going," Dylan interjected. "But it's been a blast. Thanks."

He ambled away, up the paved path, his bag swinging from his shoulder.

Sam stared after him. A bead of sweat crested on his brow. His whole body began to tremble.

Buzz sniffed. He could smell something acrid and sharp, and his throat felt scratchy. He looked down to see that Dortmeld's plastic case was melting in Sam's grip. Dortmeld did not look happy about it.

There was a yelp followed by a curse, and looking up, Buzz saw Dylan throw his bag to the ground and begin to stamp on it.

It was on fire.

CHAPTER TWO

WATCH YOUR BACK

Buzz had seen enough strange things on his quest to find the Runes of Valhalla to know when magic was being used. And he was fairly sure that this magic was coming from Sam. He grabbed his friend by his shoulders and shook him.

"Stop it, Sam," he hissed as he dragged his friend to one side of the path. "Whatever you're doing, stop it." Sam's skin was furnace-hot beneath Buzz's palms. Buzz could feel the fierce heat even through the thickness of Sam's jacket. "You're going to hurt Dylan or yourself."

Sam blinked for a moment, then dropped Dortmeld to the ground. The charred case bounced across the grass, then rolled to a stop in a smoking heap of twisted plastic.

Buzz looked over at Dylan. The older boy didn't look hurt, and the flames in his bag were swiftly dying down. A small audience of park visitors had gathered around him, and a few of them were helpfully emptying their water bottles over Dylan and his bag. Sopping wet and shivering in the spring sunshine, Dylan tipped what was left of his bag upside down, and a very melted iPad flopped onto the grass.

Sam was still blinking hard, as if he had just emerged from a dark room. "W-w-what happened?" he stuttered.

"You tell me." Buzz kept his voice low. "I'm pretty sure you torched Dylan's bag and you nuked Dortmeld."

Sam shook his head. "I just wanted to wipe that smile off Dylan's face. He said that he'd had a blast and it really made me want to blast him."

"Okay, well, you did that," Buzz said, "and a bit more besides. But how?"

"I don't know." Sam was hugging his arms. "I don't know why this is happening to me."

Buzz felt a tingle of excitement go up his spine as he stared at his friend. At last, something *extraordinary* was happening. It felt like he was waking from deep hibernation.

"Mate, quit looking at me like that," Sam said. "I'm not some kind of raffle prize." He scooped up the melted Dortmeld with a little mew of distress and shoved it in his bag. "I've gotta get out of here."

"Wait, I'll come with you. We can talk about what happened. Try to work out what's going on."

Sam whirled around to face him. "You should be freaked out." His eyes were large and panicked. "A normal person would be freaked out. Why aren't you freaked out?"

Buzz shrugged a shoulder. "Maybe it's not the first time I've seen magical stuff like that. So you don't have to panic."

"I knew it." Sam's hands clenched into fists. "I knew something strange had happened to you, and you told me there was nothing going on."

"Come on, you didn't tell me you could make fire appear out of thin air," Buzz pointed out. "We both had secrets. We're even."

"This thing." Sam's whole body shook. "Whatever it is. Only started a few days ago, and it's never been like this. So no, we're not even. You've been lying to me for months." He took a step backwards. "I'm going home."

"Fine, let's go."

Sam shook his head. "I meant what I said before. Leave me alone. I'm done with you."

"Sam, come on. I'm sorry. I'll tell you everything that happened," Buzz said. "Just let me help you."

"I don't need your help. Just stay away, Buzz. It will be safer for you."

Sam turned and ran from the park, his duffle bag slapping against his side.

"Sam!" Buzz cried. *"Wait."* But Sam was already a small, retreating figure on the other side of the common.

Buzz sank back on the bench, wondering what he should do. *Sam will calm down,* he thought. *And when he does, we'll talk.*

Buzz's mobile bleeped. Taking it from his pocket, he saw a text message from Mari.

Just landed. Can't wait to see you. Need a proper catch up.

Buzz felt a stab of guilt. He hadn't exactly been avoiding Mari's calls and messages but he hadn't exactly been available either. Talking about the runes or their adventures was just too depressing. Now she was actually coming to Crowmarsh, and there was nowhere to hide.

Yeah, see you later, Buzz texted back.

But first I need to get Sam some help. And he knew just the person. *Dad.* Buzz jumped to his feet and grabbed his bike. His father was a world-famous professor of mythology after all, and he'd been the human host for Odin, father of the Norse gods, while Buzz had been searching for the Runes of Valhalla. Dad had experience with magical powers, he understood what it was like to have them and he'd know what was going on with Sam.

Buzz quickly left the park and pedalled hard down the high street. The shops, cafés, and banks of the town became a blur as Buzz made his way home.

He'd almost reached the end of the road when a huge black jeep shot out from an intersection and swerved in front of him. Just before he squeezed the brakes, Buzz caught a glimpse of the driver: white-blond hair pulled back into a ponytail and a high-necked collar pinned with some kind of ivory, fang-shaped brooch that shone brightly. His bike skidded out from beneath him and the paved road rushed up in greeting, followed by a shooting pain in his hip.

Buzz groaned softly and turned to see the bike lying beside him, wheels still turning but now with a pitifully weary creak. He forced himself to his feet. He hurt, but lying in the middle of a road was not going to improve the situation, especially if a car ran him over. Hobbling forwards, he wheeled his bike onto the pavement.

"Young man, are you okay?" a deep-sounding voice asked.

Buzz nodded, doing his best to keep the surprise from his face as he noticed that the man speaking to him was wearing a thick, velvety blue cloak with a voluminous hood. Beneath that, a furry hat with earflaps peeped out. The man's face was almost completely obscured by the shadow of the hood and it was hard to tell exactly how old he was.

"You're admiring my hat, I can tell." The man jiggled on the spot to keep warm, and it made his earflaps dance. "I'm afraid I can't lend it to you. It's far too cold in this world."

"I'm fine, thank you," Buzz said. "I'm not cold. I'm just annoyed. She didn't even say sorry."

Both the man and Buzz watched the black jeep continue to tear down the street and then screech to a halt in front of the old post office.

"She has no respect," the man said. "Coming here, taking what she wants, no doubt gathering up the payments as she goes." Buzz's companion tutted. "Some things never change."

He turned to Buzz, hazel eyes peering out from beneath the hood. "Stay away from that woman and her companions – they're dangerous. And watch your back for the whistling stranger."

"I don't understand–" Buzz began.

"And I'm afraid I can't stay and explain. It's too risky. Just watch yourself and those close to you, understood?" The man pulled his heavy cloak more tightly around him and strode away. Buzz blinked and then lost sight of him entirely.

Weird, Buzz thought. *Super weird.*

He wheeled his bike along the pavement. The axle was all bent out of shape, and his hip ached. He stopped in front of the old post office, and his anger throbbed even more than his injured side as he watched the woman who'd caused his accident striding into the building. She didn't even look in his direction. *She should apologise,* Buzz thought. *She can't go around driving like that. No wonder that man said that she was dangerous.*

Now that Buzz was closer, he could see that there were even more jeeps, most of them parked up the side of the large brick building. Each one had the word PANTHEON emblazoned on the side in large gold letters, and underneath that was a symbol of a disc under an arch of fire. The old wooden doors of the post office were wide open, and the shutters were up. The building had been closed for as long as Buzz had been alive – it was a vast, sprawling space, and no one knew what to do with it, so they'd shut it up and left it to rot.

People wearing white tunics and slacks were busy unloading

the jeeps, which gleamed like a line of scarab beetles in the afternoon sunlight. They carried several ornately carved chests into the building.

These people aren't from Crowmarsh, Buzz thought. *Who are they?*

He wheeled his bike a bit closer so he could peep in through one of the dusty windows. He wiped the glass with the edge of his sleeve and, looking in, saw that rows of tables had been set up, and yet more people dressed in white were busy carving letters into green stone discs. A huge map of Crowmarsh had been mounted on the wall, with a sea of red pins embedded in the paper.

Somewhere to his left, he heard the *click-clack* of heels on the pavement. "Can I help you?" a silky female voice asked.

Buzz looked up. It was the woman who'd knocked him off his bike.

"I— I—" Buzz found that he couldn't get his words out. He wanted to say something about his bruised hip or tell her how his bike was all twisted up because of her wild driving. Even more, he wanted to ask what was going on in the post office, but something about the intensity of her gaze robbed him of the ability to say anything at all.

The lady smirked. "No, I thought not. Run along now, boy, it's not nice to snoop, and you'll be late for dinner, I'm sure." She turned and left him, her long ponytail swinging.

Buzz wheeled his bike away obediently. It was only when

he was almost at his house that he stopped. "What just happened?" he asked out loud. The trees that surrounded his home swallowed up his words but gave no answers. *How did she make me do that? Just walk away.* A shiver went through him as he remembered the warning he'd been given by the strange man on the street. Maybe when he'd called her and her people dangerous, he hadn't been referring to her driving at all.

CHAPTER THREE

GONE

From further up the garden path that led to his house, Buzz heard his front door slam and the sound of whistling. He spotted a man doubled over with age. His clothes were worn and dirty and his hair was wild and white. The man's whistling stopped, and he looked at Buzz with green eyes that were eager and excited.

There was a frantic scrabbling at the latch and then the front door was yanked open to reveal Buzz's mum standing in the doorway. Buzz was struck for a moment by how tired and thin she looked. When had that happened? Why hadn't he noticed before? His mum was glaring at the old man, but beneath the anger Buzz could see that his mum was scared.

"We had a deal," she said. "Get out of here."

The old man inclined his head, began whistling again, and then stepped off the path and into the trees. In a second he had completely disappeared from sight.

"Mum, what's going on?" Buzz demanded.

Natasha Buzzard rubbed roughly at her face with both hands. "Nothing. Well, not nothing. A big thing, actually, but we're going to sort it. We will. We have to."

"Sort what?" Buzz pressed.

"Please just get in the house." She peered into the woods, her dark eyes wide with fear, and Buzz could see her pulse jumping at the base of her throat.

"Mum, tell me!"

"Okay, okay. Just get in here." Her voice was choked with tears.

Buzz tried to prop his bike against the front garden wall but it kept falling over because the wheels were so twisted.

"What on earth happened to your bike?" his mum asked, and for a moment she sounded like her normal self. "Oh, it doesn't matter. Just bring it inside."

Buzz had already been worried, but now he was properly freaked out. His mum never allowed bikes in the house. She always said that the only mud she wanted to deal with was the soil she sifted through when searching for a rare plant. He picked up the bike and brought it into the house. His mum slammed the door behind him.

He noticed right away that the house smelt earthy, and the floor was covered in a thick layer of leaves and vines.

"Okay, Mum, you need to start talking. I know you sometimes bring work home with you, but this is ridiculous. And who was that whistling guy?"

Whistling. Wait. He'd been warned about that, too.

His mum sank down onto the stairs in the hallway. "Buzz, do you believe in magic?"

Buzz felt a bolt of surprise go through him. "You know about Sam? How?"

"Sam?" Buzz's mum repeated. She looked confused. "This has nothing to do with Sam. It's to do with me and a stupid promise I made so that I could get home to you all."

Buzz sat down next to his mother, noticing that the vines on the ground were actually alive. And not just alive – they were slowly creeping up towards the stairs. No normal plant he knew of grew that quickly.

"That man you saw outside is called El Tunchi," his mother explained. "He is a spirit of the rainforest." She gave a hollow laugh. "That sounds crazy, doesn't it? But it's true. When I was lost, he offered me a way home." She reached for a long wooden stick that was propped against the balustrade of the staircase. Buzz had never seen it before, but he couldn't pull his gaze away from the intricate carvings on it.

"He gave me this, and it guided me towards help – but at a price – and now he has come to collect payment."

"What kind of payment?" Buzz asked.

His mum dropped the stick, then took his hand and squeezed it. "That's not important, love, because neither your father nor I are going to let it be collected. Dad's got a plan, and I've managed to buy us some more time."

"Got a plan?" Buzz repeated. Part of him couldn't believe they were talking so calmly about a rainforest spirit with loan-shark tendencies.

His mother's grip tightened on his hand. "Listen, for the last two weeks, El Tunchi has been coming to me in my dreams. Telling me he was coming for his payment. I told your father. I thought he'd laugh at me – tell me that there was no such thing as magic or rainforest spirits – but he didn't. Instead, he went to a sorcerer, who has come up with a solution."

"What's the solution?" Buzz asked. *And who is this sorcerer?*

"He wouldn't say. Said it was safer that way." His mum released his hand and rubbed at her face again. "But he did promise that when this was all over, he'd tell me all he knew about magic, about the worlds that exist beyond this one. He told me he was sorry he'd kept any of it a secret from me."

Buzz felt a stab of guilt. He and his father had decided to keep their involvement in the quest for the Runes of Valhalla a secret. They'd been wrong to do that.

"Dad's gone?" Even as he said the words, Buzz felt panic surge up inside him. There was so much he needed to discuss with his father. Sam's strange abilities, the black jeeps that had descended on Crowmarsh, and now this El Tunchi guy. And what exactly was the rainforest spirit demanding in payment?

His mother nodded. "He said phones won't work where he's going, but he left you a letter in your room." She jumped to her feet and began to pace. "I really thought we'd have more time before El Tunchi came to collect, but then I heard that whistle." She twisted the gold band of her wedding ring. "I got us more time, though. That's what your father said I must do. And I did."

"How?" Buzz asked.

His mum scooped up the stick again. "El Tunchi told me to use this staff to find the most precious thing in our house. He said if it was precious enough, he would take it and give me more time before collecting his prize, but if not, he'd take his payment straightaway. What else could I do?"

Buzz felt a prickle of unease. "You used the stick?"

His mother nodded, and her fingers absently traced the carving of the compass that was there. "The staff took me upstairs, to your room and a box with some stones in it." She shrugged helplessly. "I was desperate, Buzz. We needed more time and you'd never mentioned the stones before and so I gave them to him. He seemed pleased and—"

"No, Mum, tell me you didn't." Buzz scrambled to his feet and raced up the stairs to his room before she could answer. He threw open the door to his room and saw right away that the box where the Runes of Valhalla had been kept these last six months was empty. The runes that could awaken the sleeping Norse gods and their powers were gone.

Next to the desk was an envelope with his name on it, written in his father's characteristic messy scrawl. Buzz tore it open.

Dear Buzz,

I'm sorry I didn't get a chance to tell you in person what was happening, but time was against me and you have seemed so sad of late, I did not want to burden you more. A great evil plagues your mother and our family, and I must stop it. She will tell you more, but you must know that I am going to find a suitable payment for our tormentor. If I fail, or if time runs out, you must awaken the Norse gods and ask for their help. It is not something to be done lightly. Our world almost ended last time they were awoken. But you must if my plan does not work. Look after your mother and sister and I will return with good news and a solution. This I vow.

All my love to you, my son,
Dad

Buzz's hand tightened on the paper, and it crumpled in his grasp.

"Buzz, are you okay?" his mother asked from behind him. "Did I do something wrong?"

Buzz turned to face her. His mother was gnawing her bottom lip, and she couldn't seem to keep her hands still. It was like she didn't know what to do with them.

How could he tell her that she'd given away the Runes of

Valhalla – the only objects that could awaken Odin and the rest of the sleeping gods? *How can I tell her that she's given away our best chance at stopping El Tunchi at all?*

He couldn't. It was another secret, but one he was determined to keep. "No, Mum, it's okay. You bought Dad more time, and that's the important thing."

They heard the front door slam downstairs.

"Mum," Tia hollered after about a nanosecond. "What is all this funky plant stuff on the floor? I'm supposed to have Marissa over later. How am I supposed to have friends visit when you've got attack of the Triffids going on in our hallway?"

"I better go downstairs." Buzz's mum gnawed on her lip even more furiously. "I'll need to explain this to Tia as well."

Buzz winced. Tia wasn't going to take any of this well. Rational was her middle name. She even got irritated when people asked her what her star sign was.

Buzz's mum must have seen some of what he was thinking on his face, because she gave him a wan smile. "Don't worry, I'm not going to lay it all on her, just enough for her to understand a little of what is going on so that she can stay safe." She came forwards and kissed his forehead and took his face in her hands. "I'm really sorry I gave away your possessions without asking you. I only did it because I was desperate. You do understand that, don't you?"

Buzz nodded and did his best not to think about the fact that with the runes gone, they had no plan B. *And how am I going to get them back? I'm supposed to be guardian of the runes.*

His ringtone, the theme music to his favourite TV show, filled the room, and a furrow appeared between his mother's eyebrows as he reached for his phone. "I don't want you going out," she said. "We don't know where El Tunchi may be lurking or what his next move is. We should all stay together safe in the house."

Buzz didn't say anything. He didn't want to lie to his mum, but he didn't think he could promise to stay in the house, either – not while the runes were gone. He looked down at the phone and saw Mari's name flashing up on the screen. *She must have just got here.* The tight fist that felt like it was gripping his heart eased a little bit. Mari would have a solution. She could be bossy for sure, but she'd know what to do about Sam and El Tunchi.

"Mum, it's Mari. I've gotta get this. She's back in Crowmarsh."

His mother was still frowning at him, but she left the room as Tia began hollering for her once again. Buzz hit answer on his mobile.

"Mari, boy am I glad you're he—"

"Oh, Buzz, I need your help." Mari was all choked up. "It's my grandmother."

"What's wrong?"

"She was supposed to meet me at the airport but she wasn't there. I got the bus to Crowmarsh instead and now I'm here and . . . and . . ." He heard her swallow. "You need to come and see this."

CHAPTER FOUR

PANTHEON

Buzz's bike made a protesting squeak as he tried to direct it in a straight line towards the picket fence in front of Mari's grandmother's house. The streetlamps illuminated the small front lawn, which was as neat and tidy as ever.

Buzz leant his bike against the fence and quickly checked his phone. No missed calls from his mum. She couldn't have noticed that he was gone yet. The conversation with Tia wasn't going so well, he guessed.

He knocked on the muted grey front door and waited.

Mari pulled it open, grabbed his arm, and yanked him inside.

"What took you so long?" she demanded. Her hazel eyes looked huge behind her glasses, which were no longer wing-tipped, but large and square and an emerald-green colour. On anyone else they would have looked ridiculous (because they kinda were), but somehow Mari managed to pull them off.

"Nice to see you as well," he said, allowing himself to be dragged along the hallway. "Thing is, I had to sneak past my mum and then I had to ride my busted-up bike over here." Buzz tugged on Mari's arm to slow her down. "It's been kind of full-on today and—"

"It's about to get a bit more full-on." Mari's hand was on the door handle to the living room. "Ready for this?"

"Ready for what?"

"This." Mari opened the door.

The normally pristine room was strewn with papers and books. The white walls were covered with arch-shaped symbols with a disc inside each one. The arches looked like they had been drawn on with ash.

Mari's grandmother stood at the far end of the room, fingers sooty with the cinders from the wood burner. She was furiously drawing yet more arches on the wall and her normally neatly pinned hair had escaped and curled around her head joyfully. She was urgently muttering something under her breath.

"What th—" Buzz began.

"I found her like this," Mari explained. "She won't talk to me. Just keeps drawing these symbols and then going back to these books." Mari bent down and scooped up one of the leather-bound volumes. "*Realms, Dimensions, and Parallel Worlds*," she said, showing him the cover. "Not normal reading for my grandmother."

"Have you told your parents?" Buzz asked.

Mari shook her head. "I know Grandmother can be a pain, but she wouldn't want them to know about this."

Buzz grimaced. "Mari, don't take this the wrong way, but your grandmother is getting old. Maybe she's getting confused as well."

"No, something else is going on here." Mari's face had set along stubborn lines. "Something really odd."

"Come on, you can't know that for sure, and—" Buzz broke off.

Mari's grandmother was still muttering under her breath as she scrawled on the wall, but Buzz finally caught what she was saying: *Pantheon.*

"Pantheon," Buzz repeated. He knew exactly where he'd come across that word before. He felt the hairs on his arms stand up on end.

"Yes. It's a word she keeps coming back to," Mari explained. "It has several meanings, I'm sure you know. It can mean a set of gods belonging to a particular religion, mythology, or tradition. Or she could be referring to a temple to the gods in Ancient Rome." Mari wrinkled her nose. "She might even be talking about the mythical red deer that appears on Tudor flags."

"No, that's not it," Buzz said.

Mari crossed her arms. "Actually, I think you'll find I am completely correct with my definitions."

Buzz ignored her and walked over to Mari's grandmother. "Um . . ." He stopped, realising he didn't even know her name. Mari's grandmother hadn't ever been that friendly, and she barely acknowledged him when they saw each other in town.

"It's Esther," Mari said, as if reading his mind. Buzz had forgotten how good she was at doing things like that.

"Esther." Buzz took one of her ash-covered hands. It felt very frail in his grip. "Pantheon, who are they? I think I saw them, too."

"You saw them?" Esther's unfocused hazel eyes had suddenly cleared, become piercing in their intensity "Where?"

"At the post office. They were moving in."

"What's going on, Grandmother?" Mari asked, coming to stand on her other side. "Who are Pantheon?"

Esther was wiping at her hands. Her face twisted in distaste as she examined how mucky they were. She looked around her and began to tut.

"Amaryllis, how could you let a stranger come into my house when it looks like this?"

Mari sighed. "It's no time to be house proud, Grandmother, and Buzz is not a stranger. When I got here, you were a wreck. Buzz was the only person I trusted enough to help. And I was right. He brought you back to yourself. Now, what is Pantheon?"

Esther tucked several coiled strands behind her ears and adjusted her half-moon glasses. Buzz could see that her hands were shaking. "You should sit down. I'll do my best to explain." She sank into the high-backed armchair by the fire and clasped her hands in her lap. "You must understand that I haven't spoken about this for many years, and the only reason

I'm telling you is so that you stay safe – the Pantheon are dangerous." She plucked at the collar of her frilly blouse. "You must not think me crazy but know what I am about to tell you really happened."

Buzz thought about what he'd seen Sam do earlier today and then the strange El Tunchi who had been whistling on the garden path. He would have said that things couldn't get much stranger. He'd be wrong.

"I moved to Crowmarsh when I was just six years old," Esther began. "My father came here to work as a scientist at one of the labs at the university – it was quite an honour. I was very homesick for our homeland in the Caribbean. Everything here felt grey and cold, but I had my older brother and he could always make me smile."

"Brother?" Mari squeaked. "I never knew you had a brother."

Esther peered at Mari over her glasses. "Amaryllis, please don't interrupt, this is hard enough already."

"Sorry, Grandmother," Mari murmured.

"Crowmarsh was a very different place then. Not much to do except play in the woods or climb the ruins near Larkscross." She swallowed. "The season was changing and so was my brother. I saw him do things that shouldn't be possible. He could move things with his mind. Create fire out of thin air." Esther hugged herself. "I didn't trust the powers. I didn't like how they were changing Benjamin." She dabbed at her eyes. "Then one day my brother said that he had met some very kind people from a travelling circus that was passing through Crowmarsh. They'd set up camp near the ruins." She pointed to one of her scrawled symbols on the wall. "They had flags everywhere with this insignia on it, and they promised to teach him how to harness his abilities properly if he could demonstrate his power." Tears escaped the half-moon glasses and Mari's grandmother began to rock backwards and forwards in her chair. "The next night he went to them, but it was a trap. A terrible trap. The circus was a cover for Pantheon."

"But who are they?" Buzz knew he wasn't supposed to interrupt, and Mari was glaring at him, but he couldn't help himself. The story of Benjamin sounded very similar to the story of Sam.

Esther took a shuddering breath. "Mainly gods, forgotten ones, and a few hard-core believers. It's Pantheon's job to seek out new gods and decide on their fate."

"New gods?"

"Yes. Individuals, normally children, who are manifesting strange powers."

"So this circus, which was actually the Pantheon, only comes to Crowmarsh to lure a new god out?" Mari questioned.

Her grandmother nodded. "I believe the new god always manifests in Crowmarsh, and then there is some kind of battle to see who will claim them."

"Okay, so what happened to Benjamin when he got to the ruins?" Buzz asked.

"I didn't see it all." Esther looked haunted by the memory of what she'd seen that night. "I'd followed Benjamin without his knowledge and only caught glimpses of what transpired." She chewed at her lip. "There was a terrible battle for him." She shuddered. "Such carnage. Such hunger. And then he went through an arch, crossed into the light with the victor, and I never saw him again."

"What did you tell your mother and father?" Mari asked.

"I told them the truth. But when we went back to the ruins nothing was there." Her fingertips dug into the armrests of her chair. "They thought me crazy. Sent me away to an institution to rest. I even began to believe that I had imagined the whole thing and that the story about what had happened to Benjamin was some kind of fiction I told myself because the truth was even worse." She sighed. "I buried it all deep down, but when I grew up, I moved back to Crowmarsh. I half hoped I might see my brother again, or some sign of the Pantheon. But there was nothing. Not until today. Until I saw her. The high priestess. She had not aged a day."

"Blond hair, tall, really intense eyes?" Buzz asked.

"Yes, yes, that's her."

"How'd you know that, Buzz?" Mari asked.

"I'll explain, I promise. But we don't have time right now. We need to talk to Sam."

"Sam?" Mari was looking even more bemused. "What's he got to do with any of this?"

"I think he might be the next manifesting god, and that means the Pantheon are going to be after him." Buzz took out his phone and dialled Sam's number. He cursed as it went straight to voice mail.

"I'm going to have to go to his house and warn him."

"No, you mustn't," Esther said. "What if the Pantheon are there? I told you, they're dangerous."

Buzz was reminded of the strange man he'd spoken to after his bike crash avoiding the jeep. He'd said exactly the same thing. "Sam is my friend. I have to go."

"Don't worry, Grandmother," Mari reassured her. "We'll be careful, but we do need to find him. It's the right thing to do."

Esther smiled sadly. "You remind me of him, you know, Amaryllis. Benjamin was always so very brave and always believed in doing the right thing. He'd have liked you."

Mari bent and kissed her grandmother's cheek. "I think I'd have liked him, too, and I know if he was here he'd want us to help Sam."

Esther nodded. "You're right. Go. Go save Sam."

CHAPTER FIVE

RUINS

Buzz heard Mari release a pent-up breath as they pulled shut the door to Esther's house. He could feel the relief coming off her in waves. It felt good to be leaving behind the pain and secrets that Mari's grandmother had been holding in all those years.

"What is it with this place, Buzz?" Mari sounded tired. "You told me once that Crowmarsh was boring. You lied."

"It wasn't a lie. I just didn't know any better." Buzz gripped the handlebars of his bike. Back then, when they'd first met, Mari had just been the odd girl with purple sneakers and spider-web leggings. Now Buzz knew that Mari was far more than that. During their quest to find the Runes of Valhalla, they'd discovered she was the mortal host for the goddess Hel. It meant she could read what people's greatest fears were. He wondered if that was why she'd seemed so comfortable with going back to normal life after their quest. Because she'd known that she was far from normal or boring.

"Buzz, are you listening to me?" Mari shook his arm. "What are we going to do? We've got gods setting up camp in Crowmarsh, and now Sam is caught up in this mess as well."

Let's not forget the spirit from the rainforest who is looking for payment and has taken the runes, Buzz added silently, wheeling his bike down the street. *But one thing at a time. Sam's in trouble.*

"I mean, stuff like this doesn't happen in New York." Mari looked thoughtful. "It must be the World Tree. When Odin planted it in Tangley Woods all those years ago, he changed Crowmarsh for ever. It's like the barriers between the town and all those other realms is thin—"

"Hey, look, it's Dumb and Dumber," a familiar voice yelled from across the street.

Buzz looked over and saw Theo at his front door. The other boy held up a hand in greeting and then jogged over to them, grinning widely.

"Theo, you do know we're supposed to be your friends now, right?" Mari pointed out. "We stopped an angry god and saved the world together, and that means we have a bond that cannot be torn asunder, et cetera, et cetera."

"Yeah, of course," Theo said. "I know that stuff."

"Well, you don't call your friends Dumb and Dumber," Mari chided. "Especially if you haven't seen one of them for months."

Theo actually looked sheepish. "Ah, sorry, Mari. It's just habit." He nudged her shoulder with his. "It's good to see you."

"Yeah, you too."

Theo looked down at Buzz's bike and let out a low whistle. "Man, your ride's busted. What happened?"

"A jeep happened, but forget that. We really need to find Sam," Buzz said.

Theo ran a hand over his short hair. "Hey, I'm really sorry about that whole Dortmeld thing." He grimaced. "Liam can usually get his hands on anything, and I was trying to be helpful. I didn't mean for Sam to get pranked like that."

"Whatever. You can apologise to Sam yourself, but we've got to find him first."

"Oh." Theo waved a hand dismissively. "I've tried saying sorry already, but he's having none of it. Told me he had more important things to worry about than my petty mortal actions." Theo rolled his eyes. "I mean, Sam does like to be dramatic, but I thought that was a bit over the top, even for him. I think he was trying to impress his new friends."

"What friends?" Buzz stopped wheeling his bike. "And when did this happen?"

"About an hour ago," Theo said. "I was on the high street and bumped into him. He was coming out of the post office with these strange-looking guys in white." He shook his head. "Like, seriously, what is up with that whole tunic thing? And they were super intense."

"Pantheon," Buzz and Mari said at the same time.

"Panther who?" Theo repeated.

"We'll explain in a minute." Buzz took his phone out again and tried Sam's number, but it was still going to voice mail. "What direction were they walking when they left the post office?" he asked.

Theo shrugged. "They were heading over to some jeeps." His eyes widened. "Hey, wait a second. Was it one of those tanks that bashed up your bike?"

"Yes, but that doesn't matter."

"It matters to me," Theo growled. "If you've got people messing with you, Buzz, you can tell me. I've got your back."

"Theo, thanks, but Sam's the one we've got to worry about."

Mari looked at her watch and pressed a few buttons.

"What's up?" Buzz asked.

"Just making sure the GPS is working. I've made some upgrades to the watch and there might be a few glitches." She wrinkled her nose in thought. "Okay, if they were going in their jeeps, then they must be planning on going at least a little distance," she reasoned. "How far are the Crowmarsh ruins from the high street?"

"About a ten-minute drive," Buzz replied.

"I bet that's where they'll be heading." Mari rubbed her arms. The balmy spring night was quickly becoming chilly. "They're going to make him demonstrate his power just like they did with Benjamin."

"Then we need to get to him before it's too late. Before they make him go through the arch."

Theo was looking at the two of them with an utterly bemused look on his face. "Hey, I don't know what's going on, but it sounds like you need to get going, Buzz. Me and Mari will catch up with you. I'll take my brother's bike and Mari can take mine. We'll be right behind you."

"I'll see you at the ruins." Buzz jumped on his bike and pushed off. It protested as he tried to steer it in a straight line, but Buzz pedalled harder until he convinced the bike to pick up speed.

The Crowmarsh ruins were right on the edge of Tangley Woods, past Larkscross and on the very margins where the forest opened up into rolling fields. Staying close to the trees for cover, Buzz peered through the gloom and into the ruins. He could see firelight coming from within the stone walls, and as he crept closer, he heard the low murmur of many voices, and then applause and the stamping of feet and maybe even hooves. A shower of sparks shot up into the air.

Leaning his bike against the stone of the ruins, he scrambled up the wall, his hands and feet searching for any gaps or crevices that would give him a hold. He finally pulled himself up onto one of the parapets to peer through an arched window of the ruin.

Down below was the strangest combination of individuals he'd ever seen, gathered around fires that dotted the interior. A giant badger sat next to a creature with a man's face but the body of a tiger with nine tails. A rainbow-coloured serpent was hissing at a fearsome-looking woman who was perched on the backs of two lionesses. A powerfully built man with an axe that sparked with lightning was stooped down to speak with a tiny woman whose skin was as rich and dark as the earth, and who had the tiniest of snakes around her shoulders. A feathered dragon prowled backwards and forwards in front of a stone arch with a pyre of silver branches at its base. Buzz shuddered as he saw the beast. Memories of Nidhogg, the dragon who had kidnapped Sunna, Norse goddess of the sun, all those months ago, were still too fresh. This dragon didn't look as big as Nidhogg, but its eyes were scarier. More human-looking and mean.

A woman in a cowl hood stood apart from them all. It was almost as if the others did not want to be near her. The cloak she wore squirmed about her as if it were a living thing and, looking more closely, Buzz saw that the material appeared to be writhing with maggots. Very slowly the figure pulled back her hood to reveal skin covered by more maggots. Her eyes were enveloped by them but this did not stop her from staring intently at the tall woman in white who stood right in the centre of the ruins.

It was the high priestess. The woman whom Esther said hadn't aged a day.

She didn't have her silver hair pulled back into a ponytail any more. It was loose and wild, and it whipped in the wind like the long white dress she now wore. The fang brooch she'd been wearing earlier now glowed eerily in the moonlight. To her left, standing on some broken steps that no longer led anywhere, Buzz could see Sam. He looked very small, somehow, as he surreptitiously tried to look at those gathered around him. His chest rose and fell very quickly as he took in a silver-skinned god whose wings spread at least eight feet across and a woman who shifted from young to old to giant crow as quickly as you could blink.

Buzz wished he could tell his friend that everything was going to be okay. *But that would be a lie,* he admitted to himself for the first time. He had no idea how he was going to get Sam away from these people. *Correction. How he was going to get Sam away from these gods.*

CHAPTER SIX

THE NEW GOD

The high priestess held up her hands for quiet. “First, I’d like to thank those who have paid their fee for entry to the Pantheon already, and kindly remind others that payment is required for full participation. Team Pantheon will circulate to collect final payment. Please have your jade discs ready.” She brought her hands together. “Now, I know a disc has not been the only cost for many of you. Your entry to this realm, be it by the World Tree or by the Ash Arch before us, will have sorely depleted your powers. But my friends, my comrades, it is worth it.” She looked out at the crowd. “We are gathered here to celebrate the manifestation of a new god and to begin our contest.” She gazed over at Sam on the ruined stairway with a pleased and possessive smile on her face. “Samraj has already proven that he has the power to create fire from nothing, and his abilities will continue to grow and multiply under the right tutelage.”

Her voice was melodic but powerful. "Therefore, in our age-old tradition, we must now determine which pantheon this new god should join."

Buzz saw the deep lines of Sam's frown even from a distance. His friend opened his mouth but then closed it again as a ripple of excited chatter went through the crowd. The gathered gods seemed to sit up a bit straighter and lean in a bit further.

"Quiet, comrades, and listen." The high priestess raised her hands once more. "Like the world around us, we must evolve or perish." Her voice took on a fevered pitch and her hands clenched into fists. "The appearance of a new god has become rarer and rarer, and such an opportunity must not be wasted." Her face twisted with disgust. "We all remember what happened with the last manifesting god that came from Crowmarsh. We cannot afford another mistake like Benjamin."

"Mistake!" Buzz heard a voice mutter furiously from below him. He looked down and saw that Mari and Theo were already halfway up the wall. "My uncle Benjamin was more than just some mistake, and if they—"

Buzz put a finger to his lips. Mari glared but managed to swallow down the rest of her words so she wouldn't give away their position.

Back through the arched window, Buzz saw that the priestess had dropped her arms and was staring out at her audience once again. "Every generation, fewer people believe in the gods who are gathered here today. Many of you are forgotten or are about to be forgotten, and live in the Forsaken Territories scratching out a life. Some of our number have disappeared entirely already." She fell silent for a moment, her eyes downcast as if paying her respects to the gods they had lost. "You all know, then, that gaining a new god for your particular pantheon is the lifeblood you need to survive." She lifted her chin. "But it could be so much more than that. It could be the catalyst we need to make it the age of gods once more. This means it is even more essential that this precious prize is well won."

Buzz saw Sam give a startled movement at this.

"Hold up." In the firelight, Sam's face shone with sweat. "I'm not a prize to be won, and I don't want to join any pantheon. You said you'd help me contro—"

"In previous contests, we have often focused on tests of power." The priestess spoke over Sam as if he had not opened his mouth. "But this time I will need to see more than strength to decide who will claim this young god, and I have decided that the whole of Crowmarsh will be your arena." She made a steeple of her fingers. "Over the coming days, until the arrival of the equinox, you must use all your ingenuity, all your cunning and persuasive powers, to create new believers. And, when night and day are in exact balance, you must show me the number of followers you each have gathered . . . They will fight for you."

A broad man with majestic antlers rose to his feet. "Berchta, you have no right to change the rules of the game." He took a step forwards, his massive shoulders rigid with fury. "Mortals today know little of belief. The contest should remain one of strength as it has always been."

The high priestess considered him for a moment like a scientist examining a strange species of insect. Almost lazily, her hand went to the brooch pinned to her collar, and her eyes began to glow icy bright. There, under the moonlight, her skin became translucent, and Buzz could see the cool blue fire that burned inside. Behind her, the pyre of silver branches within the arch caught fire and the flames knitted together to make a shimmering sheet of amber.

The man with the stag antlers took a step back. "No, no, I'm sorry, my Lady of Winter. I did not mean to speak out of turn. I was just eager to win, that's all." He fell to his knees. "Please don't make me go to that place. I'll do anything."

Berchta studied him. "Many years ago, the gods gathered here, and it was agreed that I should be the custodian of this contest. You all put your belief in me, and so it is my gods-given right to change the rules as I see fit. Understood?"

The horned god nodded, not daring to meet Berchta's eye.

"Now, let it not be said that I am not benevolent. That I am not kind. I will not send you to that place you so fear, Cernunnos, but you are forbidden from taking part in the contest." She rubbed the brooch again and the flames in the arch faded. "'Tis a shame, Lord of the Forest. You have the ability to charm and inspire when you wish, and those qualities would have been useful to make new believers." She placed her hands on her hips. "There is no doubt that this is a challenging test. You forgotten gods must make people believe in you again. The time has come to take control of this realm once more."

Mari and Theo had now joined Buzz on the ledge that overlooked the amphitheatre.

Theo lot out a low whistle. "Man, I thought I'd seen some strange things before, but this takes the biscuit. Is that a man with four heads talking to a giant rabbit?"

"I think it might be a hare," Mari corrected. "Look at the ears."

"It doesn't matter," Buzz said. "And can you guys keep your voices down?"

Theo gave a swift nod.

"It's not very nice, is it?" Mari said in hushed tones. "Making all these forgotten gods compete against one another for the prize of a new god, just so they have some chance of surviving. Some of them look so tired and weak. How horrible to be forgotten."

"Mari, have a word with yourself." Theo did not look impressed. "That ice woman with the silver hair has basically just said that these gods have got permission to go running around Crowmarsh making new believers. What happens if people don't want to believe in a giant badger?" He raised an eyebrow. "Not to mention, that Berchta woman is making moves to take over the world. And how about your great-uncle

Benjamin – the big mistake? Where is he now? What did they do to him?"

Mari set her jaw. "You're right, this is not a time for sympathy. It's a time for action." She pushed her glasses up the bridge of her nose. "Okay, let's think about how we're going to get Sam away from that priestess."

The three of them stood in silence. The seconds felt like hours.

"Well say something then!" Theo exclaimed. "You two are the smart ones."

"I've got nothing." Mari sounded mournful. "And even if I did, where do we hide Sam once we have him? These gods aren't just going to give him up."

Buzz nodded. "I wish we had time to go to the World Tree and ask Ratatosk. He'd know what to do."

"That squirrel and that tree both have an attitude problem," Theo grumbled. "Let's just use the Runes of Valhalla. These jokers won't stand a chance against Odin and the others. Their powers will be all juiced up."

"Er—" Buzz began.

"No," Mari said at the same time. "We already have enough gods in town and shouldn't be adding to the problem. Last time the Norse gods were awake, the whole world got stuck in the Unmorrow Curse." She shuddered. "Things started to decay, people became meaner. We can't let that happen again." She tucked a braid behind her ear. "Besides, Hel is fast asleep inside me and it's staying that way. This body is mine."

"I agree with Mari." The words were out of Buzz's mouth before he could stop them. He knew he was a coward for not telling his friends the truth about El Tunchi, but he didn't want to tell them he'd failed in his task of being guardian of the runes. "Better not to bring the runes into it. Not until we know we're out of options." He shrugged. "Anyway, it's not like we have time to get them."

"Okay. Okay." Theo cracked his knuckles, the sound made Buzz wince. "You're right. We don't need backup. We'll just get this sorted ourselves."

Buzz nodded even as the voice in his head continued with its admonitions. *Oh, Buzz, you're better than that. Tell them the truth. You were supposed to be looking after the runes and now they're gone. . . .*

Berchta clapped her hands, silencing the voice and everyone else in the arena. "It is time, then, for this young man to pass across the veil until a worthy winner has been chosen."

The priestess rubbed at her brooch and the branches in the arch caught fire once again, but this time they produced a smoke that was emerald green and streaked with red.

"No!" Sam pulled at the neck of his T-shirt like it was choking him. "I'm not going anywhere. You told me you could help me control my powers. You didn't say anything about sending me away."

Berchta held out a hand to him. "You are a great prize, Samraj." Her voice was soothing but firm. "Having you in

Crowmarsh will only distract those here from the task at hand." She gazed out at the crowd. "I warrant we all remember the blood that was shed the last time we allowed the prize to remain in this realm whilst the trials were performed?"

There were some nods and murmurs of acknowledgment. Some of the gods even looked sheepish.

"You're not listening to me." Sam's voice had thunder in it. "I'm not a prize to be claimed, and I'm not going anywhere." He lifted his hands and flames appeared at his fingertips.

Berchta raised an eyebrow. "It pleases me so to see your fighting spirit, Sam. A god should have fight." She smoothed down the folds of her dress with slim, elegant hands. "But I have been a goddess for over a thousand years. You do not get to refuse a command from me."

She clicked her fingers, and a clawed hand made of thick green smoke crawled forth from the arch and plucked Sam from the ground. He was held there for a moment, suspended in the air, as if the claw wanted to show off its prize, and then he was dragged towards the arch.

"Get off me!" Sam yelled. "Let me go!" He wriggled and bucked but his arms were pinned to his sides.

"Use your time away well, Sam," Berchta called. "Train and improve. For when you are finally won by your pantheon, you will need to be strong enough to survive that which lies ahead of you. Go. You will be well looked after."

"No!" Buzz cried. His voice echoed around the ruins. "Leave

him alone." But it was too late. Sam had disappeared into the smoke.

Berchta had gone very still, but now she turned slowly from the arch and looked up to where Buzz stood on the parapet of the ruins with Mari and Theo.

All around the crumbling amphitheatre, gods and goddesses were rising to their feet, their gazes also fixed on Buzz and his friends.

"Nice work," Theo hissed. "Anyone else you want to tell that we're hiding up here?"

"Theo, now is not the time for sarcasm." Mari was already scrambling down from her perch. "We've gotta move."

Berchta's eyes glowed icily once more as she pointed in their direction, and she bared her teeth. "Get them, get the intruders," she snarled.

The silver-winged god who Buzz had noticed earlier spread his glimmering wings and soared into the sky. With a smoky belch, the feathered dragon followed, and both gods raced towards them.

"I really, really, *really* hope you've got a plan, Buzz," Theo called out as he scuttled down the wall. "You have a plan, right?"

"Yep," Buzz replied. "Run!"

CHAPTER SEVEN

JUST RIDE

"You're kidding. That's the plan?" Theo squawked.

"Not all of it." Buzz scrambled to find the next foothold on the wall. "We need to get to the World Tree. Ratatosk will help us."

Mari grinned at him in the moonlight. "Exactly what I was thinking." She landed on the ground with a *thud* and sprinted for her bike. "And if we can get into the forest, it'll be harder for them to track us from the air."

"Why, oh, why did I say hello to you guys?" Theo complained even as he straddled his bike. "I'm an idiot. I could have just put my key in the door and gone into my house, but oh no, I had to say hello, and now we're being chased by a giant budgie man and some kind of dragon with feathers."

"They won't be the only ones," Mari said. "That badger will probably be after us, and badgers have excellent senses of smell and hearing. We won't be able to hide from him for long in the forest."

"What do badgers eat?" Theo asked. His voice was tremulous.

Mari wrinkled her nose. "Well, badgers are omnivorous and—"

"I'm looking for an answer here, not big words," Theo snapped.

"They eat everything," Mari snapped back. "And I imagine a giant badger eats large quantities of everything."

"Just ride, Theo!" Buzz pulled his bike upright. The front wheel still looked bent. He hoped it would last until they reached the cover of the forest. Theo nodded, and soon his feet were a blur as he began to pedal after Mari.

Buzz pushed off after them and was soon level with Mari, even as he heard the powerful flap of wings and a high screech from above his head. Looking up, he saw the feathered dragon speed downwards, its powerful body a deep blue in the moon's silvery light. It weaved in deftly between their bikes, swooping and swirling elegantly through the sky.

With another gleeful screech, the dragon flicked its tail out at Mari.

"Watch out!" Buzz shouted. He skillfully angled his bike into a skid and it caught Mari's wheel. She was thrown from her seat and went tumbling to the ground, the dragon's tail missing her by centimetres.

"Whoa! That was close. Thanks." Mari gave a small groan

as she picked herself up and climbed onto her bike once more. "I hate dragons. Why do we always end up with a dragon?"

"Wish I knew," Buzz yelled over his shoulder as he pushed off once again. "But we know from experience that they don't give up."

"Well, neither do we." Mari was right behind him. "I just hope this one doesn't breathe fire."

Buzz clenched his jaw and pedalled harder. *Nope.* He didn't fancy being turned into a dragon's kebab today, either. They had far too much to do. He focused on catching up with Theo, who had now almost reached the edge of Tangley Woods.

Mari had just drawn up level beside him when a gust of foetid air washed over them. Looking up, Buzz saw the glint of razor-sharp talons flash in the night sky. The feathered dragon was close. Buzz could even see the scaly underside of the dragon's belly and the dirty feathers of its wings crawling with insects as it continued to circle them.

Mari glanced up and then gritted her teeth and overtook Buzz. "Come and get me if you dare, you scaly rooster," she shouted up at the sky. "Or are those feathers just for show?"

"Mari, what are you doing?" Buzz cried as the dragon focused its gaze on his friend. She was now at least three bike lengths ahead of him.

"Your bike isn't going to make it, Buzz," she said. "I'm buying you some time. Go!"

The feathered dragon wheeled in the sky and surged towards

her with a piercing cry. It swiped out viciously with its talons.

"Duck!" Buzz cried.

Mari did, her braids flying over her shoulder, as she dipped forwards. The talons just missing the top of her scalp.

The woods were just a few metres away now and Buzz could see Theo waving at them frantically from the trees. "Come on!" his friend was shouting. "You can do it."

Buzz pedalled faster, but his bike was not cooperating. He could feel the twisted front wheel buckling from the strain it was under. The safety of the trees was close, but not close enough.

The steady beat of wings filled the air. The feathered dragon was still hovering in the night sky, as if working out the best way to attack. Making up its mind, the dragon shot down again. This time it came at Mari low and slow, and it blew thick smoke from its mouth.

Buzz knew that in seconds it would be impossible to see, and so he did the only thing he could think of – he grabbed his mobile from his pocket and hurled it at the dragon. It spun through the air, the phone's blue light twinkling like a strange star, and struck the god sweetly on the side of its temple before bouncing off into the darkness.

The dragon choked on its own smoke in surprise. Looking dazed, it tumbled to the ground and landed with a thump and a raspy-sounding wheeze.

Theo was cheering from the trees. "Nice one, Buzz!"

Mari turned and grinned. "Quite a throw you've got there. Shame you all don't play baseball in this countr—" She broke off and her eyes went wide as she looked at something over Buzz's shoulder.

And then Buzz was airborne, an arm like a vice around his chest. His bike clattered to the ground as he was pulled further up into the air. He looked up to see the silver-winged god. The wings were spread wide, magnificent and gleaming as they beat against the night sky.

"Let go!" Buzz wriggled and bucked.

"Most certainly," the winged god replied. "Right after I deliver you to Berchta. Now, be quiet. I've got more prey to catch, and the more you squirm, the more likely it is that I will drop you and I'm supposed to bring you in alive."

The wind stung Buzz's cheeks as the god swooped downwards and headed for Mari.

"Run!" Buzz shouted, but instead his friend stared straight at the winged god and glared. Like a daisy being picked from the earth, Mari was taken from her bike and swept upwards.

The god chuckled. "Why, that was far easier than I thought. I was watching as you gave Tiamat quite the runaround. Poor dear stuck in her animal form for all these years. I'm surprised I caught you quite so easily."

"I let you catch me," Mari explained. "I wasn't going to let you fly off with my friend, now, was I?"

Buzz shook his head. "Mari, you should ha—"

"What loyalty," the winged god interrupted. "I don't think I've seen anything quite like it since sweet old Fides."

"Who was Fides?" Mari asked. Despite everything, she sounded curious. Buzz knew that every opportunity was a learning opportunity when it came to Mari.

"She was the Roman goddess of loyalty," the god explained. "She was so loyal, she refused to leave Rome even as the empire crumbled. Now she is dust." The god wrinkled his nose. "Loyalty is a fool's game, and clearly your other friend agrees. He's run into the forest without you."

Buzz peered into the gloom. The god was right. Theo was no longer on the fringes of Tangley Woods. *He's gone to get help,* Buzz thought. *At least, I hope that's what he's done.*

The winged god clucked his tongue. "Oh well, two is better than none, and I don't know how I would have carried another person anyway." He tutted. "What are they feeding mortal children nowadays? You're both so hefty."

"Aren't you supposed to be some kind of supreme deity?" Mari asked. "Surely two little mortals can't be that heavy."

"Judge me if you will." The god flapped his wings and banked to his left as he turned away from Tangley Woods and headed back towards the ruins. "But it has cost me dearly to leave the Forsaken Territories and come through the Ash Arch." He shrugged, jerking Buzz and Mari upwards. "Luckily, once I give you to Berchta, she is bound to look on me favourably. It will help me win the contest."

"Do you really believe that?" Mari scoffed. "From what I heard, you need to gather new believers to win the contest. Giving us to her isn't going to help you do that."

"You heard an awful lot, didn't you?" the god observed. "What were you doing there?"

"We were lost," Buzz said quickly, knowing that they could not reveal their relationship to Sam. "We didn't mean to see what we saw."

"Tell the truth, Buzz," Mari said.

Buzz glared at her. "I am telling the truth."

"No, you're not," Mari replied. "But I'm going to and you're not gonna stop me."

CHAPTER EIGHT

THE DEAL

Buzz's chest felt tight. *Why is she doing this*? Then Mari winked at him, and he felt a little of his tension leave. She had a plan.

Mari tilted her head back and looked up at the god. "The truth is, a few months ago, I discovered that I am the host for the goddess Hel. Her life force sleeps inside of me."

"You mean Hel, Norse queen of the underworld, Hel?"

"That's the one," Mari said.

The god let out a low whistle. "Gracious, she has been missing for centuries. Thought she'd gone the same way as Fides."

"No, she's right here with me. When I heard about the Pantheon, I guess I wanted to learn more about the gods. I convinced Buzz to come with me."

The winged god went quiet for a moment. "I never really agreed with the whole host-god thing. It's why I chose to go to the Forsaken Territories when I lost all my believers. The whole idea of sharing the same space like that seems very strange to me."

"It is," Mari confessed, and Buzz was surprised at how sad she sounded. "Sometimes, I don't know where Hel begins and I end. I need to keep reminding myself that this is my life to live and no one else's. I'm the one who gets to make the decisions."

"Do you have any of her powers?" the god asked.

"No, not really," Mari replied. "I can tell what people's greatest fears are, but that's about it."

Buzz glanced over at his friend, finally understanding what Mari was doing. She was getting the winged god to see them as more than just prey. And the more he talked, the more likely it was that they could distract him and escape. Buzz gave her a silent round of applause. *She's doing a really good job of sounding sorry for herself,* he thought. *I never knew she was such a good actor.*

"What a useful skill," the god mused. "A bit like the power I used to have to identify a person's deepest desire. All gone now, of course, along with most of my other powers." The god sounded glum.

"I bet you're still great with your bow and arrow," Buzz said. *Ha! Mari's not the only one who can charm a god.*

"Bow and arrow," the god repeated. "What in all the realms are you talking about?"

"You're Cupid, right?" Buzz looked up at the god. "You were talking about Rome, and you've got the wings and everything . . ." He trailed off.

"How dare you," the winged god squawked. "I am not a

Roman god, and certainly not that pot-bellied teenager, Cupid." He thrust his shoulders back and spread his wings as wide as they could go. "I'm Zelus, one of the four protectors of Zeus, father of the Greek gods."

"Zelus," Mari repeated the name. "Nope. I'm really sorry, but I've never heard of you."

"Well, of course you haven't," Zelus huffed. "That's why I'm a forgotten god." The wind ruffled his feathers as if trying to soothe him. "I have a brother and two sisters: Kratos, god of strength; Bia, goddess of force; and Nike, goddess of victory. We are Zeus's constant companions and enforcers of—"

"Oh, Nike, yes, I've definitely heard of her," Buzz chipped in.

Zelus sighed deeply, the beat of his wings becoming slower. "Of course you have. Someone names some sneakers after you and you're worshipped all over the world, even if those silly mortals don't really understand who you are." His voice was raw with pain. "They say your name and wish desperately to wear clothes with those letters on it. They give offerings of coinage and wait in lines just to be first to have the same adornments as everyone else. It's just not fair." Zelus had now come to a complete stop, flapping his wings dejectedly as he hovered in mid-air.

"What are you a god of, then?" Buzz asked. He was curious, but more than that they had to keep on distracting the forgotten Greek god.

"I'm the god of enthusiasm," Zelus said, not very enthusiastically. "And on a bad day, envy."

"Ouch," Mari said. "And no one knows who you are?"

A nerve jumped in Zelus's cheek. "That's why I came to the Pantheon. I'd normally avoid it like the plague, or rather, the goddess of the plague, Lovathar." He shuddered. "Did you see her there in her cloak of maggots? I really hope I haven't caught anything. Plague takes ages to shake off." The spring breeze ruffled his long, silver hair. "And seriously, you really can't trust anyone at gatherings like that. Some of the behaviour from the others! Especially the tricksters. It's scandalous." He shook his head disapprovingly. "But things are getting desperate." His voice was becoming more and more bitter. "Nike sends a bit of power my way. I'm family after all. But I'm barely surviving in the Forsaken Territories. I don't have one single mortal worshipping me."

"Well, we could help with that," Mari said.

"We could?" Buzz questioned.

"Of course," Mari replied. "We're mortals. And think how grateful we'd be if you were to let us go. We'd give you thanks every day, and when we tell others in Crowmarsh of your kindness, they'll thank you as well. It would be a good start for you in the contest."

"A good start, yes," Zelus murmured. "And Berchta wouldn't need to know I'd let you go. I could just say I couldn't find you."

"Exactly!" Buzz said. "And remember, Tiamat didn't see you take us. She was still knocked out."

Zelus looked extremely tempted. "It's still a risk. If I do this, I'm really going to need a bit of worship."

"Sure," Mari said. "We could definitely give that a go. But you'd need to release us first."

"Hang on." Buzz looked down for a second and really wished that he'd used a different phrase. "What would worshipping you actually involve?" Mari did not look impressed, but Buzz wasn't about to make a promise to a god without understanding the terms of the deal. That was how his mother had ended up owing El Tunchi his mystery payment.

"Not much," Zelus said eagerly. "Just a few offerings once in a while, and the general exaltation of my virtues."

"Exaltu— what?" Buzz asked.

"We just need to talk about Zelus enthusiastically," Mari explained. "But we can only do that if you let us go."

Zelus bit his lip. "All right, mortals, you have a deal. Where shall I drop you?"

Buzz flinched.

"Sorry, not literally drop," Zelus reassured. "I need your worship, after all."

"Take us to the World Tree please," Buzz requested. "We need to find my friend Ratatosk, and the tree can be tricky to find sometimes."

Zelus snorted. "You're a mortal, of course the tree is difficult for you to find. We gods see the world a bit differently. Hold on."

Zelus folded his wings back and dove downwards. The force of the descent pushed Buzz's cheeks back, along with the scream in his throat. The ground was coming up at them. Fast.

He could even see frost on the blades of grass in the moonlight. Just centimetres from the floor Zelus went from vertical to horizontal and sped onwards. They were so close to the ground, Buzz's nose was almost touching the earth.

Mari gulped in a deep breath. "This is all a bit close, Zelus."

"I'm just having some fun." He laughed. "Not bad wing control for an old forgotten god like me!"

"No, not too bad," Buzz admitted. His voice came out as a hoarse croak.

Zelus laughed again. "You need to work on your exaltation, young man, but it's a start. I feel stronger already. Let's see what else I can do."

He shot into Tangley Woods, weaving between the trunks in an elaborate dance that left Buzz feeling dizzy.

At last, the trees began to open up, and Buzz could see a shimmering silver light.

The World Tree. It was as tall and regal as ever. Its bark still charcoal grey slashed with red.

It stood all alone, and the soil around it pulsed with power. Buzz could feel that energy in the air as well. It made everything thrum.

Zelus gently placed Buzz and Mari on the ground and rose up into the air again.

"Thank you, Zelus." Mari was waving. "Thank you for everything. We won't forget what you've done for us."

The god inhaled, as if drawing in her words like a sweet

scent. He inclined his head. "I should go. I don't want Berchta to get suspicious." He looked around him. "I do hope your friend Ratatosk is here. I've heard from others that he can be somewhat unpredictable."

"If by unpredictable you mean sometimes grumpy and sometimes not, you're correct," Mari said. "But he's as loyal as Fides."

"He'll be here somewhere." Buzz peered around the clearing. "He takes his job as guardian of the World Tree very seriously . . ." He trailed off. Now he was up close, he could see that the World Tree was suffering. The branches were sparser than before, and there were several ragged stumps where limbs had been ripped off. Sap seeped from the wounds, and now that he was right next to the trunk, Buzz realised that the silver-and-red bark of the tree appeared pale and sickly.

A strong gust of wind and the flap of wings made him look upwards, and he saw that Zelus had risen into the sky.

"Farewell, mortals." Zelus held up a hand. "And remember our deal. Give me thanks and tell others to do the same." Then the god was gone, weaving swiftly through the trees once more.

CHAPTER NINE

I SMELL BADGER

There was a swish of leaves and then a scrabble of claws on silver bark. A furry red face appeared out of the foliage. Long whiskers twitched, and big dark eyes peered out at Buzz and Mari suspiciously.

"Ratatosk!" Mari said. "Am I pleased to see you!"

"Pigeon man's gone, then, has he?" Ratatosk asked with a sniff. His body was still hidden by the leaves of the World Tree.

"You mean Zelus?" Buzz questioned.

"Yer shouldn't of brought him 'ere."

"Sorry, Ratatosk," Buzz said. "It wasn't exactly planned. Listen, we need your help."

But Ratatosk's head had disappeared into the foliage once again, and all they could hear was the sound of chomping.

"Ratatosk!" Mari looked like she was very close to stamping her foot. "There's no time to eat. We need your help."

"Well, I need to help myself first." The squirrel appeared on one of the silver branches, his cheeks bulging. "Need to keep my energy up in case those interlopers try their luck again." His red tail was held high, but by the glow of the silver tree and the moon, Buzz could clearly see the stump where the tip of his tail had once been. Ratatosk could be infuriating, but Buzz could never stay angry for long. This brave squirrel had lost part of his tail trying to protect Mari and Buzz from Nidhogg the dragon.

"What do you mean, help yourself first?" Buzz glanced over his shoulder. Was that the crunch of something underfoot in the inky darkness of the forest?

"Well, that lot are here, aren't they?" Ratatosk said with a jerk of his head. "Your mate Zelus is one of them."

"You mean the Pantheon!" Mari exclaimed. "They aren't our friends. But they are why we've come."

"That Berchta should know better." Ratatosk's whole body was stiff, and his red fur stood on end. "But she just came along and started snapping off branches." He leapt up to one of the tree's weeping wounds and sniffed the sap mournfully. "In all my years, I've never seen such a thing. Sure, occasionally she'd take one or two branches to use for the Ash Arch, but in the past she always asked first."

"Wait a second, you know about the Pantheon?" Buzz asked.

The squirrel shrugged a shoulder. "Odin and his lot never had anything to do with it. The All-Father decided to put his powers in the runes after his followers began to disband.

Most of the other Norse gods did the same." The squirrel turned to face them once again. "They were already fast asleep when Berchta came to me for the first time centuries ago and asked if she could take a couple of branches from Yggdrasil." Ratatosk shook his head. "I said yes. That was my first mistake. Now her and her cronies take and don't even ask, and the tree is hurtin'."

"Ratatosk, I'm sorry about the tree, but they have my friend Sam," Buzz said. "And we need to get him back."

The squirrel's eyes went wide. "He ain't the new god, is he?"

Buzz nodded.

"And they 'ave him over at the ruins?"

"No, he's already gone through the Ash Arch," Mari explained. "We don't know where they've sent him."

"But Berchta knows that we saw." Buzz raked a hand through his hair. "She sent Zelus, Tiamat and some others after us. We managed to stop Tiamat."

"At least for a bit." Mari looked out into the undergrowth. "We had to make a deal with Zelus to help us, but there are definitely more of them coming for us."

Ratatosk was rubbing at his furry forehead. "This is bad. Real bad."

"That's not all of it." Mari's voice was low. "Theo was with us, but we got separated. He's in this forest somewhere all by himself."

Ratatosk sniffed the air, his whiskers bristling. "Fret not. He's alive and on the move." The squirrel began pacing backwards and forwards on his branch. "All right. I know we're not really supposed to, but we need to get them runes and wake up Odin. Berchta will respect the All-Father's word."

"We can't." Buzz's throat felt like it was closing up. "The runes are gone."

"Gone!" Ratatosk and Mari said as one.

Buzz looked over his shoulder. There was that noise again.

"There's no time now, but there's this guy called El Tunchi, and my mum gave him the runes. She didn't know what she was doing. She was just trying to buy herself some time."

"Crikey, this is worse than bad," Ratatosk said. "El Tunchi's a wandering forest spirit. And a powerful one. It's gonna be impossible to get them runes back."

"I know, I'm sorry, okay," Buzz said. "I've failed at being guardian of the runes, and I've failed Sam."

"Don't say that," Mari said. "We don't give up, ever, and we don't let others choose how this is all gonna end. We get those runes back and we'll find Sam as well." She turned to Ratatosk. "How exactly do we do that?"

Ratatosk puffed out his cheeks. "It ain't gonna be easy. They'll have hidden Sam somewhere secure, and the only person who can help you find him is the Myth Keeper."

"Myth Keeper?" Buzz turned the name over in his mouth. "Where do we find him?"

"Or her?" Mari interjected.

"At the end of the wisdom path, of course," Ratatosk said.

"Stories hold power. They teach us lessons. The Myth Keeper would live nowhere else. You'll need to find the Keeper's temple, but the longer you take to find it, the harder it will become to see it."

The sound of something moving through the tress was even louder now.

Ratatosk raised his nose to the air and sniffed. "I smell badger," he said matter-of-factly. "And a bit of feathered dragon."

Buzz and Mari shared a look.

"They've found us," Mari said. "We need to get to the wisdom path."

"The tree will transport you." Ratatosk galloped up to one of the upper branches – flying from limb to limb like a furry acrobat. "Now, normally, I'd say you should discover the branch that leads to the portal yourself. The magic works better that way. But we ain't got time for all that." He tapped one of the thick silver branches with a claw and Buzz saw it turn into solid metal. "Well, get up here, then. We ain't got all day."

Mari started climbing.

"What about Theo?" Buzz called as he pulled himself up to the first limb of the tree.

The squirrel sniffed the air again. "He's close. I'll find him."

"Ratatosk, listen, that badger you can smell, he's really big." Mari was now level with the squirrel.

Ratatosk snorted. "It's probably that Celt, Moritasgus. I'm not worried about him, and I've taken on a dragon before, remember?"

Buzz decided it wasn't time to remind the squirrel that he'd lost that battle.

"Promise me you'll find Theo." Buzz stared into Ratatosk's dark eyes as he reached the metal branch of the tree. "Swear on Yggdrasil." The air here smelt of electricity, and Buzz's skin pricked as he saw a portal begin to open up at the end of the branch. The night sky was there but not there. The air had folded in on itself leaving an absence. Making a door.

"I promise you, Buzz." The squirrel met his gaze steadily. "Yer just focus on finding Sam. Bring him back, and all our problems will disappear."

"How?" Buzz asked. "It's all such a mess."

Down below, the sound of snuffling was even louder, and it was punctuated by a familiar loud screeching. Looking into the undergrowth, Buzz could see two pairs of eyes glowing like floodlights in the undergrowth. The badger and Tiamat were here.

"Look at me, not them," Ratatosk demanded. "With Sam's new powers he can take on El Tunchi, and we can get those runes back. Odin will deal with Berchta. No problem."

Mari was nodding from her perch on the branch. "It's a good plan, Ratatosk." She turned to face the portal, her braids a swirl around her head. "Here we come, Myth Keeper." She darted across, her feet a blur as they crossed the metal branch, and then flung herself forwards.

Buzz found himself grinding his teeth as she disappeared through the portal. "She always goes first."

Ratatosk laughed even as his eyes scanned the ground below. Two dark shapes were moving towards the tree. "It's her way of coping, and yer'll find yours. Good luck, Buzz. The Forsaken Territories ain't a place to dilly-dally in. Remember the gods there are desperate and forgotten. Get yerself home as soon as yer can."

Buzz nodded.

The squirrel broke off two twigs from the ash tree and gave them to Buzz. "Use these to get back if yer need to. They'll make yer a portal, but yer'll need to find an ash tree to plant them next to. They can only be used once, and only by you and Mari."

"Keep safe, Ratatosk."

"Always."

Buzz slid himself along the cold, smooth branch and then fell into the darkness.

PART II
THE WISDOM PATH

CHAPTER TEN

CAUGHT UP

Buzz was on a mountain path of stone and red dirt. The ground to either side of them was thick with scrubby-looking grass.

The sun was high and the air was humid and heavy.

A little further ahead, Buzz could see Mari. She was staring up at a crossroad signpost that had three arms, with a frustrated look on her face.

"You really need to stop running off like that," Buzz said.

Mari raised an eyebrow. "You really need to keep up." She pointed at the tall signpost and its three arms. "This is not helpful. Not helpful at all."

"This Way. That Way. Another Way," Buzz read out. "It seems clear to me," he said. "We go Another Way."

"Why?" Mari asked.

"Because This Way or That Way won't lead us to the answer. They're the normal way. They're not the way of adventure."

"Buzz, this isn't about having an adventure. It's about saving Sam."

"I know that." Buzz could feel himself bristling. "I don't need a lecture on what this is all about. He's my friend."

Mari looked hurt. "I wasn't lecturing you. I just . . ." She trailed off and looked up at the signpost again. "Doesn't it annoy you that this is even here? Why can't we choose for ourselves which way we go?"

"Because that's not the way it works." Buzz tried to keep the impatience from his voice. "You know that by now."

Mari shoved her hands in her pockets. "I know that ever since we finished our quest for the Runes of Valhalla, you've been down in the dumps." She bit her lip. "That you've been avoiding me."

"That's not true," Buzz protested.

"Yes, it is," Mari insisted. "Try being honest with yourself."

Buzz was grinding his teeth again. "Try minding your own business. How about that?"

Mari narrowed her eyes. "You're excited to be on another quest. Admit that at least. Admit it's made you happier than you've been in months."

"I didn't choose this." Buzz's cheeks were beginning to burn.

"No, but I think you'd stopped choosing the real world months ago, and that's scaring me, Buzz. There's nothing wrong with normal."

"How'd you know?" Buzz muttered.

Mari's brows knitted together. "What does that mean?"

"You've still got a sleeping goddess inside you. That's not normal. I'd say that's pretty unique actually." Buzz's gaze followed the path for Another Way. He could feel it pulling at him.

Mari snorted. "Trust me, I'd love a big dose of normal. Do you know how weird it is to share your headspace with someone else? To not know if something is your doing or theirs? To lose your power of choice?" She chewed her lip. "You need to start appreciating what you've got, Buzz, or all the things you care about will be gone by the time you realise their importance."

"Okay, thanks for the pep talk," Buzz said. "Can we get going now?"

Mari threw up her hands. "Another Way it is, then," she said. "Let's just hope it's not the Hard Way."

They walked along the path in frosty silence, and apart from the occasional tree or rock, there was nothing to distract Buzz from the fact that they weren't talking. He studied one of the trees. Thick vines hung from the branches and they appeared to pulse with energy. They reminded Buzz of the vines El Tunchi had left behind in his house, and he suddenly felt very far away from his mother.

He stepped off the path and reached out to touch one of the creepers.

"Wait!" Mari grabbed Buzz's arm and pulled him back onto the trail.

"What's wrong?" Buzz demanded.

Mari tutted. "We're in a strange place with zero knowledge of how things work. You can't just go walking off touching things. You know better than that." Mari was so angry she was shaking.

"Wait a second. Why's it okay for you to run off through portals, but I'm not allowed to step off the path?" Buzz asked.

Mari opened her mouth and then shut it again. "Those are merely details. The important thing to remember is that we need to work together, okay? We make decisions together and we—"

"Help," a raspy voice cried from further up the path. "Help me, please."

Buzz and Mari glanced at each other. Arguing was going to have to wait. They sprinted forwards.

"Help!" The raspy voice was getting louder.

"Over there." Mari pointed to a tree up ahead. They edged towards it. The sapling was dimly lit by the glowing, pulsating vines that covered it, and wriggling within the creepers was the biggest, ugliest spider Buzz had ever seen. Its black skin glinted in the light of the strange vines, and its eight long legs kicked furiously as it tried to escape the writhing green tendrils that were gripping it tight.

"Eh. Don't just watch!" The fangs at the side of the spider's mouth were bared. "Get me outta here."

Buzz glanced at Mari. She looked totally creeped out – exactly how he felt. Saving a spider the size of a large gerbil was not exactly what he expected when he ran over here.

"Um," Buzz said.

Twelve inky-black eyes regarded Buzz and Mari with mounting annoyance. "Be quick, now. These vines are gonna strangle me."

"We should help," Buzz finally said.

"Look at the size of it." Mari's lip was curled with distaste. "And it's probably poisonous. What if it bites us?"

"Eh. I don't bite . . . much," the spider insisted. "And I have many names, but none of them are 'it'. You can call me Ayiyi."

"Come on, Mari, we can't leave him like this," Buzz pressed. "And remember, you said that we have to make decisions together. So, are we going to do this?"

Mari hesitated but then nodded. "You're right, we should help." She stepped a bit closer to examine the vines. "How exactly did you get tangled up in this stuff?"

"It's a very short story," the spider said. "I was walking past this tree and stopped to get a bit of shade when—"

There was a sound like an elastic band snapping and a vine whipped forwards and wrapped around Mari's arm.

"Hey!" she exclaimed. Mari tried to shake off the vine but another tendril grabbed her other arm.

"Yep," the spider said. "That's exactly what happened to me."

"Why didn't you warn us?" Buzz shouted. He ran forwards to grab Mari, but a vine immediately snaked towards him and snatched at his arm.

He jumped back. *I'm not gonna be able to help anyone if I get caught as well.* He scanned the ground for some kind of weapon and spotted a large, jagged rock. He scooped it up and circled the tree. Taking his chance, he smashed the rock down on one of the waving tendrils and cleaved it right off.

The vine juddered from the impact, and then the thick green plant rippled with a surge of energy before healing the jagged mess Buzz had made.

Buzz raised the rock again and smashed it down on another part of the vine. The plant healed itself even faster in response and whipped out another tendril to try to catch Buzz.

"They're getting tighter." Mari yelped. "Do something!"

"I'm trying." Buzz panted. His limbs felt tired and heavy, and sweat made the rock slippery in his palm. He raised it again, ready to bring it down on the vine, but a beeping sound stopped him.

The vines around Mari's left hand and wrist were suddenly parting. She wiggled her fingers as the vines released more of her arm.

"Wait, how did you do that?" Buzz asked.

Mari frowned. "I didn't do anything."

"You definitely did," Ayiyi said. "I saw it with all twelve of my eyes."

The watch on Mari's wrist began to beep again, and then a tiny comb and brush on the end of a long metal arm popped out of the device and attacked the vines, swiftly untangling them until Mari's whole lower arm was released.

The comb and brush swivelled on its axis and the metal arm extended even further and began to work on the vines that bound Mari's upper arm.

"What is that thing?" Buzz asked.

Mari was looking rather pleased with herself. "You know I said I upgraded my watch? Well, this is one of the adjustments."

"You added a comb?"

"It is more than just a comb. It's a mechanical unbraider," Mari explained. "It's genius, actually. I really should patent it."

"Right," Buzz said.

"You're not convinced, but ask your mom or sister," Mari said. "It takes ages to unbraid your hair when you have lots of braids. My unbraider could be a hair revolution."

"Okay, fine," Buzz said. "I'll tell them all about it once we've found the Myth Keeper, saved Sam, got rid of those gods in Crowmarsh, and dealt with El Tunchi." He edged closer to the vines to see what they would do. They lay perfectly still; they seemed to be pulsing a lot less. The unbraider swivelled again and the vines shrank even further back, as if scared of the comb and its sharp teeth.

"The vines must have activated the watch when they caught my wrists," Mari mused. "Then the unbraider did its job and began unbraiding." She was now completely free and stepped away from the vines, shaking the last of them off her leg.

Ayiyi was also wriggling free, and with a few more jerks and tugs managed to extricate himself entirely. He waggled a skinny leg at the vines as he scuttled away from the tendrils. "Eh, you didn't like that, did you? You twisty turny menaces." He cackled loudly. "A bit of technology and you got scared." He turned to Mari. "Girly, I'd shake your hand and say thanks, but I don't know what else that watch does." He eyed it suspiciously. "Does it squish spiders?"

Mari laughed. "No, but it does play music and have a flashlight."

Buzz coughed. "You can thank me if you like, Ayiyi. I mean, I've only been leaping all over the place with a heavy rock for the past ten minutes."

The spider took a bow. "Brother, I am forever in your debt." He peered quizzically at him. "Buzz, isn't it?"

"That's right."

"Let me help you. Both of you. I may be an old forgotten god, but the Forsaken Territories are not a safe place for a couple of young mortals. I know that much." He looked out over the horizon. "I heard you say earlier that you're looking to find the Myth Keeper."

Buzz nodded. "We need the Keeper's help to find our friend Sam. We're looking for the wisdom path."

Ayiyi stroked his chin (at least Buzz thought it was his chin) with one of his hairy legs.

"The Keeper won't help you for free," the spider pointed out. "She'll want payment."

"Ha, I told you the Keeper was female," Mari crowed.

Buzz ignored her. "Payment?"

The spider nodded. "But all I see are your two long hands."

"Long hands?" Mari examined her own palms in confusion. "They're average-sized, to be fair."

"He means empty-handed," Buzz explained. "My mum says that sometimes. It's an old Jamaican saying." His chest suddenly felt tight as he thought about his mother. It was like his ribcage were suddenly too big for his body. He'd left Mum and Tia alone in Crowmarsh. What if El Tunchi had been back to the house?

"Eh, no matter," the spider said. "You'll just have to hope that you collect some good stories along the way. The Myth Keeper loves stories. Whoever tells the story holds the power – remember that. Come, I will show you the way."

They walked further along the mountain path. The air gradually became cooler as the sun began to drop in the sky. The spider was fast, his eight legs making easy work of the path ahead of them, and Buzz and Mari had to trot to keep up with him. Buzz winced as a stone in his shoe continued to cut into his foot, but he refused to say anything. *I'm not going to be the one to slow us down.*

Rolling slopes stretched out before them. He could see patterns of deep grooves cut into the ground, filled in with white chalk. To Buzz, the land looked like an army of sleeping giants covered in grass and small alpine flowers. It was beautiful, but there was no sign of anything other than more grass and more flowers.

"Ouch!" Buzz swore under his breath as the stone in his shoe jabbed him again.

Ayiyi stopped. "The hunter in pursuit of an elephant does not stop to throw stones at birds."

"What?" Buzz asked.

"Don't get distracted," Mari translated. "Get rid of the stone in your shoe and keep up."

Hopping on one foot, Buzz removed his sneaker and tipped the stone out. "How long will it take to get to the Myth Keeper anyway?"

Ayiyi looked him up and down. "Even with both of your legs on the ground, a long time."

"We don't have time." Mari kicked at a pebble on the path. "Why didn't the World Tree get us closer to the Keeper's temple?"

Buzz laced up his shoe. "Ratatosk said the tree was suffering because Berchta stripped it of so many branches. Maybe this was the best it could do?"

Ayiyi had wandered away from them and was watching, with increasing concentration, a strange-coloured bug that had landed on one of the purple flowers. He pounced on it and stuffed the insect into his mouth.

"I thought we weren't supposed to get distracted," Buzz reminded him.

"Who says I'm distracted?" Ayiyi was still chewing. "What

I do know is that we don't need no World Tree to help us." The spider swallowed the last of his meal. "However, we do need to move faster, or you'll never find the temple." He waggled a leg at them. "The long way round can sometimes be the shortest route to success."

"That makes no sense." Mari was looking a bit queasy as she watched Ayiyi pick an iridescent wing from his teeth.

"You'll see," the spider replied. "Come now, we go this way."

CHAPTER ELEVEN

THE FORGE

I -ya-a ya-o sa, nom-be,
ya-o, ya ya-o sa-a nom-be,
a nom-be, sa-ka be-ne sa-bi-na,
nom-be ya ya-o sa, a, nom-be

Ayiyi's voice rang out in song as the green of the rolling slopes gave way to a narrow causeway of rough stones and scarps. To Buzz it almost looked like someone had taken a mallet and smashed a hole through the mountain. The path was so narrow that he, Mari and Ayiyi had to walk in single file.

They escaped the causeway and found themselves on a hilltop. A cool breeze gusted here, and it chased away the humidity. At the base of the hill, Buzz could see what appeared to be an abandoned settlement. The huts looked tired and unloved, their thatched roofs threadbare. Looking to his left, he could see ancient hills crisscrossed with silvery strands of water and a few horses standing on the bank of one of the streams.

Buzz sniffed. Wood smoke and the smell of hot metal travelled on the wind. It filled the air. Following his nose, Buzz turned around and saw one small hut standing alone. Smoke pumped out from the hole in the top of the thatched roof, and the pounding rhythm of metal on metal filled the valley with its strange music.

"Good, good." Ayiyi rubbed two of his spidery legs together. "He's still going. Stubborn as they come that one."

"Who?" Mari asked.

"Gu," Ayiyi answered. "God of iron to some, but alas not many." The spider licked two of his legs and began smoothing down the bristles on his head. "That's why he makes his home here in the Forsaken Territories."

Ayiyi focused his twelve eyes on Buzz and Mari. "Now listen up," he warned. "It's no coincidence that a god of iron is very often a god of war as well. They are two sides of the same coin."

"Okay," Buzz said. "But what are we doing–"

"So we go carefully. He might be a bit spiky." Ayiyi paused and then began to chuckle. "Yes, spiky like the weapons he makes."

Buzz pinched the bridge of his nose. "Ayiyi, why are you bringing us to meet a god of war, a god of iron? A god of anything? We don't have time for this."

Mari put a hand on his arm. "I think I know," she said. "Look around. What do you see apart from that hut with the smoke?"

"Nothing," Buzz said. "The settlement is abandoned except for a few horses."

"Exactly," Mari replied. She turned to face Ayiyi. "That's why you've bought us here. For the horses."

"Like I said, the long way round can sometimes be the shortest route to success. But we have to convince Gu to lend them to us first."

The sound of pounding metal suddenly stopped, and looking down the hill, Buzz saw a towering figure emerge from the hut. The man wore an iron breastplate, the deep brown skin of his arms was overlaid by a fine mesh, and in his hand he held a heavy hammer. His face was entirely covered in metal, and through the metal grids Buzz could see two red eyes.

"Ayiyi, you sly old rascal, what do you want?" Gu's voice was deep and slow and not friendly.

"Sly old rascal." Ayiyi sounded indignant as he scuttled down the hill. Buzz and Mari raced to keep up. "Old friend, you mean."

Gu's grip tightened on his hammer. "If you say so."

"I need your help, Gu." Ayiyi beckoned for Buzz and Mari to come and stand next to him.

The god's steady gaze travelled over to Buzz and Mari. "What are a pair of mortals doing in this place?"

"They are on a quest," Ayiyi explained. "The details aren't important but the—"

"We're looking for the Myth Keeper," Buzz interrupted.

Gu shook his head and muttered something under his breath about timewasters and silly games.

The hairs on Ayiyi's body bristled and he raised his front two legs as if to attack, his pedipalps fully extended in the air and his thorax lifted. "I didn't completely catch what you said, God of Iron," Ayiyi growled. "Maybe that's for the best. We share a story, you and I. I would hate for that story to be at an end."

Gu met the spider's gaze but broke eye contact first. "You are right. That was rude. I haven't had company for a while. A quest is a quest."

Buzz frowned. He didn't understand how the gerbil-size spider had managed to put Gu in his place, but he had.

The God of Iron turned to face Buzz as Ayiyi lowered his legs. He seemed a whole lot less scary now. If anything, Buzz thought he looked weary, but it was hard to tell under the metal mask the god wore.

"Welcome. If you are friends of Ayiyi, then you are friends of mine." Gu flung his hammer over his shoulder and Buzz ducked just in time. "I'm guessing you want me to endow you with some magical gifts, a dance sceptre, perhaps, or snake iron." Gu's dull red eyes lit up. "It has been a while since I have been asked for help by mortals, but the God of Iron is as skillful as ever."

"Um . . . " Buzz began.

"Actually," Mari said, "we just want to borrow some of your—"

"Your knowledge and expertise," Ayiyi interrupted. "We

would never presume to ask for anything else." The spider opened all twelve of his eyes very wide. "Although brother, if you were to forge a mighty sword or axe for my friends, we would surely be humbled by such an auspicious gift." Ayiyi bowed low, his hairy head touching the ground.

"Wait a second," Mari said.

Buzz trod on her foot. "We're on a quest. We need stuff," he hissed.

Mari closed her mouth.

Gu nodded and beckoned with a battle-scarred hand for them to follow him into his hut. His forge was dark and smoky, and Buzz could see rusting iron hoops, dangling metal rods, swords, daggers, and axes hanging from the thatched roof. As he looked for longer, Buzz could see horseshoes with carefully painted patterns and beautiful pieces of jewellery dotted between the sharp blades and rods of metal. In the centre of the room there was a heavy block of iron with a smooth flat top. *An anvil.* The sides of it were covered with symbols that were etched into the metal.

"I try to keep busy," Gu said, and in the dark of the hut it felt like a confession. "The number of those that worship me has dwindled, but still I smelt and cast and hammer. If I stop doing this, I might disappear entirely."

"Why didn't you go to the Pantheon?" Buzz asked.

Ayiyi shot him a warning look, but it was too late. The question had been asked.

"Stupid games," Gu spat. "That's what Berchta likes – has always liked. But guess what? I'm not playing." He carefully placed his hammer next to the anvil, his fingers tracing the symbols he found there. "I'll stay here with the honesty of my iron and anvil, not the two-facedness of that rabble."

Gu reached out and plucked a simple belt made of interlocking metal links from the wall. He ran a hand over it, and the dull metal began to shine like black gold.

"It's beautiful," Buzz murmured. "What does it do?"

Gu laughed. "Well, that depends somewhat on the person who wears it. But each link is connected to the intrinsic magic of iron ore."

Mari frowned at it. "The intrinsic magic of iron ore. What does that even mean?"

"Take it and you'll find out." The belt dangled from Gu's calloused hand.

Mari looked unsure but took the belt from the god's outstretched hand and looped it around her waist. "Thanks."

Gu turned in a slow circle, looking at the other strange objects that lined the walls of his hut or hung from the thatched roof. Buzz followed his gaze, taking in a three-bladed sword, an iron rod shaped like a snake, and an axe with a broad flat edge that shone.

Gu suddenly nodded and took two thick metal cuffs from a shelf. They were rough-looking, and the iron was green and mottled with age. "Oh, man," Buzz muttered.

Gu's red gaze rested on him. "Disappointed, mortal?"

"Well, it's a bracelet." Buzz couldn't even be bothered to pretend.

"Eh, these children," Ayiyi said from behind them. The spider shook his head. "So ungrateful. And they're armlets, not bracelets, boy."

"I'm not ungrateful. It's just that there's a three-bladed sword up there and–"

"Stop." Gu pointed to his anvil in the centre of the room. "Think you can pick that up?"

Buzz stared at the hunk of metal and its strange carvings. "No."

"Try."

"Can I have the sword if I lift it?" Buzz asked.

"If you still want it," Gu promised.

Buzz stepped forwards and squatted down like he'd seen weightlifters do on TV. Gripping either side of the anvil, he yanked upwards and . . . completely failed to budge it even a centimetre.

"Hee, hee, ho," Ayiyi chortled. "You should see your face."

"It's not funny." Mari came and tried to lift the anvil with Buzz. It made no difference.

"The metal's getting warm." She released the anvil. "Can't you feel it?"

"No, not really." Buzz tried again. The anvil still refused to move, but beneath his palms Buzz could feel a sudden flare of heat. The symbols on the anvil glowed red, and the metal became scorching hot.

"Ow!" He let go of the anvil with a yelp and blew on his hand.

"Are you okay?" Mari examined Buzz's palm and then glared at Gu. "What's your problem? That's gonna blister."

Gu held out the armlets to Buzz. "Now try picking up the anvil with my . . . what was it you called them? Bracelets."

Buzz shook his head. "No, thanks." He continued to blow on his hand.

"Things will be different this time," Gu said. "Trust me. Take the armlets and pick up the anvil."

"Go on, Buzz." Ayiyi's twelve eyes were piercing. "Think of the stories you will tell if you can lift that hunk of metal." The spider's voice pounded in Buzz's head like Gu's hammer, and he found himself taking the cool armlets from the god. They were heavy in his palm but weighed nothing once he slipped them on his wrists.

"Buzz, you'll hurt yourself," Mari hissed, low enough that only Buzz could hear. "We still don't know if we can trust these guys. Whatever they say, they're players of the game, just like Berchta."

"I know," Buzz whispered. "But if we're going to get Sam back, we've got to learn the game and beat them at it."

He took hold of the anvil. It was warming up again, but this time the heat did not scorch his hands – it seemed to pass straight into the armlets. The metal cuffs began to tingle with the anvil's heat, and then the warmth passed up his arms and through his whole body. The tingling around his wrists became more intense as the symbols on the anvil glowed brightly, but still Buzz felt no pain in his hands. He felt nothing.

No weight at all as he lifted the anvil clear off the ground.

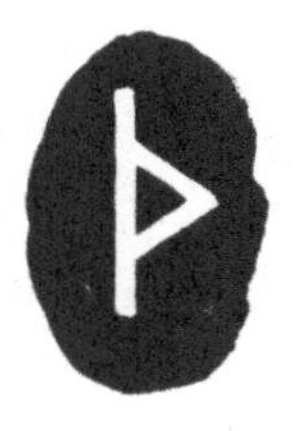

CHAPTER TWELVE

GIFTS COME IN ALL SHAPES AND SIZES

Buzz dropped the anvil with a clang. "Whoa!" he breathed. "I literally have superhuman strength."

"Super-*god* strength," Ayiyi corrected him.

Mari was looking at her belt again. She was scowling.

"Gifts come in all shapes and sizes," the spider reminded her.

"Maybe I don't want this gift," Mari murmured. "Maybe I don't want to be enhanced or changed. Maybe magic isn't always the answer." She crossed her arms. "We just wanted to borrow his horses."

Buzz bit the inside of his cheek. *Why is she trying to ruin it? What if Gu makes me give the armlets back. They're mine.*

The God of Iron looked at Mari for a good while, his face impassive, and then he began to chuckle. "You dislike magic.

You distrust it. But it is a part of you, and from that there is no escape." He pointed at the belt. "You and that belt are going to get on well. It's made of strong stuff, just like you." Gu lifted the anvil and moved it back to the middle of the room. "And you may have come for horses – and by all means, have them – but your true destiny, your true story, brought you to me for a purpose, and I have fulfilled it." He placed a hand on the smooth top of the metal block and closed his eyes. "In the days that have passed, heroes would come to me and make an oath of loyalty right over this very anvil. In return I would help them on their quests. It is the way it should be between gods and mortals."

"But we've made no oath of loyalty to you," Mari said.

"Are you sure?" Gu questioned. "You both put your hands on the anvil. That is oath enough for me."

"That's sneaky!" Mari exclaimed. "You tricked us."

"I'm no trickster." Gu sounded genuinely offended. "But you're right to be wary of them."

Buzz's gaze met Mari's as she glanced over at him. They knew far too much about tricksters. The Norse trickster god, Loki, had ended up helping them with their quest for the Runes of Valhalla, but that didn't exactly make him a friend, and certainly not someone they could ever trust.

"Eh, come children," Ayiyi's voice was waspish. He suddenly seemed impatient to leave.

"Yes, you have the Myth Keeper to find, after all," Gu said softly. He handed them two beautifully made saddles that creaked with newness, and some reins. "Take the two horses closest to the hut, the grey and the sandy-coloured one. They will look after you."

"Thank you," Buzz said, "for everything."

"You may not thank me in the future," Gu said. "The armlets are not without cost. Try not to overuse them, or you will feel it. Do not become too dependent on them for they will only work in this realm." Gu took a step back. "Remember, both of you, your gifts are iron. Too much exposure will make you hard."

"Yes, yes, yes." Ayiyi scuttled out of the hut and over to the two horses that Gu had described. Buzz and Mari followed straight behind. The horses gave a whinny of fear as Ayiyi came close. The spider tutted and crossed his two front legs. "Fool horses. What have they got to fear from a little old spider like me?"

"You're not exactly little," Buzz said. "But these horses are. They look more like Shetland ponies than horses."

"They're lovely." Mari held out a hand, and the sandy-coloured horse came over to nuzzle it.

Buzz threw the saddles over the ponies and began to fasten them, one after the other. "Ayiyi, you can ride with me."

Mari was grinning as she watched him get the horses ready. "You ride? How did I not know that?"

Buzz shrugged. "There are some stables just up the road from me." He placed the bridle over the grey horse's head. "I actually used to ride quite a lot but when Mum went missing, I stopped."

"Why didn't you start again when she came home?" Mari was staring at him hard.

Buzz shrugged a shoulder, hating the feeling that he was under a microscope. "I don't know. Somehow, it just didn't feel like it mattered that much any more." He attached the second bridle. "How about you? Had lessons?"

"Just one," Mari revealed. "In Central Park." She frowned as she looked at the sandy-coloured horse, who was still nuzzling her hand. "I'm not sure that's going to cut it."

The horse lifted his head. "Don't worry. I've got this."

Mari dropped her hand like she'd been burnt. "You talk!"

The horse blew a forelock of hair out of his eye. "Yeah. When I can be bothered." The horse nodded his head over to the grey pony. "She doesn't talk at all. I'm Skip and she's Dora."

"Nice to meet you." Mari rubbed the horse under his chin. "I'm Mari, and this is Buzz."

"And Ayiyi," the spider chipped in.

"We're trying to find the Myth Keeper," Mari continued. "Any chance you know the way?"

Skip nodded. "I can help you find the wisdom path for sure, but we won't go beyond it. Not safe for horses. Not safe for mortals." He glanced at the spider. "He'll probably be okay."

Buzz stared at the sky. The sun was dipping lower on the horizon. "Will we get to the end of the wisdom path today?" he asked.

Skip shook his shaggy head. "No, we need to ride for a good

few hours. We'll leave tomorrow at first light."

"We can't wait," Buzz insisted.

The horse gave a nicker of protest. "We only have five moons here, you know. And we're horses, not owls. How do you expect us to see in the dark?"

"Five moons," Buzz repeated.

"Obviously," Ayiyi said. "There are many moon gods or goddesses who have ended up in the Forsaken Territories. Now forgotten, they've surrendered their human form."

"Right," Buzz said. He wondered what other gods might have lost themselves in this place.

"Wait," Mari said. "We can use the flashlight on my watch. I can put it on its floodlight setting."

"Floodlight," Skip repeated. "What's flood water got to do with light?" The horse gave another nervous-sounding nicker. "Mixing them sounds dangerous."

Mari laughed. "It's got nothing to do with mixing light and water," she said. "Look. It'll be easier to show you." She flicked a button on her watch and a beam of light shot out from it. In the amber glow of dusk, it illuminated the path ahead.

"Wow," Skip's eyes had become large. "That's powerful magic, but it's still a bad idea to ride at night." His ears were stiff and twitching. "All kinds come out at night."

The other horse gave a nicker of agreement.

"We're going." Buzz wasn't going to back down.

Skip sighed and tossed his head. "Fine, we'll go with you,

but only because Gu said. First sniff of trouble and we're out of there. Right, Dora?"

Another nicker of agreement.

"Like I said, she's not much of a talker," Skip explained. "But I can tell you she's not happy."

The two horses set off into the valley. Buzz and Ayiyi rode on Dora, and Mari on Skip. From high up on his horse, Buzz could see more deep grooves, lined with chalk, cut into the ground. He squinted and tilted his head, and realised that the chalky grooves formed a giant figure – a giant *naked* figure – which had been carved into the landscape. Buzz sniggered, imagining what Sam and Theo would say if they were here.

They rode on, and the steady movement of the horse beneath him brought with it memories of past riding lessons. The stocky pony was different from the taller horses Buzz had ridden back home in Crowmarsh, but Dora had a calmness that he liked. She reminded him of his old horse, Cody. Dora had grey in her mane and looked older than Cody and Skip, but Buzz could still feel strong muscles moving under her shaggy coat.

Buzz suddenly realised how much he missed riding. Before his quest to find the Runes of Valhalla, playing soccer, hanging out with Sam and going to the stables had been the stuff he'd looked forward to.

But it hadn't been enough. Not after the quest.

Homesickness swamped him. He wanted Sam back, and for his mum to not be scared of El Tunchi any more. He wanted his dad to return from his mysterious mission, and he wanted to know that Theo was safe.

The hours of twilight were far behind them now. Ayiyi filled the silence with story after story. Song after song. And still they rode, winding up the mountain path. The five moons gave off an eerie glow and as Mari's light cut a path across the dark hillside Buzz noticed yet more white chalk and deep grooves cut into the ground to form a large figure.

"Look! It's a naked giant," Buzz called over to Mari. "I bet he's cold."

"You should not mock," Ayiyi rebuked. "The giants in these hills are ancient deities. Just because they are forgotten does not mean they should be disrespected."

Dora gave a nicker of agreement.

"I just said they should put some clothes on," Buzz protested as they trotted into a gorge. "It was a joke."

"Well, it's not funny," Ayiyi said. "You never know who is listening."

"Ouch!" Mari exclaimed from up ahead.

"What is it?" Buzz asked.

Skip had stopped, and Mari turned in her seat, clutching at her cheek. "I just got hit by a piece of rock. Not sure where it came from."

There was a whistling sound as a lump of rock shot past Buzz's ear. He looked up, scanning the top of the rocky gorge. The moonlight revealed a hunched-over figure that almost looked like it was part of the landscape. "Up there," he shouted, pointing. "There's someone up there throwing rocks."

Mari aimed her watch at the top of the gorge. In the beam of light, there was a flash of green moss; a wide, staring eye; and hands the size of dinner plates.

"Oh brother, we're under attack," Ayiyi shouted. There was a creaking sound and then a rumble as a boulder began to thunder down the hillside.

"From who?" Buzz asked.

"A giant." Ayiyi sounded grim. "I told you not to insult them. More will be coming, and we're stuck in this gorge. We need to ride."

"Oh no!" Skip wailed. "We're gonna be squished by a boulder. Like, completely flattened."

Dora's tail was up high and swishing backwards and forwards furiously. "Quit grumbling and get moving," she commanded. "We go forwards. And we don't stop."

Skip's ears pricked up. "No way! You actually speak," he said. "I can't believe it. After all these years."

"Just go," Buzz, Mari, Ayiyi, and Dora said as one.

Skip sprang forward with a fierce whinny, his shaggy, messy mane flying out behind him. "Here we go," the horse cried. "Hold on tight!"

CHAPTER THIRTEEN

EVERYBODY'S STORY ENDS

Buzz hunched over Dora, his heels pressing into her flanks as she galloped after Skip.

More rocks slashed down at them. Small and large missiles ricocheted off the sides of the gorge, but by now Skip had found his stride and the younger horse was pulling away.

"Buzz! Come on!" Mari cried over her shoulder.

"We're coming. Just don't slow down," Buzz yelled back. "Come on, Dora. Stay with them."

"I'm trying, boy rider." The pony's voice came out as a pant. "I'm no spring chicken, you know."

Buzz laughed despite himself. "That's lucky. I'd be in real deep water if I were riding a chicken."

"Well, you've got an old nag instead." Dora sounded mournful. "I don't think that's much better."

Buzz patted the horse's neck. "Not old. Experienced."

"What? Me?" Dora sounded unconvinced.

"Yes, and wise," Buzz added. "The wisest and cleverest of horses I've ever met." *Not that I've actually had a conversation with another horse before,* he confessed silently. But Dora did actually seem pretty smart.

"And the wisest will always find a way," Ayiyi added helpfully.

"Exactly," Buzz said. "Dora the wise, I just need you to ride like you never have before. Think you can do that?"

Dora dropped her head. "Boy rider, I will do my very best."

She surged ahead, her hooves sending up a shower of gravel.

"That's it, Dora." Buzz leant right over the pony's body, making them as streamlined as possible. "Go, go, go!"

Dora lengthened her stride, and Buzz felt the wind lash his face as he clung on, holding tightly to the horse's neck.

From up above, he heard another creak, followed by an even louder rumbling. Looking up, he saw two massive boulders rolling down the side of the gorge.

Dora threw her head back, her mane whipping and flecks of froth flying from her mouth. "We won't make it past them. I'm too slow."

"Don't stop," Buzz cried. "Don't stop."

Dora galloped even faster along the causeway, the chasm becoming narrower and narrower as they rode. Buzz heard one boulder smash onto the path behind them. And then the second one landed. Looking over his shoulder, Buzz saw this boulder bounce once and then spin out towards them. He jerked his body left and Dora did the same. Buzz cried out as his left thigh was dragged across the wall of the narrowing gorge.

"Eh, brother, be careful. I almost lost some legs," Ayiyi complained from behind them.

Dora's step faltered, as further along the gorge another boulder began rolling down the hillside. It landed just a few metres in front of them. Dora reared up onto her hind legs, her front hooves flailing.

"Easy, easy." Buzz gripped tightly with his legs as he tried to stay in the saddle. With a whinny, Dora's hooves came back to earth, and she came to a weary stop.

Buzz adjusted his position in the saddle and tried to ignore the pain in his leg. He could no longer see Mari and Skip. The way ahead was completely blocked by the boulder that was wedged between the two walls of the gorge.

They got away, Buzz thought. *Wish the same was true of us.* The giants had them trapped. No way forward and no way back.

"Sorry, boy rider," Dora wheezed. "I tried, I really tried. I hope you know that."

Buzz ruffled her mane. "You were amazing."

In the distance he heard the thump of heavy footsteps.

"They're coming." Ayiyi sounded resigned. "The giants are coming."

Buzz swallowed. Three hulking figures. Three *naked* hulking figures made of moss and grass were silhouetted against the moonlit sky. They'd left their boulders and were lumbering down into the chasm. The earth shuddered with each step.

Why, oh, why did I mock them? Buzz thought. His mouth went dry, and he realised he was making a strange wheezing sound.

"Calm yourself," Ayiyi said. "Hope is the power to see light even in the darkness. Hope is the power to find an answer when there appears to be none."

"So be it. I hope Skip is okay wherever he is." Dora pawed at the ground, creating a cloud of dust. "And his girl rider."

Buzz looked over his shoulder at the spider. "What are the giants going to do to us?"

Ayiyi shrugged. "Grab us, crush us. Turn our bones to dust." The spider laughed. "Not that I have any bones. Not like yours, anyway."

"I can't believe you're laughing about this." Buzz ground his teeth.

The spider shrugged. "Everybody's time comes. Everybody's story ends."

"Not mine," Buzz said. "Not yet."

"So, what are you going to do about it?" Ayiyi's head was tilted to one side.

"I DON'T KNOW!" Buzz's voice was loud in the chasm. "Can't you do something?" The ground continued to tremble as the giants approached.

"I'm just a spider. What happens next is in your hands."

Buzz stared down at his lap, willing an answer to come into his head. The iron armlets caught his gaze.

Of course, he thought. *I'll move the boulder. Just like I did with that anvil.* He swiftly dismounted and placed his hand on the rock. It was rough beneath his palm, and cold.

"Think you can budge it?" Ayiyi sounded intrigued.

"I don't see why not," Buzz replied. The thundering footsteps were getting closer now. "I should have thought of it before."

Both of his hands were on the boulder now. *Shift.*

Buzz could feel the warmth of the armlets on his wrists. They were lending him their power.

But the boulder would not move.

Come on! Shift. Buzz pushed again, and the armlets heated up even more, the metal searing his skin. The pain brought tears to his eyes. But still the boulder did not move.

"It's no good, boy rider," Dora said. "You can't move mountains. That boulder is properly wedged there and you are hurting yourself. I see it in your face."

"See it? I can actually smell your pain," Ayiyi commented. "Smells a bit like bacon. Those armlets getting too hot for you?"

"No," Buzz shot back, but the truth was, his wrists were in agony.

"The answer is not always strength." Ayiyi almost looked bored, sitting there on the horse. "A great warrior needs more than one strategy."

Buzz stopped pushing, more because of the pain in his

wrists than because of what Ayiyi had said. The armlets cooled down immediately and soothed the burns they had created. He stared at the boulder, which filled his vision. He had to tip his head back to see the top of it. Now that the pain in his wrists was fading, he could think. *Okay, perhaps it's not about moving the boulder aside,* he thought. *Perhaps it's about getting us over it.*

"Ayiyi, shift over, will you?" Buzz climbed back onto the pony. He leant forwards. "Dora, you're not ready for your story to end, are you?"

"No, boy rider."

"Then you need to get us over this boulder." Buzz scooped up the reins. "You need to jump."

"Eh, brother, now we're talking." Ayiyi began to cackle. He settled himself comfortably in the saddle and held on to Buzz's waist. "We're going flying. I *love* flying."

Dora snorted. "Wait one trotting second! I'm not Pegasus, you know."

"I know—" Buzz began.

"I mean, I don't have his wings for one," Dora went on. "And I certainly don't have his massive ego."

Buzz could hear the raw envy in Dora's voice, and her ears were twitching furiously. Someone was jealous. Buzz knew what needed to be done.

"Yeah, I guess I'm asking too much." He had to shout to be heard over the approaching footsteps of the giants. "I just wish Pegasus was here. He'd get us over that boulder no problem."

Dora pawed angrily at the ground once more. “Pah. He isn’t that special. It’s more hype than anything else.” She tossed her head. “Watch this.”

CHAPTER FOURTEEN

BETWEEN GIANTS

The horse trotted backwards as far as she could go and then raised her head and stared at the boulder. Her whole body pointed towards it like an arrow. "Boy rider, hold on!"

She cantered forwards, her stride soon lengthening to a full gallop. Buzz could feel how hard she was working, the muscles beneath her coat bunching up as she shot upwards and soared into the sky.

The pony's jump was good. But even as they hurtled through the air, Buzz could see that the boulder was just too tall.

"Come on, Dora," Buzz whispered. His wrists began to sting as the armlets heated up once again. He felt the power build there for a moment and then it was gone, passing through his fingertips and evaporating into the reins in his grasp.

Dora suddenly arched her body even further, and they cleared the boulder. Crashing down on the other side, the horse did not even break her stride. With the end of the gorge now in sight, she hurtled forwards.

"Dora, that was amazing!" Buzz yelled.

"We did it together," Dora replied, laughter in her voice. "I was tired, so tired, and then you helped me. You sent me strength."

Buzz looked down at his armlets. They had cooled once again, soothing the skin beneath the metal. He realised that Gu's gift not only had the ability to make him strong – he could also lend that power to others.

There was a crashing sound behind them, and Buzz realised that another boulder must have rolled into the chasm.

"Eh, those giants are stubborn," Ayiyi commented.

"Come on, Dora." Skip's voice drifted into the canyon, and Buzz saw Mari and Skip waiting for them at the end of the gorge.

Buzz patted Dora's neck, feeling the dampness of her coat. "We're going to mak—"

He stopped as he heard heavy footsteps right behind them.

Buzz turned to see a giant figure made of stone, soil, grass, and grit lumbering towards him with massive steps. That last crash hadn't been a boulder. It had been a giant jumping over the huge rock. He felt the air leave his lungs as another giant strode down the side of the chasm and climbed over the boulder that was still wedged there.

Dora let out a rasping, wheezing breath as she tried to go

faster. Her whole body trembled, and Buzz knew that if he pushed the pony any further, it would be the end of her.

The giants aren't going to stop, he thought. *They want me. Just me.* Buzz stared down at his armlets. *Well, they can have me.*

"Ayiyi, get Dora to safety." Buzz scrambled to dismount.

"No, we won't leave you," Dora cried, coming to a stop. "It's a giant, for the gods' sake."

Buzz stared at the horse. Her brown eyes were wide, scared, and stubborn. "I won't be long," he promised. "Now go!"

"Don't argue with him." Ayiyi gathered up the reins. "Good luck."

Buzz held up his armlets. "I don't need luck. I've got these."

Ayiyi wagged a leg at him. "Remember, strength is not the only strategy." The spider snapped the reins and Dora galloped down the gorge.

Buzz turned to face the first giant. He beckoned him forwards with one hand. "Want me? Come and get me, then!" The giant's green, mossy face twisted with rage, and his mouth opened, showing teeth that were spikes of rock. He reached out, but Buzz easily skipped to one side. The armlets began to warm on his wrists, and he felt power surge through his body. Buzz felt great. Unstoppable. *Shame I don't have a plan.*

The giant came at him again, and Buzz pushed off the ground, somersaulting through the air for the first time in his life. He trusted the strength and skill the armlets gave him and did not look down as he landed, his feet instinctively finding a safe foothold on the side of the gorge. He started to race up the slope, the strength in his hands and feet propelling him upwards.

I'll take the giants away from the others, he thought. *It's a start, at least.*

Buzz heard a roar of rage, and then something large whizzed past his ear. He turned to see both giants chasing him, and they were shooting sharp-looking flints from rocky hands thick with moss and decaying leaves. Buzz dipped his head just in time as a stony missile hit the side of the gorge. It smashed apart. The pieces struck at his face like glass.

As the giants shot more rocks from their fingertips, Buzz carried on scrambling up the wall of the gorge. "Buzz, watch out!" Mari's voice seemed very far away, but he turned to see that one of the giants was almost upon him. He ducked as a massive hand of stone and moss swiped at his head. The giant growled with fury, and his left hand lashed out much faster than should be possible for a creature so big, and engulfed Buzz.

"Let go of me!" Buzz yelled. He tried to wriggle out of the giant's grasp, but the massive hand just squeezed him tighter.

Stars popped into Buzz's vision and blended with the grey, the green, and the brown of the hand that held him.

He could feel a tide of black washing over him, but he pushed against it. *If I pass out, I'm not waking up again.*

He tried to focus on the armlets, wishing for the now familiar strength to come, but it was difficult to think with no breath in his lungs. There was no tingling around his wrists. No heat. Everything felt very far away and not real any more. He was tired. *I'll just close my eyes.*

A guttural snort and then a growl brought him back from the edge of unconsciousness, and from between the mossy fingers that held him, Buzz saw that the two giants were facing each other. The second giant was pointing furiously to where Buzz was gripped. He clearly wanted his share.

The first giant pushed the second giant with his free hand. The second giant pushed back.

Buzz felt the grip around him loosen just a little as they continued pushing each other. He took a deep breath and focused on the armlets. He called the strength to him, and it rushed from the armlets in a flood. The power coursed through him, out of him, and he burst free from the giant's grip.

Buzz slammed to the ground with a thud, the impact winding him for a moment. The two giants ignored him even as Buzz staggered to his feet. They had stopped pushing each other and were clenching and unclenching their fists, their faces full of marvel.

Oh no, Buzz thought. *I've given them the armlets' powers.* He clenched his hands, ready to fight them, but the giants were only interested in fighting each other.

Growling, they started pushing each other again, and then they each pulled an arm back and struck the other with all their strength.

It was like a stick of dynamite had exploded. Buzz threw an arm up and covered his head and face as fragments of moss, leaves, rock, and chalk rained down from the sky. Then all was quiet.

Buzz uncovered his face. The giants had gone, replaced by two piles of rock and leaves.

"Whoa," a familiar voice said from behind him. "What happened?"

Buzz turned to see Mari, Skip, Dora, and Ayiyi standing there.

He held up the armlets, which were cool once more. "These did." He explained how he'd accidently given the giants his strength.

"And then they destroyed each other." Mari let out a low whistle. "We came to help as soon as we could, but it looks like you got it sorted out all by yourself!"

Buzz shook his head. "I didn't do it on purpose."

"Doesn't matter," Ayiyi said. "The result is the same, and you learnt something, no?"

"I guess. I learnt not to insult giants."

The spider laughed. "Not just that. You learnt that sometimes one has to give power away to win the day."

"If you say so." Buzz frowned. "But I'm never giving these armlets away. Not ever." He looked at the remains of the giants. "Poor guys. If I'd just kept my mouth shut, they'd be alive."

"Eh, don't worry about that. They'll pull themselves back together soon enough," the spider said ."We'd just better be far away from here when they do."

Buzz looked more closely at the two hillocks of stones, moss, and leaves. They were vibrating, fizzing with energy, drawing together.

He jumped on Dora. "Let's get out of here."

FIFTEEN

THE TROUBLE WITH PIGS

"Buzz, slow down a bit, would you?" Mari said. "Skip and Dora have been through a lot."

"We can't." Buzz continued to look ahead. "The longer we take to find the wisdom path, the less likely we are to find the Keeper's temple. Ratatosk warned us."

"I know." Mari's voice was sharp. "But these horses are in our care. That means we look after them."

Buzz didn't reply, just urged them onwards as the sun began to climb in the sky. The mountain pass sloped steeply and led them to the edge of a valley that curved inwards like a basin. It was lush with grass, tall fruit trees, and flowers. On the other side of the valley, Buzz could see several black slabs standing tall and proud against a crisp blue sky. They adorned the mountainside like sculptures in an art gallery.

"Look!" Buzz pointed ahead. "I think we've found the

wisdom path. We just need to cut across the valley."

"I wouldn't go that way if I were you," a voice said from above them.

Buzz tipped his head back to see a small man with rosy-pink skin sitting on a stone ledge above them. Next to him were several piglets, all trying to squash up against him for comfort.

The man clucked his tongue and brought out an old blanket that Buzz could smell even though he was several metres away.

"Here you go, lovelies," the man cooed to the piglets, as he laid the blanket over their small, pink backs.

"Why not?" Buzz was doing his best not to breathe through his nose.

"Why not what?" The small man was still busy tucking the blanket around the squiggling, downy bodies of the piglets.

"Why shouldn't we go across that valley?" Buzz could hear the impatience in his voice.

"Got two of my biggest pigs, Erym and Caly, down there, haven't I?" the man explained. "And they don't like strangers. Go around the rim of the crater."

"Okay, thanks for the warning," Mari said. "It won't add that much time." She clucked her tongue. "Come on, Skip, let's go."

But Buzz did not move. "We're going into the crater," he said. "It's the faster way to the wisdom path."

The small man sighed deeply, got to his feet, and began to lower himself from the ledge. He landed on the path, and as he did so, Buzz noticed that instead of feet, the man had trotters.

He was not wearing much – just a ragged cloth around his waist and quite a lot of mud. The small man lifted his chin as he came to stand in front of Buzz and Mari. His eyes were a piercing blue against the muck that was smeared all over his face. "You're not listening. I'm Priparchis, the god of piglets, and—"

Buzz snorted despite himself. *The god of piglets,* he thought. *No wonder this guy's in the Forsaken Territories.*

The small man lifted his chin. "You find something funny, clearly," he said. "But you won't be laughing if you go down into that crater."

"We can deal with a couple of piggies," Buzz said. "Especially if they're in the way of our shortest route."

"Eh! Are your ears for listening or decoration?" Ayiyi asked from behind him.

Buzz hand's tightened on the reins. "I'm not looking for input right now. I'm looking for results. Come on, Dora." He snapped the reins, and the horse moved gingerly down the slope into the crater. From the stiff line of her body, Buzz could tell she wasn't happy about it.

He heard the sound of galloping hooves from behind him, and Mari appeared at his side. Her face was flushed. "Buzz, that wasn't very nice of you."

"I didn't do anything!" Buzz exclaimed.

"You laughed at that poor god." She frowned at him. "And then just rode off. What's going on with you? You've never been a mean person before."

"I wasn't mean."

Mari didn't say anything for a moment as if she wanted to choose her words carefully. "Listen, I know you've got a lot on your mind," she said, "but we'll sort this out. All of it. We'll save Sam, we'll get those runes back, and stop El Tunchi and Berchta."

Buzz gave her a thumbs-up.

"Wow, now I'm getting the sarcastic thumb treatment."

Buzz ducked his head. "Okay, maybe that was mean."

"Perhaps it's to be expected." Mari almost sounded like she was talking to herself.

"Excuse me?"

"It's those armlets." Mari was looking at Buzz's wrists. "They're changing you. Gu said they might."

Buzz's neck and shoulders felt tight. "That's rubbish. These armlets are what saved me from the giants." He adjusted his position in the saddle. Ayiyi really took up a lot of room for a spider. Buzz wished he could just ride by himself. "I mean, you were nowhere to be seen."

Ayiyi tutted and Mari's jaw dropped. "I couldn't get to you," she said. "Me and Skip tried, but the boulder was in the way."

"Sure, sure," Buzz said. "All I'm saying is that the armlets were there to help me when it counted. They're a part of me now, so quit criticising them."

"Brother, don't get too attached," Ayiyi chirped from behind him as they moved further down into the crater. "Gu said they'd only work in this realm. Remember?"

"Will you both just stop talking?" Buzz's annoyed voice echoed across the hollow. It was answered by a loud guttural roar.

"Eh. That didn't sound good," Ayiyi said.

Skip had become skittish. "What was that? What made that noise?"

Mari pointed directly ahead. "That did."

Out of a dark cave appeared a large creature with a thick, bristly body and long tusks that glinted in the sunlight. It stood very still, watching them.

"Wait a second, that's not a pig. That's a monster," Buzz hissed, even as the boar began to paw at the ground.

"He's gonna charge," Mari said. "We've gotta move!"

Mari and Buzz snapped their reins. Skip galloped in one direction and Dora in another. Looking over his shoulder, Buzz saw the boar looking first at Mari and then over at him.

It flared its nostrils and made its decision. Lowering its massive head, the boar charged after Skip and Mari.

Buzz brought Dora to a stop and wheeled her round. "We need to help," Buzz said as he watched the boar's pursuit. "They're not going to be able to outrun it for long."

"What are you going to do?" Ayiyi had stood up and was resting many of his legs on Buzz's shoulder.

Buzz shrugged him off. "I'm thinking, okay?" He looked down at his armlets. Was he really strong enough to wrestle a boar?

Another roar ripped through the air, and from the other

side of the crater, emerging from the shadows, came a new boar. Buzz gulped. If anything, this one was even bigger. Its tusks were certainly longer.

"Eh, that's *really* not good," Ayiyi said.

Thanks for stating the obvious, Buzz thought. The second boar charged towards Mari from the other direction. At any moment she was going to be trapped between them.

What should I do? What should I do? Buzz's brain just wouldn't work.

The earth beneath his feet suddenly gave a massive jolt, and then another. The movement uprooted several of the trees that surrounded him and sent them hurtling towards the ground.

Dora rose onto her hind legs, but Buzz managed to stay in his seat. Ayiyi was not as lucky. He tumbled to the ground. Scrunching himself up into a ball, the spider rolled away from Dora's flailing hooves.

Earthquake, Buzz thought. *This day just keeps on getting better and better.* The ground beneath his feet seemed to be expanding and contracting, almost as if it were alive and charged with energy.

He searched for Mari. The ground that she and Skip were standing on had risen to a majestic peak, leaving the two boars scrambling to get up its sides. One of the boars already had its front trotters stuck in the earth, while the other tried gouging at the mound with its curling tusks, only to get their razor-sharp length caught there.

Mari was quite still, almost as if unaware of the devastation around her. From where Buzz stood, he could see the fear in Skip's face, but Mari's eyes were closed. Her whole being was bathed in a ruby light as the belt around her waist gave off a fierce red glow. And she was smiling.

Up ahead, Buzz saw more trees toppling like wooden bowling pins as everything within the crater writhed and flexed again, sending a huge reverberation through the ground.

Mari's doing this, Buzz realised, *with the help of that belt. And she can't sto—*

The thought was broken as Buzz saw a giant tree hurtling towards Ayiyi, who was still curled up in a ball.

"Ayiyi, watch out!" he cried. The spider tried to scuttle away, but he was not quite quick enough. The tree slammed down on top of him.

"NO!" Buzz rode forwards, even as trees continued to fall all around him. As he got closer to Ayiyi, he saw a couple of hairy legs poking out from among the branches, but there was no movement.

"Ayiyi?" Buzz whispered.

The spider let out a small groan.

Buzz dismounted and tore at the branches to reveal the spider's face. Ayiyi gave him a small smile. "Well, get the rest of this tree off me, then."

The crater gave another shudder and Buzz was thrown to the ground. He lay on the floor for a moment, his head ringing.

The vibrations of the ground went straight through him, wave after wave, like the sea, unending. Mari had become a force of nature.

"Eh, brother, don't sleep on the job. Get me out of here," Ayiyi yelled. "Before another tree drops on my head."

Dora was making scared little snorting sounds but hadn't galloped away.

Buzz flipped himself onto his hands and knees and crawled back over to the spider. He grabbed the tree and lifted, feeling a surge of strength in his hands. He threw the trunk to one side.

Ayiyi lay quite still.

"Hey, you all right?" Buzz asked.

Ayiyi nodded. "Just nice to have breath in my chest again." He flexed his legs gingerly. "But something needs to be done about that girl. She's out of control."

Buzz looked over at Mari. Her eyes were still closed. She was completely lost in the power of the belt.

Another fierce tremor went through the crater, toppling more trees. Soft, round fruits that looked a bit like plums scattered as the trees hit the ground.

Buzz picked one up. It was mushy in his hands.

"Wakey, wakey, Mari," he said softly and, calling on the strength of his armlets, he hurled the fruit at her.

He missed.

"Come on, you've got to do better than that," Ayiyi complained. "You're relying too much on the armlets. They give you strength, but the rest is up to you."

Buzz remembered how he'd thrown his phone at the feathered dragon. *He'd managed to find his target then and that was before the armlets.*

He threw another piece of fruit. He missed again.

Mate, you're overthinking it. You gotta kind of squint at it and then lob it. The words were Sam's. *They were a memory.* He'd say this whenever they played basketball. It'd been a while since they'd done that.

Buzz narrowed his eyes and lobbed another piece of fruit at Mari. It hit her on the shoulder with a wet squelching sound.

"Bull's-eye," Ayiyi crowed.

"Gross!" Buzz heard Mari cry. Her eyes were open and she was blinking furiously.

The tremors had stopped entirely, and the belt no longer glowed. She was looking down at the boars, still trapped in the mound she had created, like she wasn't sure how it had happened.

Buzz swiftly clambered onto Dora, and Ayiyi slipped on behind him. They cantered over to Mari. The boars began to thrash even more wildly as they came closer, but they could not free themselves.

Wisely, Dora still gave them a wide berth. Mari looked down at them and then pointed to the squished-up fruit on her top. "I'm guessing this is your doing?"

"I didn't know how else to stop you," Buzz confessed.

Mari scrubbed at her face. "I glad you did. Thanks, Buzz. I don't think I could have stopped myself. The belt was too powerful. It felt too good."

She urged Skip down the mound, careful to avoid the trapped boars.

"How did you even get the belt to work?" Buzz asked as Mari drew alongside him.

"I'm not exactly sure," she admitted. "I was trapped and needed a way out, and the next moment, the belt had taken over. It was like I knew how to access its power, or at least some part of me did."

"Gu did say the belt held the power of iron ore," Buzz reminded her. "I guess that means it can control the earth."

"But who's controlling me?" Mari asked. "I'm sure Hel helped me activate the belt. She must have been there. Steering me."

"Did you feel her?"

Mari shook her head.

"Maybe it was just your instinct and not the goddess," Buzz said. "You should trust it. It saved you."

Mari ducked her head and then looked behind her at the boars as Dora and Skip galloped across the interior of the crater. "Do you think they'll be all right?"

"You really care?" Buzz asked.

"We came into their territory, Buzz, not the other way round. We were warned."

Buzz felt the weight of someone's gaze on him. He looked

up and saw Priparchis staring down at them from the rim of the crater. The god's blue eyes were still piercing, even from this distance, and Buzz could feel their judgement. "They'll be fine," Buzz said. "Priparchis will make sure of that."

CHAPTER SIXTEEN

RIDDLES

As they finally reached the top of the crater, they were greeted by the wisdom path, which stretched out before them. Black stone slabs stood regally alongside the path as it curved steeply up the mountainside. The peak looked close and although the summit was thick with white mist, Buzz could see the shadow of something behind it – a temple just visible. *The Myth Keeper.* They were close.

Skip gingerly put his front hooves on the steep mountain path but immediately began to slip and scrabble to stay upright.

Mari drew him back. "Careful, Skip."

Dora was shaking her head. "I think this is where we will have to leave you, boy and girl rider," she said. "We can't climb that path, as much as we'd like to."

"Wait!" Skip said. "Maybe we can try and—"

"You've both been amazing," Mari interrupted. "And we

thank you for that." She reached out and stroked their shaggy manes. "But we're not going to risk your lives any more than we have already."

Buzz felt a flicker of annoyance. Mari was right. But why did she always feel the need to take charge?

Buzz dismounted and rubbed Dora's neck as Ayiyi got down as well. "Thank you," he said. "For everything."

The horse gave a wheezing laugh. "This is the most fun this old nag has had for years. Thank you." She butted her head gently against Skip's side. "Come on. Time for us to go."

Mari got down and hugged both horses. "We'll miss you. Make sure you avoid those giants and those boars, okay?"

"We'll take the long way round." Dora looked over at Ayiyi. "You look after them," she said.

"As much as they'll let me," the spider replied.

"I guess that will have to do." Dora didn't sound that impressed. "Come now, Skip."

The horses turned and walked back down the winding trail. Before long, the path curved and took them out of sight completely.

"And then there were three," Mari murmured.

"Not for long," Buzz said. "Come on – the sooner we find the Myth Keeper, the sooner we find Sam."

They climbed the path, Ayiyi scuttling along easily while Buzz and Mari puffed and panted with every step up the mountainside. Buzz focused on keeping his feet moving, one after the other, as they climbed the steep trail, passing the stone slabs as they went. But his legs were tired, and his thigh still ached from where he'd injured it on the side of the gorge. He no longer bothered to check where the Keeper's temple was, as it never seemed to get any closer.

His fingers went to the armlets; he touched the cold metal. If he just called on the armlets' powers, he'd have the strength to bound up this mountain in no time at all.

"Don't even think about it," Mari said. She wiped a bead of sweat from her brow. "We need to save the magic for when we really need it, or it will take us over."

"But we do need it," Buzz said. "We're running out of time, and we're not getting any closer to that blasted summit."

"Wait a second." Mari stopped. "You know what? We're not getting closer, are we? Something's not right here."

Ayiyi scuttled over to them. "Eh! It took you a long time to figure that one out. Thought you'd never look up from your feet." He gave a cackling laugh. "You need to look ahead to get ahead, dum-dums."

"Honestly, Ayiyi, you could have given us a clue." Mari scanned the path carefully as she moved forwards.

"Why didn't you tell us we were missing something?" Buzz demanded. "And don't call us dum-dums."

Ayiyi was laughing, wiping the tears from his many eyes. "This is the wisdom path, dum-dum. I can't tell you what to do or you'll never get to where you need to get to."

"Then what exactly is the point of you being here?" Buzz asked.

"I'm your companion," Ayiyi said. "I thought I was your friend."

"Well, you thought wrong. All you do is laugh at us and tell silly stories, and then you end up needing to be saved. You're a waste of space."

Ayiyi's shoulders slumped. "Oh, I see. I'll go then, shall I? If I'm so useless."

"Yep, you do that. Crawl back to whatever hole you came from."

"Farewell then, brother." The spider sniffed and then turned around and began to drag his eight legs back down the path. He glanced over his shoulder. "I'll see you, then."

"Perhaps." Buzz turned his back on the spider. He knew he was being harsh, but he couldn't stop himself.

"Hey, Buzz, you need to come and see this." Mari was a little bit further along the path.

He arrived at her side.

"Where's Ayiyi?" she asked. "He'll like this."

"He wandered off. Think he saw a bug he liked the look of." The lie fell easily from Buzz's lips. "What have you found?"

"There's a riddle carved into this stele," she said, pointing to one of the stone slabs at the side of the path. "Think you can solve it?"

"'My first is in earthwards but not in hardhearted,'" Buzz read out. The riddle continued:

My second is in helps but not in spell.
My third is in devoid but not in divide.
My fourth is in toughness but not in unsought.
My fifth is in solve but not in sole.
My sixth is in raider but not in raid.
My seventh is in unstressed but not in untested.

He shook his head. "I don't get it."

Mari was grinning at him. "Lucky you've got me, then, even if you don't appreciate it. Each part of this riddle is trying to get you to identify a letter." She pointed to the first line. "You see the words *earthwards* and *hardhearted*? They both have exactly the same letters except for the letter *W*."

Buzz studied the next line. "Okay, so the answer to the second line must be *H*."

"Exactly," Mari said. "And the answer to the third line is *O*."

"'Who,'" Buzz said. He scanned the other lines. "'Whoever'. Once you work out all the letters, it spells out 'whoever'."

The stele flashed once as if to say, *Well done.*

"Quick work," Mari said.

"Well, we did have a lot of practice solving riddles when we were looking for the runes," Buzz reminded her.

"I remember. We made a great team." Mari's voice almost sounded wistful.

Buzz felt something twist in his chest but ignored it and looked up ahead. "Do you think there is a riddle on each of these slabs?"

"No, I don't think so," Mari said. "There's a pattern. Look, the next stele is over there. It was blank but now it has words on it. We needed to be looking ahead this whole time. Ayiyi was right." She looked over her shoulder. "I hope he catches up with us soon."

"Come on," Buzz said. "Let's not waste time."

They raced over to the next slab. "The answer is 'tells'," Mari said after studying the stele for less than a minute. It flashed once in response.

"The answer is 'the', Buzz said on the third stone slab. This stele flashed, too.

They stopped in front of the fourth stele. Buzz saw right away that the riddle here was in a different format from the first three.

I can bore or amuse.
I can teach or entertain.
I can be long.
I can be tall.
I can be true, I can be false,
I can be about nothing at all.

"I can't work this one out." Mari chewed her lip. "Where's Ayiyi? He must have finished hunting for bugs by now. We need his help."

"Won't I do?" Buzz raised an eyebrow.

"I didn't mean it like that, Buzz," Mari said. "I'm just saying Ayiyi has a way with words. He's always telling stories and singing songs. Haven't you noticed?"

"Of course I've noticed. It's really irritating." Buzz wrinkled his nose. "He's gone now, though."

Mari stared at him. "Gone?"

Buzz scrubbed at his face. The armlets were cool against his cheeks. "I kinda lost my temper with him and told him to go, and he did."

Mari sighed. "Dum-dum. We could use him now, couldn't we? Do you think he's coming back?"

Buzz shrugged. "I don't know, and I don't care." He looked up at the stele. "Let's get on with this riddle."

"Okay, we don't really have any other choice, do we?" Mari sounded unhappy. "'I can bore or amuse. I can teach or entertain,'" she read out.

"It sounds a bit like my teachers," Buzz said.

"But would you ever describe your teachers as being long?" Mari questioned. "Or of being nothing at all?"

"No, not even Theo would say that," Buzz admitted. "The only thing this is describing is one of Ayiyi's stories."

Mari grabbed his hand. "That's it." Her eyes were wide behind her glasses. "The answer is 'story'. It can be long, it can be tall. It can be about anything at all." The stele flashed at them, letting them know they were right.

They raced from the stele and swiftly solved the next two riddles. The low shape of the temple could be seen more clearly now behind the thick mist, but as they came to the last stone slab, Buzz saw that the path had run out. There was only air and cloud between where they stood on a rocky ledge and where the Keeper's temple hovered.

"How are we going to get to the temple?" Buzz asked. "There's no path."

"I don't know," Mari said. "But I think the answer has to do with this stele. I just don't understand why no words are appearing on it."

"Okay, let's try to finish this sentence we've put together so far from the clues," Buzz said.

Mari pushed her glasses up her nose. "'Whoever tells the story holds the . . .'"

"Key," Buzz said.

The stele remained blank.

"The secret?" Mari asked hopefully.

Still the stele remained blank.

"This is hopeless," Mari said. "What hope have we got of solving a blank riddle? It's not fair."

"Hope is the power to see light even in the darkness," Buzz murmured, Ayiyi's words from the canyon coming back to him. "Hope is the power to find an answer when there appears to be none." Buzz looked at the stele. "The answer is 'power'," he whispered. "Whoever tells the story holds the power."

Buzz knew what he had to do. He clenched his fist and punched the stone. The sound of cracking filled the air and the stele crumbled. As it did so, the fragments of rock flew up in an arch and knitted together to form a narrow bridge to the temple.

"How did you know what the answer was?" Mari asked, as Buzz stepped onto the stone bridge that now stretched across the sky.

"It doesn't matter now." He held out a hand. "Be careful, this stone is slippery."

They inched along the length of the bridge, and beneath it, Buzz saw only clouds. He decided that looking forwards rather than down definitely made the most sense.

They stepped off the bridge and arrived in front of the temple.

"Wait." Mari's voice was full of amazement. "I don't think this is mist."

Buzz reached out. She was right. The substance around them was thick and sticky.

He tore into it, grabbing handfuls at a time. Mari did the same. White tendrils clung to their fingers, but still they grabbed and pulled and tore, and soon they had created a hole big enough for them both to wriggle through.

Within the white cocoon, the air was very still and quiet, but there was a golden light all around them. Ahead stood a dome-shaped edifice built from multicoloured brick with eight channels leading from it. The channels were filled with light – light that seemed to pulse with the same golden glow as the steles that had lined the wisdom path.

"I think this is it," Buzz said. "The Keeper's temple."

"Then what are we waiting for?" Mari said. "Everything we need to know to save Sam – to save all of us – is in there."

They took a step towards the temple, but Buzz stopped when he heard a crunching sound underfoot. Looking down, he saw that the floor was lined with what appeared to be the torn pages of books. He bent down and scooped up a page. The script on the page was in a language he did not understand, but it was beautifully drawn.

They resumed their walking, and soon they were almost at the door of the temple, and Buzz could see that the building was not made of bricks at all, but rather books – books that shimmered. Some big and some small. Some thin and some fat. Some new and some old. They were piled one on top of the other, so high that Buzz had to tip his head all the way back to be able to see the smooth, rounded pinnacle of the building.

Stairs made of yet more books led up to the arched doorway, and the door itself – which was made of something like thick, aged papyrus – stood ajar.

They climbed the stairs of books and entered the temple.

CHAPTER SEVENTEEN

MYTH KEEPER

It was dark. Buzz's eyes ached as he tried to search out any pinprick of light. In the darkness he could hear a low swell of voices, but it was as if they were coming from under water.

A beam of light cut across the dark and then widened, illuminating the whole room.

Buzz looked over to see Mari holding her watch aloft and light flooding from it.

They were in a sparsely furnished room. A simple table with an inkwell stood in the centre, shelves full of stone tables rose up one wall, and freestanding mirrors lined the edges of the chamber. Looking closely at the mirrors, Buzz saw that many of them were dark or clouded with age and showed no reflection at all. Low voices seemed to come from each one, and the words rolled and tumbled over one another so that all Buzz could hear was noise.

"It was like this in the beginning," a woman's voice pierced the cacophany. "There was just noise. No stories. No meaning. No wisdom. Just noise."

Buzz and Mari both turned in a circle, but neither could tell where the voice had come from. It did not speak again.

Buzz found his reflection in one of the mirrors and came to a halt. He looked tired and bruised. The Forsaken Territories had taken their toll. He was studying the purple bruises streaking his face when suddenly he saw someone standing behind him. It was a woman with deep brown skin and a towering headscarf. She was wrapped in swathes of brightly coloured fabric and held a large book in the crook of her arm.

Buzz whipped around, but there was no one behind him.

"What the—"

"What's wrong?" Mari asked.

"I saw a woman," Buzz said. "She was standing behind me in the mirror. I think it was the Myth Keeper."

He looked back at the glass, willing the woman to reappear, but all he saw was his reflection and its wide, anxious gaze.

Mari let out a gasp.

"What? Did you see her?" Buzz asked.

"No, something else." Mari was still staring at the mirror in front of her. "I thought I saw Ayiyi. But I'm not sure."

Buzz shoved a hand through his thick, curly hair, fingers snagging for a moment. It hurt, but he didn't care. "Stop playing games," he said to the room. "We answered your riddles. If you are the Myth Keeper, show yourself."

The glass in one of the mirrors shattered at his words, and the lady in the long colourful robes stepped into the room.

She dusted some shards off her shoulders, and the glass tinkled as it hit the floor. "Hmm, interesting. Many of the people who seek me like the smoke-and-mirrors stuff." She came and stood directly in front of them. "I guess you're not one of them."

"Are you the Myth Keeper?" Buzz asked.

"I am," the lady replied. "I have many other names besides. But you can call me Aunt Nancy."

"Aunt Nancy," Mari repeated. "Why does that sound familiar?"

The lady gave an elegant shrug. "Maybe my reputation precedes me."

Buzz held out a hand. "I'm Buzz, and this is Mari."

Aunt Nancy inclined her head but ignored the outstretched hand. "Welcome to the chamber of stories. My home."

Mari was scanning the room with a puzzled look on her face. "I was kind of expecting more books," she said.

Aunt Nancy smiled. "Young lady, did you fail to notice that my temple is *built* out of books?"

Mari looked sheepish. "I wasn't criticising. I just thought there'd be more books, especially if this is the chamber of stories."

"Mari, does it really matter?" Buzz began.

Aunt Nancy held up a hand. "There is nothing wrong with being inquisitive," she said. "It is one of the ways we acquire wisdom. Another is through stories." Aunt Nancy readjusted the large book that lay in the crook of her arm. "We told those stories with our voices first of all and then we wrote our stories on stone. That is what this chamber preserves. Behind each mirror lives an early storyteller."

A sharp tapping suddenly came from behind one of the mirrors.

Aunt Nancy tutted. "Please ignore the noise. Some storytellers also happen to be annoying little critters." Aunt Nancy clicked her fingers and one of the darkened mirrors lit up, revealing a familiar spindly figure.

"Ayiyi!" Mari exclaimed.

The spider was tapping on the glass with all eight of his legs, but his little face looked strangely blank.

"Let him go," Mari demanded.

"I'm afraid I can't do that." Aunt Nancy swept across the room and placed the large book on the table. Its title, *The Book of Wonders,* was emblazoned in gold on the spine. "I'm the Myth Keeper. I'm the guardian of stories. All stories. That spider has been telling tales for centuries, and they were never written down. His place is here in the chamber of stories, where he can be protected along with the others." She clicked her fingers again and the rest of the darkened mirrors around the room lit up. Buzz could now clearly see other figures behind the panes of glass. A man with a harp sat alone, plucking the strings, his mouth open in song. An old woman wrapped in furs sat cross-legged in front of a fire, and her hands drew shapes in the air. Buzz saw another who wore a mask and told a story while dancing. "He and all the rest are my wards," Aunt Nancy explained.

"Prisoners, you mean." Mari's fingers went to her belt and grazed the iron.

"Never," Aunt Nancy replied. "Here, at least, they are safe and never forgotten. If we lose our stories, we lose ourselves." She sighed. "Ayiyi's place is with me – he knows that. He should never have left."

Buzz looked at those behind the mirrors. All the other storytellers did look happy – not even aware that their world existed behind glass. All except Ayiyi. He continued to tap on his mirror.

He's not my problem, Buzz thought. *Don't get distracted.*

"We'll buy his freedom," Mari insisted. "There must be a price."

Aunt Nancy gave a husky laugh. "Come now. You didn't come here to buy this arachnid's freedom. Forget about him and tell me why you are really here before I lose patience."

"We're not leaving without Ayiyi." Mari whirled round to face Buzz. "Right?"

"We need to stay focused," Buzz said. "We're here to find Sam. Ayiyi isn't our responsibility, and it's not like he's in danger."

"But he doesn't want to be here." Mari was looking at him like he was a stranger, and Buzz hated it. "We need to do something."

Aunt Nancy drummed her fingers on the table. "A story would do it. Perhaps. The better the story, the more currency you have to spend, but ultimately it is the book that will decide if you are worthy of help." She opened the tome and began riffling through its gilt-edged leaves, until she came to some blank pages. She then took a black feather quill from the inkwell on the table.

"Buzz, we have to try," Mari said. "Our story will be enough to save both of them."

"But what if it isn't?" Buzz shot back. "You'd endanger everything to save that spider? You didn't even like him at first." Buzz twisted one of his armlets. The skin beneath felt like it was on fire. "What about Sam? What about getting the runes back from El Tunchi and stopping him? What about defeating Berchta and the rest of the Pantheon before they try to take control again?"

"It's okay," Mari said. "The Book of Wonders will find our story worthy. Because it is."

Aunt Nancy looked up. "So certain, Mari." She tapped the quill gently on the edge of the inkwell. "The Book of Wonders will need more than just a retelling of your quest so far. It will need more than flowery descriptions of friends and foes. It has plenty of those. It has the best of those. Scheherazade, Hercules and Gilgamesh. Beowulf and King Arthur. No, what the book needs from you is a story full of drama. It needs heart. It needs truth and a little bit of pain."

"We understand," Mari said.

"But first we need to know if you can help us," Buzz said. "Help us find our friend Sam."

Aunt Nancy inclined her head. "I know where they are keeping the new god. And I can get you both there. Right into the heart of the Jade Pavilion."

Buzz expelled a deep breath. "Is he all right?" he asked. "Do you know if he's safe?"

"Of course he is safe," Aunt Nancy said. "He is the new god. They want him to start the revolution. He is precious."

Precious. The word jabbed at Buzz's insides. A stab of jealousy that he couldn't ignore. *Sam's a god,* Buzz thought. *Mari has a sleeping goddess inside her. And I'm the guardian of the runes, with no runes to guard. A joke.*

"Buzz." Mari's voice was coming from far away. "Buzz! Come on, we need to start."

He blinked. "I'm sorry, start what?"

Aunt Nancy adjusted her robes with an angry flick of her wrists. "I said tell me your tale. Let's discover whether the book considers it worthy."

Buzz looked at Mari. "Let's begin."

So Buzz and Mari did. They told Aunt Nancy about Esther and the Pantheon. Buzz did his best to explain how he had felt when he saw Sam disappear through the arch and when the giant had him in his grasp. Mari described how it had felt to use the belt for the first time. The rush she experienced at seeing the very earth obey her command.

The whole time, the Myth Keeper wrote down their words. Laughing at points and looking worried at others.

"And that's the story up to now," Mari said at last. "Here we are in the chamber of stories, and we really hope the Book of Wonders will find our story worthy, because we need to save Sam."

The Myth Keeper placed both hands on the open book. She frowned.

"Oh dear. I'm afraid the book is not speaking to me." She looked at them with pity. "It does not want to help you."

CHAPTER EIGHTEEN

THE OTHER SIDE OF THE MIRROR

"What?" Mari said. "Why?"

"I don't know for sure. I wonder if you've given the book enough drama. If the heart of your story has really been revealed."

"Of course it has," Buzz said.

"Tell me, why are you saving Sam?" The Myth Keeper asked.

"That's obvious. Because he's my friend."

"But he didn't tell you what was happening to him." Aunt Nancy tipped her head to one side. "Surely a friend would share that?"

"I don't know why he didn't tell me," Buzz confessed.

"Such a shame," Aunt Nancy continued. "Because if he had told you, Berchta may have never got hold of him."

"You're not being fair," Mari interjected. "Why are you attacking him?"

"And tell me, Mari, why are *you* looking for Sam? He's not your friend."

"No, he's Buzz's friend, but—"

"But if you find him, you get the Runes of Valhalla back, and you get to stop Berchta. Maybe even find out what happened to your great-uncle Benjamin all those years ago. Revenge would be sweet, no? You're sick of all these gods taking control of mortals. Taking control of you."

"Listen—" Buzz began.

Aunt Nancy turned in his direction and wagged a finger at him. "Admit it, Buzz. Sam was a friend once, but now you are searching for him because you want to get the runes back and stop this El Tunchi and the threat he holds over your mother."

"No, that's not true." Buzz stopped for a moment. *The book wants truth.* "Okay, yes, we need him to get the runes back from El Tunchi, but that's not the only—"

"I see."

"No, you don't," Buzz said. "Because even if Sam wasn't able to help us, I'd still be here. I'd still be trying to save him. Because he is my friend, and I don't care what you think."

Aunt Nancy put her quill down. "Okay, let's say that is true. Aren't you fed up? Don't you wish you could do it all yourself? Stop Berchta, stop El Tunchi? Not have to ask for anyone's help at all?"

"Of course not." Mari scoffed. "Me and Buzz are a team.

He wouldn't want to do this on his own."

The Myth Keeper raised an eyebrow. "Really?"

Buzz opened his mouth, then closed it again, wishing that Aunt Nancy would stop asking questions.

"Aren't you going to answer her?" Mari asked. Her voice sounded as hard as Buzz's armlets.

"Okay, fine." Buzz frowned. "Sometimes it feels like it would be easier to be doing this by myself, okay? There, I *said it.*" He shook his head. "You always want to do things your way, Mari. Do this, don't do that. Save the spider. It's like you don't realise we have a mission here."

Mari's face looked hurt and then angry. "I apologise. I didn't realise saving the world with me was so annoying." She crossed her arms. "No wonder Sam didn't want to tell you what was happening to him. He probably knew you'd be upset that *you* weren't the manifesting god."

"Take that back." Buzz could feel heat building up in his chest and exploding onto his neck and cheeks.

"I won't." Mari glared at him. "You wish you were the one with all the power. That's why you keep trying to prove yourself and do stupid things." She'd begun pacing backwards and forwards. "You hated listening to Ayiyi, and that's why you got rid of him, and it's why you keep on using those armlets even though Gu said you shouldn't—"

She broke off as the book in front of Aunt Nancy began to vibrate and then spark with light.

The Myth Keeper clapped her hands in delight. "Oh yes, very good! That will do. That will do nicely."

"Do?" Buzz could still feel the heat on his neck and cheeks.

"Yes," Aunt Nancy said. "I told you, the book needs truth. It needs heart. It needs drama and a little pain. You have given it enough of that now."

But at what cost? Buzz wondered. *My friendship with Mari?* He shrugged off the thought. *Maybe it's for the best. Friendship just complicates things anyway.*

"What now?" he asked. "Will you get us to the Jade Pavilion?"

"Yes, the book will see to that," Aunt Nancy said.

"And what about Ayiyi?" Mari said.

"Ayiyi will remain." Aunt Nancy put a finger to her lips. "Shh, let's not speak of him any more."

Buzz caught sight of a small black tattoo on the outside of Aunt Nancy's fingertip. It was very small, but it was clearly in the shape of a spider.

"You're not listening." Mari's jaw was set. "He's coming with us." And then she was gone, sprinting over to the mirror where Ayiyi was still tapping on the glass. "Stand back," she shouted and touched a link in her belt.

"Mari! No!" But Buzz's words were drowned out as the ground beneath Ayiyi's mirrored prison began to tremble. It sent fierce vibrations out into the rest of the chamber of stories, and Aunt Nancy gave a yelp of alarm as a couple of mirrors near her began to shudder.

Buzz heard a tearing sound and then saw six more arms shoot out from the Keeper's robe. They grew longer and longer and stretched out to keep two mirrors in place and catch a few of the falling stone tablets.

She has eight arms, Buzz thought. E*ight arms.*

"Don't just stare," Aunt Nancy demanded. "Help me."

Buzz ran over to hold another mirror in place. This one contained the old lady in furs. The storyteller looked away from her fire for a moment to peer at Buzz through the glass. And then Buzz was on the other side of the mirror. Standing by the fire.

"Search for the bear," the old lady said. "And when you find him, say the prayer just like this." Her lips moved but Buzz heard no sound. The old lady smiled, and Buzz saw that her teeth were black. "Good," she said. "Good."

She gazed at the flames once more even as the ground continued to shake, and then Buzz was back in the chamber, the smell of wood smoke still in his nose. The mirror holding Ayiyi was almost a blur as it continued to vibrate in front of Mari. Then, with a cracking sound, the glass came away from the frame in a shower of shards.

Mari jumped back and the tremors stopped immediately. Ayiyi had slumped forwards and lay motionless on the floor.

"No!" Mari cried. "No! What have I done?" She sat down and scooped up the spider, cradling him in her arms. "I was just trying to help." She looked up at Buzz, tears streaming down her face. "He's not moving. He's not breathing. I think he's dead."

Buzz released the mirror he was holding and rushed over to his friend. He wanted to say or do something to make her feel better, but he didn't know what that was. He could hear Ayiyi's voice in his head. "Eh, brother, don't be silly. Tell her how you feel. Tell her you're sorry."

Buzz twisted at his armlets, where his skin felt itchy and hot, and the words of comfort seemed to flee his brain.

Aunt Nancy released her mirrors and strode over to Mari. The Myth Keeper loomed over her. "That was a very stupid and very dangerous thing to do, and all for that thing." Aunt Nancy poked the spider with her toe.

"Don't you dare." Mari batted away the Keeper's foot.

Aunt Nancy tutted. "Calm yourself, girl." She knelt down and lifted the spider by one leg. "It's not real, you know."

"What?" Mari stared at the spider.

"It's a model. A decoy," Aunt Nancy explained.

"So where is the real Ayiyi?" Mari was on her feet. "You'd better not have hurt him."

"She hasn't hurt him," Buzz said, finally putting all the pieces together. All the clues had been there: the Keeper's temple with its eight channels and domed middle, the thick white webbing that had surrounded it, the black tattoo of the spider, and Aunt Nancy's eight arms. "Aunt Nancy *is* Ayiyi. Or rather, Ayiyi is her."

Mari was looking at the Myth Keeper in bemusement.

"What? Because she has eight arms?" She peered over the top of her glasses. "Hang on. When did you get eight arms?"

"That doesn't matter." Aunt Nancy was grinning. "Buzz is right. Looks like he is starting to use his brain again and not just rely on his brawn. Mari, all is not lost." As she said this, her robes began to fall away.

Buzz screwed his eyes shut. He really did not want to see a naked spider lady.

"Eh, brother, you're okay to look." Buzz tentatively lifted one eyelid to see Ayiyi standing there with a pool of bright cloth at his feet.

"What exactly is going on here?" Mari asked. She held the dummy of Ayiyi in her hand, and it flopped about as she gave it a shake.

"I'm the Myth Keeper," the spider said simply. "I'm Ayiyi. I'm Aunt Nancy. I am Anansi."

"I know you." Buzz breathed. His mother had told him tales of Anansi when he was much younger. Anansi, the trickster spider god from West Africa and the Caribbean. The god who had stolen all the stories and given wisdom to humanity.

Mari slapped a hand against her forehead. "I knew that name Aunt Nancy sounded familiar!"

Ayiyi chuckled. "Yes, I fooled you longer than I thought, but then, you've been distracted, haven't you, Mari?"

"I guess," Mari admitted.

"Distracted," Buzz repeated. "Why?"

"Eh, brother," Ayiyi said. "You're a slow learner, but it's all part of your story." The spider shook his head. "She's worried about . . . about how you've changed."

"Still changing," Mari corrected.

"I haven't changed!" Buzz protested.

The spider waved away the words with a flick of one of his legs. "Save it." He scuttled over to Buzz and stared at him with all twelve of his eyes. "I met you on the wisdom path because I needed to know that you were worthy of my help."

"You did it because you are a trickster," Buzz retorted. "You did it because you could, and because you thought it would make a good story."

"You're wrong," Ayiyi said. "I tested you because this quest will test you. I want you to be strong enough to succeed, and you could be, but only if you take the help of others."

"Fine," Buzz said with a sigh. "Can we just—"

Ayiyi tutted. "You are not listening, Buzz. The Book of Wonders tells me what is to come as well as what has been. Your battle will be close, too close to call. You are lucky to have Mari by your side. She could tip the scales."

Buzz glanced at Mari, expecting to see a gloating expression, but she refused to look at him.

Whatever, Buzz thought. *This part of our quest is finished. That's the important thing.*

"Understood, Ayiyi," Buzz said. "I'll take that on. I promise. Now we really need to get going."

"Yes, you do." The spider gently stood the Book of Wonders up on the floor and stepped backwards. "There you go," he said.

"There you go?" Mari repeated.

"Come, come, Mari. What do you do with a book?"

Mari looked sheepish. "You open it." She stepped forwards to do just that, but then stopped and looked over her shoulder. "Unless you want to do it, Buzz? I don't want to take over or anything."

Buzz was sure she was being sarcastic, but he ignored her, and kneeling down, he yanked open the book. It shook furiously in response, and the pages began to flap wildly, cutting at his hands.

"Ouch." Buzz watched the blood seep from the papercut on his finger. It was so dark it was almost black. He sucked on his finger, tasting iron.

He heard a sound like leather stretching, and he saw that the book was growing, shooting up in height and broadening in width. Soon it was taller than Buzz and had quadrupled in width. And still it grew.

Mari was looking up at the book as it towered above them, her face filled with wonder, and it made Buzz smile. *It's like all her Christmases have come at once,* he thought. *All she needed was a giant book.* The pages of the book suddenly stopped flapping. It had come to rest on a blank page.

Ayiyi offered Buzz the inkwell and quill from the table. "Tell it where you want to go."

Buzz took the quill. It felt strangely fragile in his hand.

He tried to scratch out Sam's name on the expanse of white paper in front of him, but blobs of ink just splattered on the page. His hands felt awkward and heavy in the armlets. He couldn't even form a letter.

"How do I write with this thing?" he complained.

Mari took the quill from his hand. "I'll help you." In a smooth, flowing script, she wrote Sam's name.

"Perhaps we should do his full name," Buzz said. "Just so we're absolutely clear."

Mari nodded. "Yeah, you can never be too sure when it comes to magic."

She penned his full name, *Samraj Matharu*. "What else shall we put on here?" she asked, quill ready.

"Write 'Jade Pavilion' down," Buzz said.

Mari quickly inked the words, the quill scratching loudly against the paper. She took a step back, and the words began to move around the page. They circled one another on the paper like a cat stalking its prey, and then the words ran into each other, blurring into one dark blot of ink.

The ink shimmered there, a lake of black on the page.

"Dive in, then," Ayiyi said with a wink. "A new realm awaits. Good luck."

Buzz and Mari looked at each other, and then stepped into the darkness.

PART III

CHOICES

CHAPTER NINETEEN

THE JADE PAVILLION

Buzz coughed and the taste of ink filled his mouth. He spat to his right and then rolled onto his back with a groan. His eyes were closed, but he could hear the patter of rain on a hard roof, and he felt humid dampness all around him. He opened his eyes, but everything was still black. He reached out, but it was so dark he couldn't even see his hand. His fingers touched smooth, cold stone.

"Mari," Buzz called out. "Mari! Where are you?" His voice echoed back at him. It sounded small and worried.

"I'm right here." Mari's voice was soothing, and soon light filled the room. She sat just a little way to his left, holding her watch aloft.

"Oh," Buzz replied, feeling a bit silly. "Sorry I shouted."

"It's all right. I think you've damaged one of my ears, but I have another one." Mari got to her feet. "You sounded scared."

Buzz shrugged. "Just wanted to make sure you'd kept up."

Mari snorted. "Yeah, sure."

Buzz ignored her comment. "Come on, let's go find Sam."

"All right, but first we need to work out how we get out of here." Mari's flashlight flared even more brightly and revealed a room made of shiny green bricks. "I can't see a door."

Buzz quickly scanned his surroundings. Mari was right. He began feeling the walls, searching for some nook or cranny that might reveal how they could escape the room.

"What is this stuff?" he asked, touching the smooth, cool greenness of the wall.

"Jade, I think." Mari was busy, methodically illuminating each of the bricks in turn. "Ha! There you are," she said with satisfaction.

"What'd you find?" Buzz asked.

"See this brick here?" Mari pointed with her flashlight. "It's a bit shinier and smoother than the others."

"Like it's been rubbed at," Buzz said.

"Exactly!"

They scooted over to the brick, and Mari and Buzz stretched out their fingers at the same time and rubbed at it.

The brick shuddered and then pushed outwards so that it stood out from the rest of the wall like a handle. Green light trickled from the raised brick and then raced up the wall, etching the outline of a door.

Mari grinned. "That's more like it."

They both began to pull on the brick, but the door did not budge. “It's no good,” Mari panted.

“Let me do it,” Buzz said. “I'll use the armlets.”

Mari frowned. “Every time you use them, Buzz, you get worse.”

“Stop it, will you?” Buzz pleaded. “The armlets aren't changing me.”

“Fine, don't listen to me.” She stepped back and did a gallant bow. “The door is all yours.”

“Thank you.” Buzz mimicked her movements. Mari wasn't the only one who could bow sarcastically. He closed his eyes and called for the strength in his armlets. He braced himself for the surge of heat. The pain in his wrists. But nothing happened. No heat. No pain. No strength. He tried again. Still nothing.

“They're not working,” Buzz said.

“Really?” Mari questioned. “Are you doing it right?”

“Of course I'm doing it right.” A knot had formed in Buzz's throat. The idea of not having the power of the armlets made him feel sick.

“Maybe you've just overused them,” Mari said. “Let me try the belt. Maybe I can shake the door open.”

She put her fingers to her belt and screwed up her face in concentration.

Buzz thought she looked a bit like she had wind, and he laughed despite himself.

“What's funny?” Mari demanded.

“You look constipated.”

"I'm trying to get this belt to work." Mari put her hands on her hips. "And can I just say, you don't look so great either when you're trying to get the armlets to do their thing."

Buzz rolled his eyes. *There's no way I pull a face like Mari's.*

Mari unhooked her belt and dangled it from a finger.

"Why have you taken it off?" Buzz asked. "Try again. I won't take the mick out of you, I promise."

"There's no point," Mari said. "It won't work, and neither will your armlets."

She slumped down against the door.

"What are you talking about?"

"Gu told us. Remember?"

Buzz shook his head.

"He told us that these gifts were to help us in the realm of the Forsaken Territories. Well, we're not there any more, are we? The Jade Pavilion is a different place entirely."

"Well, that's it. They're useless."

"Pretty much." Mari placed her belt on the floor. "They've played their part in our story."

Buzz twisted at the armlet on his right arm and it released with a sticky, squelchy sound. The skin beneath it looked red and mottled. He pulled the armlet off his other wrist and saw that the skin there was the same.

He dropped the armlets to the floor with a clatter and slumped against the door next to Mari. His back grazed the bricks as he slid to the ground.

There was a creak and then a grinding sound as the door behind them gave way and swung outwards. Buzz and Mari nearly toppled over.

Buzz began to laugh, and it felt good. He realised he hadn't laughed properly in a long time. "The door was a push, not a pull. We tried everything but that."

Mari was laughing as well. "Not our brightest moment, admittedly. Let's not tell anyone about this."

"Too late for that," a familiar voice said. "You'd better come in."

"Sam!" Buzz and Mari said at the same time.

They raced through the entrance, and as Buzz's eyes adjusted to the dimly lit room, he could see that they were in a great banquet hall.

Up ahead, on a platform, was a long table, heavy with food and drink. The table was vast and ran along the middle of the room. It was surrounded by individuals who could only be gods and goddesses. A large worm lay curled on one of the chairs, its sightless head bobbing from side to side. Another figure that looked just like a scarecrow stood stiff and tall, his face a mask of deep thought. A man dressed all in black except for a crown of poppies muttered words into a silver goblet while a beautiful lady covered in scales the colour of ocean spray was talking to a moody teenage girl who wore a necklace with a familiar-looking planet hanging from it. At the head of the table sat Sam. His dark hair was pulled back off his forehead and held in place by a circlet made of jade.

There was a small, odd creature perched on Sam's shoulder, and as Buzz got closer, he could see more clearly what it was. The top part of the creature was an old man's head with a wizened face, a long beard, and pointed ears and nose. The bottom half was more squidlike, and its tentacles draped over Sam's neck, chest, and shoulders. One tentacle was even curled around his friend's ear. The tentacles writhed and curled. They looked like they might strangle Sam at any moment.

"It's rude to stare," the creature snapped.

"It's rude to climb on someone's shoulders and strangle them," Buzz snapped back. "So you'd better get off him."

The creature smiled. "Make me," he wheezed.

Sam patted one of the tentacles. "Amin is not strangling me, Buzz. He's my teacher. My friend."

"We're your friends," Buzz shot back.

Sam looked at them balefully. "Is that why you're here? Is that why you came all the way to the Jade Pavilion? To tell me that?"

Mari was looking around at the other gods and goddesses with suspicion. "We'd prefer not to say what we're doing here at this precise moment. It's rather crowded."

Sam laughed. "Mate, if you want privacy, you just need to say." He rose to his feet, and a ball of fire appeared at his fingertips. Those around the table gave a collective gasp of appreciation.

"Who wants a bit of Samster magic?" he called out.

All the gods that had hands raised them. Their eyes were large and pleading. Even without eyes the worm did a good job of looking keen.

"If you can catch it, it's yours." Sam blew on the orb and it hurtled towards one of the closed windows and tore a hole through the jade-green shutters. Each god bowed deeply to Sam before they sped off after it, exiting the banquet hall.

In a moment, only Sam, Amin, Mari, and Buzz remained.

"He needs to go as well," Buzz said, pointing to the squid-man thing.

Sam shook his head. "No, Amin stays with me." He looked Buzz up and down. "Wow, you're looking rough, mate. Try not to make too much of a mess." Buzz looked at his filthy clothes and resisted the urge to brush himself down.

"You're looking quite different yourself," Mari commented. "Some interesting accessories." Her gaze fixed on Amin. "We came to save you, but it doesn't look like you need saving."

"Well, I am a god," Sam said. "I really need to update my profile page, don't I?"

"This isn't a joke, Sam," Buzz said. "The last time we saw you was at the Ash Arch, and you were scared. We couldn't save you then, but we'll do better this time."

Sam held up a hand. "I'm glad you didn't save me, or I would never have met Amin." Sam's voice was steady. "I would have never learnt what I am truly capable of. What it means to be a god."

"So you want to stay here." Buzz let the statement hang. "You want to leave Berchta in Crowmarsh turning everyone into believers? You want the forgotten gods to take over the world?"

"Don't be ridiculous," Sam snapped. "Of course Berchta can't be allowed to do that."

Amin was shaking his head. "We must stop her. We will stop her."

Buzz felt some of the tightness in his chest go. Sam was different for sure. *And I have no idea what this Amin guy is all about, but at least we're all on the same side.*

Mari studied Sam for a moment and then leapt forwards and gripped his arm.

"Hey!" Sam tried to pull himself free. "You're hurting me."

"What is your greatest fear?" she asked.

"Get off me." Sam tried to yank his arm away again. "I could blast you into smithereens you know. Just need to click my fingers."

"Mari, let him go," Buzz pleaded.

"Answer the question," Mari demanded.

"Answer the question," Amin urged.

"Fine," Sam said. "It used to be trifle." He shook his head. "I feel like you knew that. But now it's the thought that we won't stop Berchta and the Pantheon. That they'll take over the world. That good enough for you?"

"Good. You're telling the truth." Mari released his arm. "I wasn't sure, what with the new hairdo and all, but I would have known if you were lying to me."

"Your very own magic power," Sam said. "You'll have to tell me all about it sometime. Buzz never could be bothered to tell me the full story."

"Oh, don't start that again," Buzz said.

Sam held up a hand. "It doesn't matter. I just want to get back to Crowmarsh, but even with all my powers, it's impossible for me to cross into that realm. We've tried."

"There's no way. No way," Amin repeated.

"We can sort that." Buzz took out the twigs Ratatosk had given him. "Get us to an ash tree and we'll be able to use these to open a portal."

"How?" Amin asked. His wheezy voice sounded more breathless than usual.

"Don't know, really. Ratatosk just told me that Mari and I are the only ones who can work them."

"Sounds promising," Sam said. "But before we use the portal, there is something we need to collect first. It will get rid of Berchta and the Pantheon once and for all."

Buzz and Mari shared a look.

"That's great, but we kinda have a plan as well," Buzz explained.

Sam laughed. "But I'm a god, Buzz. My plan trumps yours. Surely you see that?"

"Trump me!" Buzz couldn't believe how arrogant Sam sounded. "We're not playing cards."

Amin tapped Sam with one of his tentacles. "Let them tell

us their plan first," he wheezed. "Always better to have all the information when making a decision."

Sam pursed his lips. It looked like he'd just finished sucking a lemon, but he nodded.

"You better sit down," Mari said. "We have a lot to tell you if our plan is going to make any sense."

Buzz and Mari told Sam and Amin all about their quest to find the Runes of Valhalla – how the runes held the key to awakening the sleeping Norse gods, and how they had been stolen by El Tunchi.

Sam looked thoughtful. "You want me to stop El Tunchi and get the runes back? That's the plan?"

Buzz nodded. "Then we'll be able to stop Berchta."

Sam spread his hands on the banquet table. "Listen. I'm awesome. Fact. I mean, other gods are literally full of awe when they see what I can do, and I'm still learning. But who is this El Tunchi? How do we know for sure I can stop him?"

"It's a risk for sure," Amin said. "I know of El Tunchi – he's a restless spirit, and they're the worst kind because they're empty. Lacking." Amin's eyes became sly. "He'll be searching for something to fill that void." Amin began to cackle wildly. "Probably you, Buzz. Spirits like him often claim the firstborn son in a family."

"What is that about?" Sam asked. "That's always happening in stories. Remember issue eighteen of *Captain Phantom*, Buzz?"

Buzz nodded, but he was thinking of his mother. The fear in

her eyes when she had held his face and begged him not to leave the house. The desperation in his father's note. Amin was right. El Tunchi was in Crowmarsh for him. He was sure if it.

"Listen, mate, I think we'd better go for my plan." Sam made a steeple of his fingers. "Amin's told me of this thing called the cyphon. It can entrap gods, magical beings, spirits. You name it, it does it."

"Where is it?" Buzz asked.

"It's over in the Pearl Tower, right on the edge of the Jade Pavilion." Sam leant back in his chair. "We get the cyphon, and we'll solve our problems in one go. We'll send El Tunchi, Berchta, and the Pantheon to the Forsaken Territories for good."

"Gone, gone, gone," Amin crowed.

"It's the perfect plan. We'll even remember to get those rune things of El Tunchi before we give him the boot for good."

Mari was nodding. "But how do we get the cyphon?"

"Your job is to get us home when the time comes," Sam said, "Amin can get us to the cyphon." He looked at Buzz and Mari. "You ready?"

"Ready!" Buzz and Mari replied.

CHAPTER TWENTY

THE CARVED WALL

"The Pearl Tower awaits us," Amin said. "We must make our way there."

Mari bit her lip. "Won't we be seen?"

"I told you I'm awesome," Sam said. "None of those other gods want to upset me. They all want a bit of the Samster magic."

Amin tapped Sam on his head with one of his tentacles. "The girl is right to be cautious. They want your favour, but that doesn't mean that Berchta doesn't have eyes and ears in this place. We shouldn't go by foot."

Sam scowled. "So what *should* we do?"

Amin smiled and pointed upwards. "You show your friends here some of what I've taught you."

"You're my only friend, Amin," Sam said. "But sure, I'll show them what I can do." He walked over to one of the chamber's jade green shutters and threw it open.

Moonlight poured into the room, and Buzz realised suddenly how much he missed daylight. Almost as much as he missed Sam's friendship.

Sam held his palm flat, and an orb of smoke began to form there. As it grew bigger and bigger, he set it upon the air, where it twisted and turned until it wove itself into the shape of a motorbike.

"That's Captain Phantom's bike!" Buzz exclaimed.

"Yeah." Sam looked pretty pleased with himself. "Exactly like the one he rides in issues three through fifty-seven." He turned to Buzz and Mari. "Ready to ride?"

Mari looked nervous as she approached the window ledge. "What are we supposed to do?" she asked.

"Mate, just jump on it," Sam said. "It'll take us straight to the Pearl Tower."

Mari didn't look convinced. "Will it take our weight? I mean, it's just smoke."

Sam laughed. "Why are you worried?" he asked. "You've got a goddess inside you. She's not going to let you come to any harm."

"I told you before, she's asleep." Mari's hands were clenched. "Besides, I'm my own person. I don't need to rely on her."

Sam raised an eyebrow. "But it's thanks to her that you can read people's greatest fears. Sounds like you might need her just a little bit." He held up his hands. "Listen, I can see it's a sore topic. Let's leave it." Climbing up on the ledge, he jumped onto the bike.

The motorcycle dipped for a moment as Sam sat down and then hovered upwards again so that it was once more at the height of the ledge. Amin gave them a little wave from his perch on Sam's shoulder.

"All right, your turn," Sam said. "Just aim to land right here next to me."

Mari still did not move.

Strange, Buzz thought. *Not like Mari to be scared. Something's bothering her.*

"Look, I'll show you," Buzz said. He leapt off the ledge and landed behind Sam.

He patted the seat behind him. "There's loads of room, Mari."

She nodded, but Buzz could see that her legs were actually shaking. She took a deep breath and leapt from the ledge, her arms and legs cycling through the air. Immediately, Buzz could see that the jump was way too long. He tried to grab at her, but Mari flew straight over the width of the bike.

Fear must have strangled Mari's vocal cords, for even though she opened her mouth, no sound came out as she fell through the air.

Buzz felt a cry leave his own lips, but it was drowned out by the roar of the bike as Sam gunned the engine. They shot after Mari, the night wind slashing at Buzz's face. The bike tore through the air, gobbling up the distance between them.

She was not that far ahead now, but the ground was racing to meet her.

"Faster!" Buzz yelled.

"Don't worry, I've got this." Sam gunned the engine again and the bike hurtled past Mari to hover just beneath her. She landed on the saddle of the bike on the balls of her feet and balanced there for a moment, a shocked look on her face, before sinking down behind Buzz.

She leant her forehead against his back and took in a gulping breath. "Thanks, Sam," she finally managed to get out.

"No worries," Sam replied. He took the motorbike upwards once more.

Buzz turned to Mari. Her eyes were closed.

"Are you all right?" he asked.

Her eyes flickered open and she nodded.

"Thanks to Sam."

Buzz forced himself to ignore the stab of jealousy. "It was quite a good catch, wasn't it?"

"You're telling me." She shuffled up the seat as if worried she might drop off the back and tucked her braids behind her ears. "Please remind me next time we need to jump anywhere not to be quite as enthusiastic."

"I will," Buzz promised. He dropped his voice. "But it's not like you to mess up like that."

"Thanks, Buzz." Mari's voice was weary. "That's exactly what I want to hear right now."

"No, what I mean is that you were really scared up there."

"It was stupid," Mari mumbled. "For a moment, just

a moment, I looked at Sam and I just couldn't trust him. Or rather, I couldn't trust Sam with Amin on his shoulder." She shook her head. "Then I couldn't think straight. I certainly couldn't jump straight."

"But you checked," Buzz said. "You know from that thing you do. Sam wants to stop Berchta just as much as we do."

"I know," Mari said. "I told you it was stupid."

"Hey, what are you two talking about back there?" Sam called over his shoulder. "This engine is so loud. I can't hear anything."

"Nothing," Buzz shouted back. He noticed that Amin was staring at him with inky black eyes from Sam's shoulder. "We were just wondering how far the Pearl Tower was."

"Not too far," Amin wheezed. "Hold on, you two. We don't want any more accidents, or none of us are getting home, are we?"

The motorbike continued to race through the sky. Soon they were at the far edge of the Jade Pavilion, and the Pearl Tower came into view. It shone white under the stars and was much taller than all the other parts of the building, and it narrowed into a turret that was as thin as a blade, slashing at the sky.

The bike arrived under one of the turret's windows, but the window was sealed shut by two pearl shutters. A heavy bolt lay across its front.

"Come on!" Sam yanked at the bolt, but it would not budge.

"Let me try," Buzz volunteered.

Sam smirked at him from over his shoulder. "Don't be silly, Buzz. If I couldn't open it, I doubt a mortal like you can."

Buzz clenched his fists and wished for the strength from his armlets so he could smash through the pearl shutters. Then he remembered. He didn't have the armlets any more.

"The bolt has been enchanted," Amin said. He reached out and touched the metal, before muttering some words under his breath. He shook his head. "No, I cannot break the charm."

"What exactly are you the god of again?" Buzz asked. "I don't think you told us."

"Don't make fun of him," Sam said. "It's not Amin's fault. His power was stolen by his brother. That thief is the one who left him like thi– Ow." Sam's hand went to his neck. "Why'd you pinch me?"

Amin just glared at him.

Clearly the little guy doesn't want us to know too much about him, Buzz thought.

"Will you all stop arguing?" Mari snapped. "Let me try."

She stood up and clambered over Buzz and Sam until she was balancing on the handlebars of the bike.

"Mari, be careful," Buzz warned. He half wished 'nervous Mari' was back.

She ignored him, holding up her watch and pressing a button. The unbraider popped out, and she snapped it off the watch in one quick movement.

"What is that thing?" Sam asked.

"It *was* an unbraider," Buzz said. "Why'd you just break it?"

"You'll see," Mari replied. Still balancing on the handlebars, she began to work on the bottom two hinges that held the shutters in place. Her long fingers worked swiftly, using the sharp end of the unbraider to undo the fastenings. Once she had removed the hinges on the bottom half of the shutters, she immediately started on the top. The bike rose up until she could reach.

"That's it," Mari said as she pried out the last fastening. She opened her arms and the still-bolted shutters fell into her embrace, leaving the window wide open.

"Nice work," Sam said. A jet of grey smoke left his finger and encircled the shutters. "Let me deal with those."

Mari gently placed the shutters on the cloud that had gathered in front of her. "Thanks."

"No problem. The smoke will put the shutters back once we're all in," Sam explained. "That way, no one will notice anything strange."

Buzz gazed at the open window that led into the Pearl Tower. It was pitch black in there.

Mari must have been noticing the same thing because she activated the flashlight on her watch. "I'm going in," she said, and then lowered herself across the ledge and through the window.

"Wait!" Sam sounded put out. "I should go first."

"You'll get used to it," Buzz said. "Come on, who knows

what might be in there. The cyphon will be guarded, right? If it's as powerful as you say."

"No, I think not," Amin replied, as Sam climbed onto the ledge and dropped down on the other side. "The gods have short memories in this place. They have forgotten about the cyphon and focus on the wrong things entirely." His voice became bitter. "They laugh at me because I'm half of what I once was, but at least I bothered to do a bit of research, and I was very efficient when I did it."

Buzz followed them into the Pearl Tower. "How about the bike?" he said. "We don't want someone to see it."

Sam pointed a finger over his shoulder and a jet of smoke flew from it and straight into Buzz's face.

"Hey!" Coughing and spluttering, Buzz waved a hand to clear the air.

"Sorry, mate." Sam did not sound sorry at all. The smoke flew out of the window and covered the bike, obscuring it in cloud. The shutters, still carried by the smoke, drifted over and slotted back into place, cutting off the moonlight.

Mari's flashlight illuminated the path ahead, and Buzz saw that they were at one end of a stone corridor. Racing along it, they soon entered a wider chamber. A sundial was etched onto the floor, and the wall on the far side of the room was created by a towering series of pearl bricks, each carved with strange symbols. Lying at the base of the wall were a jewelled chisel and hammer.

Buzz heard a sound like grinding stone and, looking over his shoulder, he saw that a new wall of pearl had rolled across the entrance they had just used.

"Now hang on a second." Sam blasted a ball of fire at the wall, but the flames extinguished on impact.

"Guess they want us to stay. I wouldn't waste your time." Mari held the flashlight higher, and Buzz could see more clearly now the symbols that were carved there.

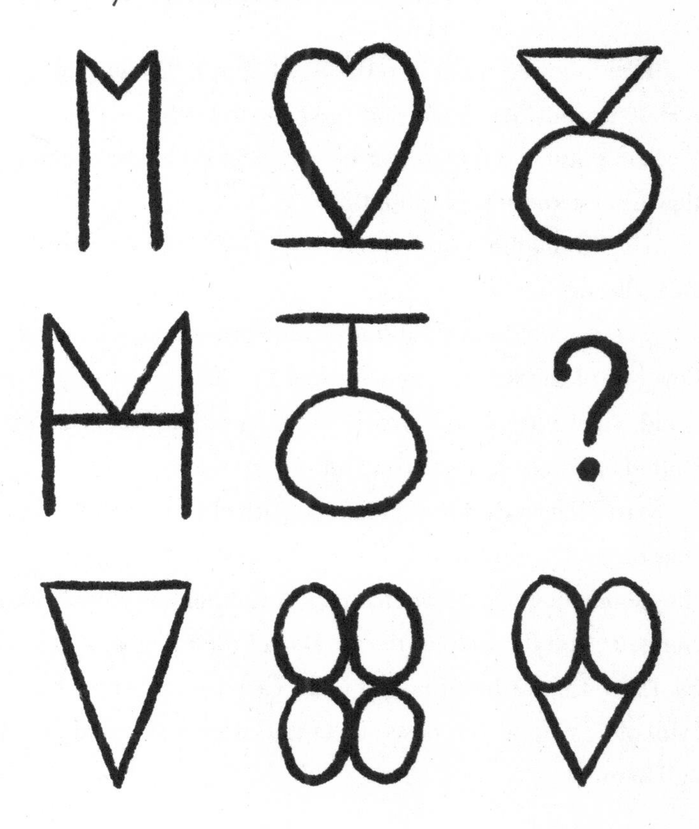

The symbols appeared in blocks of nine, repeating themselves again and again, but the only symbol Buzz recognised was the question mark. That symbol had been written on the pearl brick in charcoal while the other symbols had been carved individually into the bricks.

Amin placed a tentacle against the wall. "The cyphon is behind here. I can feel its power." He gazed hungrily at the wall, tracing the shapes and lines that were etched there.

"Do you recognise any of these symbols, Amin?" Mari asked.

Amin shook his head. "I've looked at many of the ancient texts, but I have never seen these cryptograms." He wrung his tentacles together. "I don't understand. I have read everything there is to read about the cyphon. How can I not know this?"

"Great, we're trapped." Sam began to pace, wrenching Amin away from the wall in the process. "And if we do get out, we still won't have the cyphon. How are we going to stop Berchta and the Pantheon without it?"

"Looks like your awesome powers aren't quite that awesome." Buzz knew he shouldn't have made the dig, but his eyes were still stinging from all that smoke in his face.

Sam glared at him. "My powers are still growing, thank you very much." He crossed his arms. "Besides, there's one of me and a load of them. I'd be outnumbered." He sniffed. "You certainly wouldn't be much help."

"Maybe your massive ego will help instead," Buzz said.

"I don't have a massive ego," Sam retorted.

"Are you kidding?" Buzz asked. "You've really changed."

"Must be like looking in a mirror," Sam shot back. "Now you know how I've felt for the last six months."

"Outnumbered." Mari had been quietly repeating the word to herself. She began to bounce up and down on the spot. "Mirror!"

"Um, is this what they call dancing in New York?" Sam asked, staring at her.

Mari ignored him, and with her thumb she rubbed away the charcoal question mark to leave just a plain stone. She then picked up the chisel and hammer.

"Wait," Amin said. "What are you doing?"

"You'll see." Mari began tapping away at the brick.

After a few minutes she stood back to admire her work.

The block began to tremble and then withdrew to leave behind a perfectly rectangular indentation.

"What just happened?" Buzz asked. "What did you carve into that brick?"

"The right answer, of course!" Mari said. "The number six and its reflection."

"Nice, I see what you did." Sam was looking up at the wall with a grin. "That's actually really clever."

Buzz was staring at the symbols. They still didn't make any sense.

"Each of the symbols is made from a numeral – one, two, three, and so forth – and its reflection in a mirror," Sam explained. "It's obvious, really. I'll finish this off."

A narrow beam of fire left Sam's finger like a laser, and he pointed it at each of the bricks with a question mark on it, carving the symbol into each one. Each time he carved a symbol on a brick, it withdrew to leave an indentation.

"All done." Sam dusted off his hands.

"Not quite," Buzz said. "Look, there's something up there. Right at the top of the wall." He pointed at a tennis ball-sized pearl, set in the brickwork, which was now glowing brightly. He scrambled up to it using the indentations as hand and footholds. At the top of the wall, he plucked the pearl out. It was smooth and shiny and began to glow even more brightly in his hand. It shone a spotlight on the ceiling of the chamber and Buzz saw that there was a perfect pearl-shaped hole there.

He eyed the distance. *If I stretch right out, I'll be able to slot the pearl in . . . probably.*

Taking hold of one of the indentations in the wall with his left hand, he reached out with his right and tried to place the pearl into the ceiling. Instantly, he knew he was too far away.

The smooth pearl rolled off his fingertips and tumbled downwards.

"Catch!" Buzz yelled, looking down.

Sam and Mari both leapt up for it, but it was Amin who caught it.

"Nice wor—" Buzz stopped. Looking over Amin's shoulder, he saw that a flicker of flame had ignited in the corner of the room.

Then the fire began to spread.

"Behind you," he cried. "Watch out!"

CHAPTER TWENTY-ONE

THE CYPHON

The fire flickered orange and blue as it began to blanket the floor. In the centre of the chamber, where the sundial had been etched, a thick, circular plinth was slowly pushing out of the ground. Buzz could see that the flames hadn't reached it yet. He scrambled down the wall, and as he landed, he grabbed Mari's hand. "Quick," he said. "We need to get on the plinth." He dragged her over to the rising sundial and jumped on.

"What's happening?" Mari asked.

"We need to get that pearl into the ceiling." His eyes were scanning the room for Sam and Amin. He spotted Sam shooting flames at the fire that was creeping ever closer to them.

"What are you doing?!" he yelled.

"I'm fighting fire with fire." Sam's face glowed red and orange in the firelight.

"It's not working," Buzz said. "Get on the plinth."

"I've got this," Sam insisted.

"Please." Buzz held out his hand. "Get up here. We need that pearl."

Amin dipped his head and whispered something in Sam's ear. Sam nodded and raced across the floor and jumped onto the plinth as well.

"I don't understand why I couldn't put the fire out." Sam almost seemed to be speaking to himself.

"The fire's magic was stronger than yours," Amin said simply. "But your powers will grow, I promise."

Mari tucked her braids behind her ears. "Okay, we got away from the fire, but this plinth is still going upwards." She looked up and swallowed hard. "We need to make this thing stop before we get squashed."

"Then we need to put the pearl in its rightful place." Buzz pointed at where the glowing orb needed to go.

"Easy peasy." A jet of smoke left Sam's hand, encircled the pearl that Amin held, and lifted it up to the ceiling.

As it slotted in, Sam grinned. "Much easier than having butter fingers and dropping it, no?"

Buzz did not respond. Sam was annoying, but more worrying was the fact that the plinth was still rising and the fire had not died away.

Dread coiled though him as he looked down and realised they couldn't even jump to the ground because the flames would get them. They were trapped. His gaze caught on something by his feet. Letters were appearing around the edge of the column they were on.

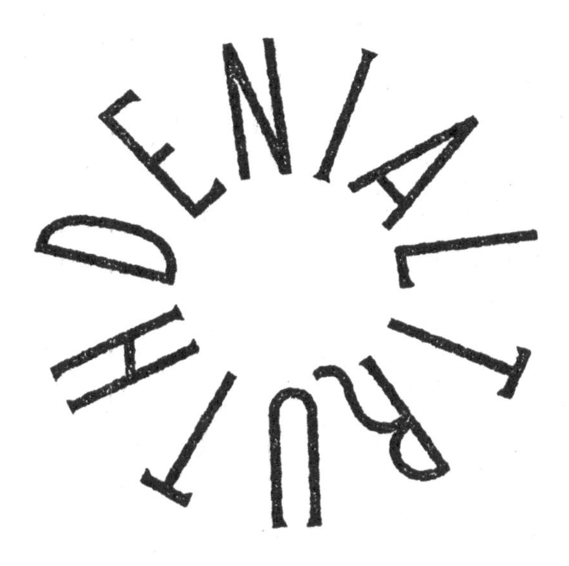

"Why isn't it working?" Mari asked, still looking at the ceiling.

"I don't know," Buzz replied. "But I think these letters have something to do with it." He pointed at them with the tip of his sneaker.

"'Denial Truth'," Mari read. "It's obviously some kind of riddle." She straightened her glasses. "We solve it, and I bet it'll stop the plinth and the fire as well."

"Exactly which truth should we deny, then?" Sam asked.

"Right now, the truth looks like we either get squashed or we get roasted."

"Truth." Buzz blinked hard as he stared at the characters. "Oh, I see," he said after a moment. "Funny. I didn't see the words. They were just a jumble of letters to me. Like Liam's anagram for practical joker."

Sam glared. "You're just bringing that up to hurt my feelings."

"No, I'm not," Buzz insisted. "I just thought—"

"Don't think," Sam said. "It will be less painful for you."

"Quit it, okay!" Mari demanded. "Me and Buzz have solved a lot of riddles, and one thing I've learnt is that things are never as they first appear. It's all about how you look at them."

"She's right," Amin said. "Perhaps the answer isn't Denial Truth. What if this is a clue telling us to deny the truth, even if the answer seems as plain as the noses on our faces?"

Sam crossed his arms. "I don't see why you're all ganging up on me."

Amin rapped his tentacles on Sam's head. "Stop feeling sorry for yourself. It is not becoming of a god."

Buzz smiled despite himself. Sam didn't look very happy with his telling off. Looking up again, he saw that the ceiling of the chamber was just a few metres away now. He dropped to his knees and quickly scanned the letters. "Let's jumble them up then," he said. "Deny the words in front of us and make new truths. New words."

Mari dropped to her knees as well. "What else could this be an anagram for?"

Buzz pointed to four letters. "Dial," he said. "That's one word straightaway."

Sam knelt down and traced some more letters with his fingers. "Turn," he whispered. "You can spell turn and dial, and still have the letters HTE left over."

"Turn the dial," Mari said. "That's what the letters are telling us to do!"

"Are you sure?" Amin's wizened face was sceptical. "There's no dial here." He looked up at the ceiling, which was now a metre away. "And we're out of time."

Buzz noticed that the old guy was subtly unwrapping his tentacles from around Sam's shoulders.

"You're wrong." Buzz slapped his hand on the etching of the sundial in the centre of the plinth. "There's a dial right here." He placed his fingers into the grooves of the sundial, and as his fingers touched the channels, he felt a pulse of power. Taking a firm grip of the carving, he exerted a bit of pressure, and the whole sundial began to rotate. As he turned the dial around three-hundred-and-sixty degrees, the plinth began to rotate in the opposite direction, retracting into the ground.

"It's working," Mari said. "We're going back down!"

As the plinth settled back into the ground, the flames died away, and the wall of symbols in front of them began to roll back.

Buzz, Mari, Sam, and Amin walked forwards together.

Directly ahead of them stood a statue of a bear. It was on its hind legs with its head thrown back, looking up at a ceiling that was also rolling back to reveal the stars and the moon.

Buzz's heart sank. They had solved two riddles and risked being squashed and burnt, just to find a statue of a bear under a night sky. He walked over to the sculpture. It was enormous and very detailed. Buzz imagined he could almost see the wind from above blowing through the bear's fur.

"No sign of the cyphon in here," Sam complained. His voice echoed around the chamber.

"No, but there is a statue of the Great Bear." Amin's voice was filled with wonder. "One of the first gods. One of the greatest."

"Humph. If he's so great, why have I never heard of him?" Sam asked with a sniff.

"He was a god to the first people," Amin said. "The god of the Neanderthals."

"They didn't make it, though, did they?" Sam pointed out. "So not such a great god. Not as great as me." He kicked at the base of the statue just as moonlight poured into the chamber.

And then came the roar.

The bear statue was no longer still. It dropped onto its legs and prowled forwards.

With a yelp, Sam sent a jet of fire from his fingertips, but it just bounced off the bear's stone pelt.

Amin cradled his head in his tentacles. "What have you done?" he wailed. "What have you done?"

The bear was pushing Sam into a corner. Saliva dripped from his stone teeth as he stretched his mouth wide.

"Stop!" Buzz cried. "Stop, please." *Search for the bear.* The voice of the old woman in the mirror came back to him. *Say the prayer.* Buzz flung himself in front of Sam and held up a hand.

"Great Bear, I seek your teachings, your wisdom and your solace. Guide me in the right direction, show me the strength I have inside and the kindness I can lend to others. Give me sight so I can see the truth, and the words so I can speak it."

The bear blinked, the wildness in his eyes replaced by a softness that was almost dreamlike.

Buzz felt some of his breath return. "He didn't mean to cause you offense." Buzz looked over at Sam. "Okay, he did. But he's sorry. Aren't you, Sam?"

Sam nodded, clearly not able to get any words out.

Mari crept forwards. "We didn't mean to disturb you, Great Bear. We were looking for the cyphon." She tried to smile but it was a bit wobbly. "It's obviously not here, so we'll get out of your . . . um . . . fur." She looked over her shoulder, and Buzz saw that there was still no door. "If you can just show us the way out."

The bear closed his gaping jaws and sank back on his haunches. He looked tired. "You are wrong. You have found the cyphon. It is right in front of you."

"You're the cyphon?" Amin's eyes were wide. "Why did the books not say?"

"Because this knowledge belongs to a time before books,"

the bear explained. "Before gods." His eyes became dreamlike once more as he remembered. "The gods came from me, and I can draw them to me again, for I am one of the nine. I am the sixth."

"That's why those numbered symbols were on the wall!" Mari exclaimed.

The bear nodded. "We ended the darkness. We cleared the skies and allowed the moon and the sun to shine their rays on the world. We even gave man the power of flame."

That explains the pearl and the sundial, Buzz thought. *And the fire.*

A tear ran down the bear's marble cheek. "I am the sixth," he repeated. "I am the only one left from the nine."

"The world you helped make is in danger," Mari said. "Those gods you made want to take control of humanity. But their time has passed."

The bear shook his mighty head. "Everyone's time passes. Even my time has passed. I cannot help you."

"You must," Buzz said. "You started all this. The world is still your responsibility."

The bear looked down at one of his giant paws for a moment and then brought it to his mouth. He began to pull at one of his claws with his teeth.

"Ow!" Buzz could hardly watch. "Stop! Why are you hurting yourself like this?"

The bear laughed, even as he finally managed to rip the

claw from his paw. "I am far beyond pain at my age. But thank you for the concern." He held out the claw. "I cannot leave this place. But I give you this. It's part of me. So it is the cyphon."

Buzz took the claw. It was surprisingly heavy, and warm.

"This claw will draw the gods into it, but it will not destroy them, and it will not hold them for ever." The bear looked at them with pleading eyes. "The gods are my children. Once they have been caught in the cyphon, they must be taken far from your world and resettled. Far, far away, or they will find a way back."

Buzz looked over at Sam and Amin. He held out the claw to them. "Coming here was your idea. You should look after this."

Sam reached out for the claw, but Amin snatched it out of Buzz's palm instead.

Amin hugged it and dipped his head. "Thank you, great bear."

The bear looked at him with an unreadable expression. "Make the right choices, half god." He lumbered back into the middle of the room. "Good luck to you all in what is to come."

The bear rose to his full height, and then he turned to stone once more.

"Wow," Mari breathed. She stepped forwards and looked up at the bear. "That was surreal. Do you think he can still see us and hear us?"

"What does that matter?" Sam was looking at the cyphon that Amin still held close. "I can't believe we've actually got it." He swallowed hard. "Thank you, Buzz" he said. "I would have been a bear's brunch if you hadn't said that prayer."

"You're welcome." Buzz glanced at his friend. "I know you don't believe it, Sam, but you mean a lot to me. I'm sorry I didn't tell you the truth about what happened to me. I'm sorry I made you feel like you weren't enough. Right now, all I want is to put things back to how they were before."

Sam swallowed harder. "But everything is so different now. I don't know if things can ever go back to how they were before."

"But we can be friends again, right?" Buzz said.

Sam opened his mouth but closed it again. "I . . . I . . . don't know," he finally managed to say.

Amin shifted his weight on Sam's shoulder. "Perhaps he'll be able to answer that question once we have got back to your realm and dealt with Berchta and the Pantheon. That needs to be our focus."

"Of course," Buzz said. "I know that, but—"

"Let's go find an ash tree," Mari said. "We've been away for too long. It's time to go home."

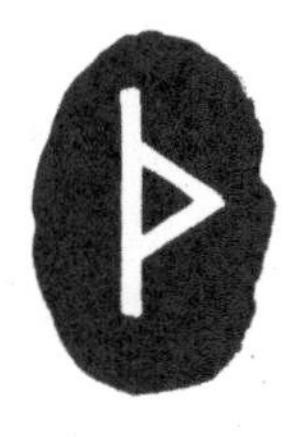

CHAPTER TWENTY-TWO

TRAPPED

The same moon that had awoken the Great Bear lit their way as Buzz, Mari, Sam, and Amin fought a path through the forest. The ground beneath their feet was uneven, thick with roots and bracken that were eager to trip them up. There only seemed to be one moon in this realm, but it was full and close and so bright Mari did not need to use the flashlight on her watch.

"How far now?" Mari asked. She swore as she tripped over another root.

"There is a copse of ash trees just a few metres from here," Amin said. "Once we're there, you can unlock a new portal."

"Ratatosk's twigs better work," Mari said, "or we're stuck here."

"Of course they'll work," Buzz said. "He's never let us down before."

"True." Mari looked worried. I hope he's all right," she said. "And Theo."

"Guys like Theo are always all right." Sam's voice was as bitter as chicory.

"Theo's not a bad person," Buzz said. "He really isn't. You should give him a second chance."

"No second chances," Sam muttered under his breath. "Not any more."

"Look, over by that hollow oak," Amin cried. "There are some ash trees."

"At last." Mari raced over to them but stopped as a loud flapping sound filled the air. "What's that?"

"Just a bit of wildlife," Amin reassured her. "Come, let's open that portal."

"Amin," Sam said. "I don't think I can do—"

"You don't need to do anything," Amin snapped.

Buzz noticed that Amin's tentacles were writhing even more than usual, curling and uncurling on Sam's shoulder. One tentacle even seemed to be in Sam's ear, just the very tip.

"He's right, Sam." Mari planted her twig next to the ash tree. "This is our job. We'll get the portal open."

Buzz couldn't pull his gaze from Sam. His friend looked ill. Scared.

He noticed something dark splattered on the front of his friend's white robes. It was blood, and it was coming from Amin. It trickled from a wound in the old man's tentacle and was now falling to the ground.

"Amin, you're hurt," Buzz said.

Amin shook his head. "It's nothing."

The flapping sound was louder. It was closer.

"Really, it's nothing." Amin was looking all around. "Please, let's just get this portal open."

Something's not right, Buzz thought. It was written all over Sam's face and Amin's as well. *Are they nervous?* Buzz knew he was. How exactly were they going to get the cyphon to work? How were they going to trap all the gods?

Buzz strode over to the silver trees. He wasn't going to let the fear of the unknown stop him. *This is my story,* he reminded himself. *We'll find the answer.*

He placed his hand on the smooth bark and then plunged his twig into the earth. Immediately the air thrummed with energy and a portal ripped itself open in the air. The gash was filled with nothing. It was an absence. It was the way home.

Buzz felt someone barge past him, smacking into his shoulder. As he turned he saw Sam and Amin shove past Mari as well, so that they were directly in front of the portal.

"No need to push," Mari grumbled. "We're all getting home."

Sam turned to face them. There were tears in his eyes. "No, no we're not." A jet of fire burst from Sam's fingertips and surrounded him, Amin, and the portal in a sphere of flame. Buzz felt his eyelashes singe and he and Mari took a step back from the fierce heat.

"What are you doing?" Buzz yelled over the roar of the fire.

Sam was already halfway into the rip in the sky. He looked

miserable and triumphant all at the same time. "You're not part of the plan, Buzz. You never were." His eyes were wild, and Amin's tentacles seemed to be all over him.

"Plan?" Mari repeated.

"We're going to capture Berchta and the Pantheon. They don't care about what I believe in or what my family believes in. Berchta didn't ask me about my faith once. Now I get to choose."

"We'll destroy them all," Amin said.

Sam nodded. "And then it will just be the two of us."

"Worshipped by all." The old man cackled with glee.

Over the roar of the flames, Buzz could hear that flapping sound again. It was very close this time.

Amin looked up and began to laugh even more wildly.

"I am going to set the strix on you. They have smelt my blood trail," he called, looking up at the sky. "They're coming for you and are far worse than those blood-sucking creatures you've heard about in stories." He stared at Buzz and Mari and his lip curled. "Thanks for all the help getting the cyphon. We couldn't have done it without you." He tugged Sam further into the portal, his tentacles almost strangling him.

Sam's eyes bulged. "Get out of here, Buzz, before the strix come." And then he and Amin were gone.

The portal closed behind them with a *pffffff* sound, the flames surrounding it disappearing.

"Those little toads," Mari snarled. "They tricked us. They both tricked us, and now the portal's gone."

"We can't worry about that now." Buzz looked up at the sky. "I don't exactly know what strix are but they are coming for us." He bent down and picked up a flat, heavy stone.

Mari raised her watch. The flashlight shone bright.

Ten wide yellow, pupil-less eyes stared back at them from the branches of the surrounding trees. Watching them hungrily were five giant birds that looked like owls but with red feathers, black legs, and golden beaks.

"The strix," Buzz whispered.

"We need to go," Mari cried. But it was too late. A tide of red surged over them.

Buzz could feel pinpricks of pain all over his body as sharp talons tore at his clothes. Heavy wings beat at his face, and he staggered backwards, catching glimpses of beaks that looked as sharp as blades.

"Get off me," he cried as the birds continued to swirl all around him. He swung out with the flat stone but the creatures were far too quick.

"There's too many of them!" Mari's face was scratched and bloodied. "We're gonna be ripped to shreds."

Buzz swung out with his stone again, but it was hopeless. They were surrounded by the creatures. He staggered backwards as two strix drove him away from Mari. *They're trying to separate us.*

"Mari?" He yelled her name at the top of his voice. "Mari, where are you?" The strix nearest to him gave a screech of pain and veered away to the left. Buzz called her name again as loud as he could, and the other strix began to shudder and screech in pain.

"I'm here, Buzz," Mari's voice sounded ragged but it was nearby.

"They don't like loud noises," Buzz shouted. "Play some music on your watch. As loud as you can."

The baseline for the song 'Wiggle' suddenly began to pound.

Buzz would have chosen something a bit more serious, but it would do. There was a cacophony of noise as the strix all began screeching and backing away from them.

"It's working," Mari shouted over the music as she staggered to his side.

"I know," Buzz said. "Keep playing the music . . ." He trailed off as one of the strix began rubbing its head in the dirt of the forest floor. The movement threw up a cloud of moss and dead leaves that clung to the strix's head and its pointed ears.

The other strix began to caw in delight and followed suit.

Mari's mouth hung open. "They're actually making ear plugs out of dirt. That's super clever." She deactivated her music. "I mean, whoever said that birds have small brains haven't met this bunch."

"We can admire them later," Buzz said. "If we survive that is."

"We'll survive," Mari promised, and grabbed his hand. "They're smart but I'm smarter."

They ran over to the massive old oak with its large tree hollow. "Get in," she said.

Buzz grabbed the edge of the hollow and then hoisted himself up before wriggling through it and dropping into the cavernous space within. He held up a hand and pulled Mari in.

"What now?" he gasped, as they both crouched down.

"We hide," Mari said. "I don't think they saw us come in here, and they won't think to look inside."

"Wait, don't owls live in tree hollows?" Buzz asked.

"Um . . ."

"Why did I trust a city girl?" Buzz asked with a groan.

They heard a scraping sound outside the tree, and it quickly turned into a fierce slashing sound. Buzz jumped back as a golden talon stabbed through the wood and ripped the front of his shirt.

"The entire trunk is getting shredded," Mari said, as the tree around them began to shake. "It won't hold out much longer."

Buzz's fingers went to the tear in his shirt. His sister had given him this shirt for Christmas, and he'd never really told her how much he liked it. He wished he could see Tia now to tell her the truth, but he wasn't going to be seeing any of his family soon. The strix had them trapped.

Buzz released the torn material, realising what an idiot he had been. He'd managed to rip his life apart over the last few months. He'd been so convinced that everything in his life was boring compared to his quest for the Runes of Valhalla that he had stopped living. And now it was too late to say sorry to any of his friends or family for how mean or cold he'd been. And the truth was, his life had been great – he just hadn't appreciated it.

There was a series of loud whistles followed by high-pitched yelps, and then the sound of talons and beaks on bark ceased. The tree stopped shuddering.

"What exactly is going on out there?" Mari asked in the gloom.

"I don't know," Buzz said. "Think we should have a look?"

"It might be a trap," she whispered. "We trusted Sam and Amin, and that was a mistake."

"You're wise, Mari, to be cautious. It was a mistake to trust Amin," a deep voice said from outside the tree. "There's nothing good about him. I should know – he's part of me. But I vow to you on all that is good and true that it is safe to come out now."

"Is this guy for real?" Mari asked.

Buzz shrugged. "Well, we can't stay here for ever. Let's find out."

Buzz and Mari scrambled to get out of the tree hollow to find a carpet of unconscious strix on the mossy floor. Their eyes were closed but their chests still rose and fell. Standing next to them was a figure in a long, dark cloak.

"Wait, I recognise you," Buzz said. "You're the guy who was outside the post office when I got knocked over by Berchta's jeep."

"Indeed." The man threw back his hood so his face was no longer in shadow; it was just like looking at a male version of Mari's grandmother. "I'm Benjy."

"As in, Great-Uncle Benjamin?" Mari's voice was hoarse. "Grandmother's long-lost brother?"

Great-Uncle Benjamin smiled. "Like I said, it's Benjy. And it is so very wonderful to meet you, Mari."

"What are you doing here?" she asked. "And what did you do to the strix?"

Benjy held up a long pipe. "I used this blowgun with darts made from the arbutus tree. They're asleep, but not for long. I suggest we get moving. I'll explain more as we go."

"We're stuck here," Buzz said. "Sam and Amin used the portal, and we can't make another one."

"Don't be so sure." Benjy unclasped his cloak. The inside was lined with black silk, and it had a map of stars and constellations embroidered onto it. Benjy lay the cloak flat on the ground, silk-side up.

"Step on and step in. It's time to go home."

CHAPTER TWENTY-THREE

EVEN MAGIC NEEDS A LITTLE DIRECTION

Stars shot past them as they fell through the night sky.

Buzz wondered if he should be scared; he didn't feel scared. They were falling slowly, and with Mari's great-uncle beside them, guiding them, he knew they couldn't get lost in this wide expanse.

"You know, I actually miss getting around by normal transportation." Mari's voice echoed in the darkness.

"I was just thinking that I was quite enjoying this," Buzz confessed.

Mari shook her head. "There's really nothing wrong with a plane or a car. All these portals are making me feel sick."

Benjy angled his body ever so slightly left as they drifted down. "You are right to be suspicious of portals. The more you use them, the less anchored you feel to any one place. You lose a grip on the real world, because all the worlds are real."

"Is that what happened to you?" Mari was floating directly beside her great-uncle. "Is that why you never came back to see Grandmother?"

"You're wrong. I visited Crowmarsh many times," Benjy said. "And I would check on my little sister often. But I could never go home." Benjy's face looked pained. "You must understand that after I went through the Ash Arch, nothing was ever the same for me again. I thought I'd learn how to harness my powers, but they consumed me. Almost destroyed me. Until I took action, and removed that angry, hungry part of myself."

"Wait a second," Buzz said. A memory had sparked within him – Amin reacting furiously when Sam began to describe how he had become half a person.

"Is that what you meant when you said Amin is part of you?" Buzz asked. "Is Amin the part of yourself that you removed?"

Benjy looked down at his hands. "I was young and a coward. I did not want to deal with who I was becoming, so I cut the bad out of me and discarded it. Then I travelled the worlds and gave away my magic to those who needed it most."

"So, Amin – the guy who left me to be eaten by some giant owls – is also my great-uncle?" Mari's voice was raised.

"I'm afraid so." Benjy swallowed hard. "He's the worst part of my nature, and I never should have abandoned him. It was dangerous to do so."

"And where exactly have you been all these years," Mari asked, "if you haven't been hanging out with your bad self?"

"Living as a wiseman in your realm some of the time, with a side order of sorcery; travelling between worlds to gather knowledge at other points. It's been my calling to help those in need when I can."

He looked over at Buzz. "Your father came to me more than once for advice. I tried to help."

"No way," Buzz said. "You know my dad?"

"Indeed; he's a mythologist, and I am a sorcerer. We have a lot in common."

"I'm guessing he wanted advice on how to stop El Tunchi."

"Ah, you know about that?" Benjy questioned.

Buzz nodded.

"Well, that's a start, at least. I told your father to tell you about El Tunchi weeks ago, but he was too scared."

"It's okay. I'm scared as well," Buzz admitted. "El Tunchi's not going to give up."

"No, Buzz," Benjy said. "Your father was scared that you'd want to go with El Tunchi. He was worried that you'd want the adventure more than you'd want a life in Crowmarsh."

"That's crazy!" Buzz exclaimed.

"Is it?"

Buzz let the sorcerer's words sink in. His father had never told him any of this. *Was I so hard to talk to? Was I that lost?* "But where's Dad now?"

"He decided to search for Ceridwen's Cauldron," Uncle Benjy revealed. "He's hoping that such a precious gift might buy your freedom, but I'm not so sure. El Tunchi's hunger is not for things. It is for feeling." Benjy looked out over the night sky and angled himself even further left. "El Tunchi has no purpose, and he has no companionship. He has nothing. But your father wouldn't listen." Benjy's gaze became steely. "I promised I'd look out for you, Buzz, and when the Pantheon turned up, I knew I needed to stay in Crowmarsh to make sure you and Mari were okay. It was just unfortunate that I lost your trail. I did not factor in Sam." Benjy reached out and took hold of their hands. "Get ready now. We're almost there."

"How'd you actually find us then?" Mari asked.

"Ratatosk told me you'd gone to find the Myth Keeper, so I followed you there. Alas, you were not easy to track down. You chose a very difficult route."

"Told you we should have gone This Way or That Way!" Mari rebuked.

Benjy landed on the ground with a soft thud, and Buzz and Mari stepped off the cloak. The sorcerer wrapped it around himself once again.

Looking around him, Buzz realised that they had landed on the high street, opposite the post office.

But things looked different.

Many of the shop windows on the high street were smashed in, and the road was covered in rubbish and graffiti. Even though it was the middle of the day, the town centre looked completely deserted.

"What happened?" Mari asked.

"I'm afraid the people of Crowmarsh have stopped working, stopped caring for the town and one another," Benjy replied. "They are far too busy worshipping gods whose time passed many moons ago."

"But where are they?" Buzz asked. "Are they safe?"

"Not exactly," Benjy admitted. "They'll be at the Crowmarsh ruins – or the Believers' Arena, as Berchta likes to call it."

"So what're we doing here? We should be at the ruins." Buzz began to pace.

"You told me that Amin and Sam have the cyphon, correct?" Benjy asked.

"Yes," Mari said. "They're going to use it on the gods to imprison them."

"Well, it won't work. Not without a little direction, at least." Benjy was busy peering across the road at the post office.

"What are you talking about?" Buzz asked.

"The cyphon will only be able to draw a god into it if it has their true name, and Berchta is the only one who has a record of all those who have come through the Ash Arch."

"The Great Bear said nothing about that." Buzz was still pacing.

"The Great Bear is old. He probably forgot," Benjy explained. "And even magic needs a little direction sometimes." Benjy rubbed his arms to keep warm. "The cyphon is powerful. It needs specific, detailed information, or we'd all get sucked into it. That's where the names help."

"You're saying we've basically got to do a mega mystical register?" Buzz asked.

Benjy nodded.

"Okay, where do we get these names from?" Mari wasn't even bothering to disguise the impatience in her voice.

"From the post office." Buzz pointed at the old, cavernous building, finally understanding. "The names are written on little jade discs. I saw Berchta's people carving them. I just didn't know what it meant at the time."

"Indeed," Benjy said. "Someone's been paying attention. Those little jade discs are Berchta's payment but they're also a record of every god and goddess participating in the Pantheon."

"Well, that's lucky. But how are we going to *get* in there?" Mari scanned the building across the street. "It looks pretty secure."

Great-Uncle Benjy unclasped his cloak. "Leave that to me. You two keep guard." The cloak fell to the ground, and Benjy stepped into it and disappeared.

"That's a neat trick your great-uncle can do." Buzz was surprised he didn't feel any jealousy at all.

"I guess, but I reckon my grandmother would have been more impressed by a visit."

"Don't be too hard on him, Mari. He probably thought he was doing the right thing by staying away."

Mari crossed her arms. "Perhaps." She looked at him

sideways. "We haven't spoken about Sam. About what he did."

Buzz knelt down and tied a shoelace that didn't need tying. "And we're not going to. Not now. We need to stop Berchta and the rest of the Pantheon first."

"Okay," Mari said. "But we can't harm any of them. We promised the Great Bear."

"And we won't need to. We'll get the cyphon, and we'll get the names. Then every god will be pulled from our world and locked away until we can find them a new home."

Mari looked down at him. "You make it sound so easy, but Sam and Amin aren't just gonna hand the cyphon over, are they?"

"Then we'll just have to take it." Buzz stood up. Pretending to tie his shoelaces wasn't going to help anyone.

Mari laughed but it sounded hollow. "We're gonna need more of a plan than that. We need ideas."

"Ideas about what?" Mari's uncle had appeared at their side again – this time with a bulging burlap sack in each hand. He gave both of them a rattle.

"About getting the cyphon off Sam and Amin," Buzz answered.

"Leave that one to me. Amin and I have a lot we need to discuss." Benjy delved into one of the sacks and brought out a jade disc. "Your job is to plant each and every one of these names in the arena."

"Why do we need to plant them?" Mari asked.

Benjy smiled at her. "You are very like your grandmother.

She was also full of 'whys' as a child. The element of earth is powerful. If you bury the names in the arena, it will amplify the magic of the cyphon when we finally call on it. Ensure that it works properly."

He threw his cloak on the floor. "Come, it's time for us to leave." He looked up at the sky. "The equinox is almost upon us. Amin will choose the point where day is as long as night to use the cyphon. He'll want everything to be perfect."

CHAPTER TWENTY-FOUR
BELIEVERS' ARENA

They arrived inside the ruins, keeping to the shadows that gathered in the corners. The arena was full. Buzz recognised many people from Crowmarsh. Mr Collins, the butcher, was deep in conversation with a god who had two or three animal skins around his shoulders.

"That's Fan-Kui, god of butchers," Benjy explained. "Looks like he managed to find himself one believer at least."

The chatter in the arena fell silent, and Buzz had to swallow a gasp. Theo, Ratatosk, and a familiar-looking giant badger were being pushed into the ring by a throng of people dressed in blue and yellow feathers and armed with sharp sticks. Berchta had also appeared, gazing down at them all from one of the highest tiers of the arena.

She clapped her hands for silence. "Moritasgus has betrayed me. Has betrayed *us*. He was sent to bring back the intruders but instead befriended them. Protected them. Now it is time for him to pay, and Huitzilopochtli's believers will be the ones to extract payment."

The people with the sticks cheered at that. Their faces were ugly with hate. The captors and their prisoners all came to a stop in the centre of the arena, and the badger instantly curled his body around Theo and Ratatosk, keeping them close.

"Theo," Mari murmured.

"Ratatosk," Buzz said at the same time. He moved forwards, but Benjy put a hand on his arm.

"Our focus must be on getting the cyphon to work," he said. "If we give away our position now, without locating the cyphon or planting the names, there's no way we'll be able to save your friends – or anyone else, for that matter." Benjy thrust one sack into Buzz's hand and the other into Mari's. "Get planting. Look, I'll show you how."

Benjy took a handful of the discs and then began stabbing away at the earth.

But Buzz couldn't wrench his gaze away from what was happening in the arena. He watched as Mrs Garrison, the florist, leapt forwards and struck Moritasgus on his side. The badger gave a howl of pain and staggered back.

"Oh, that wicked woman." Mari's hand tightened on the sack in her hand.

"She's not normally," Buzz replied. "I don't understand why she's acting so differently."

Benjy looked into the arena. "They're wearing Huitzilopochtli's colours, which means they're now true believers of the Aztec god of war." He sighed. "Berchta wants them to prove their loyalty to Huitzilopochtli by spilling blood. It's all part of the contest."

The badger let out another roar of pain as two more of Huitzilopochtli's believers sprang forwards and drew blood with their sticks.

Buzz put a palm over his mouth to stop himself crying out. "We can't just watch."

"Trust in Moritasgus," Benjy said. "He is the Celtic god of protection, after all, and is not entirely without gifts. Now, get those discs into the earth." He gave them both a little push. "I'll search the arena for Sam and Amin. They're here somewhere." He pulled his hood over his head and melted away into the throng of spectators.

Buzz knelt down and began to dig a hole with his fingers. The earth was tough and hard and tore at his skin. *This is going to take forever.* He looked to his left and saw that Mari was struggling as well, but her face was determined as she concentrated on the task.

Buzz heard Moritasgus give another cry and looking up, he saw the badger swing out with his claw, but the attackers were too quick. They just mocked him, pulling faces and jabbing out with their sticks again.

Buzz's chest felt tight. *Moritasgus is still protecting Theo and*

Ratatosk, and I'm here planting stone discs. It's not right.

"Buzz, concentrate," Mari said. "If we don't do this right, none of us are going to get out of here."

Buzz nodded. He tried to blank from his memory the sight of the badger with the whites of his eyes showing, or the whoops and hoots the attackers gave as they drew yet more low cries from the injured animal. *Concentrate.* Buzz realised he couldn't dig deep with his fingers, but he could dig faster if he did lots of little holes. Working his way around the perimeter of the arena, sticking to the shadows, he planted the names of the gods, one disc at a time. He looked up and saw that Mari had also picked up speed and was now on the other side of the arena, invisible unless you knew to look for her.

Buzz's gaze caught on Berchta. She now sat towards the front of the arena, next to several other gods and believers, and she held a clipboard, taking notes every time one of the believers attacked. One god with a headdress made of bone and feathers was studying the action intensely, while the others were just clapping in delight at the action.

Mrs Garrison raised her stick, ready to strike again, but Ratatosk was faster. He jumped forwards and covered the florist's eyes with his paws. Theo then leapt over the badger and wrestled the stick away from the florist and threw it to the ground.

"Leave us alone!" he yelled. "You're better than this. Wake up, won't you?"

Ratatosk had released the florist, and Mrs Garrison was blinking at Theo. "It is Huitzilopochtli's will that we do this." She didn't sound as sure, though.

Mr George, the owner of the local garage, growled and ran at them, his stick held high. Theo ducked low and stuck out his leg, tripping up the older man, who landed in the earth with a thud. A few in the audience began to laugh.

The god in the bone-and-feather headdress stood up. "How dare you laugh at my believers!" he thundered.

"They're not very good ones, are they?" the horned god, Cerunnos, said. "You won't win the new god with believers like that. Perhaps you should give up now."

Huitzilopochtli narrowed his eyes and swept into the arena, his cloak of blue and yellow feathers flying out behind him. His followers immediately knelt in front of him, their heads touching the ground.

Huitzilopochtli picked up the discarded stick. "There is no truer saying than if you want something done, just do it yourself." He drew the stick back and threw it at Theo like a spear.

Time slowed. Buzz's gaze went to Theo, Ratatosk, and the badger again. He could see that the badger's whole body was trembling with fatigue, but bravely he was rising up onto two feet. Opening his jaws, he let out a roar so full of fury that the arena went silent.

A powerful light shone from the badger's chest and

encircled the three of them in a protective shield. As the spear hit the golden orb, it bounced off, whipping through the air and stabbing Huitzilopochtli's cloak to the ground.

The god gave a squeak of outrage and tried to pull free, but the spear was embedded deep in the earth and had him trapped. Huitzilopochtli looked at the spear as if not quite believing it, and then, with a roar, he ripped the cloak off his shoulders. He was quite naked beneath, except for a belt of feathers and his tattoos. The arena was no longer silent. Everyone was laughing. Even the believers whose heads had quickly tilted back towards the ground were snorting with mirth.

The god of war looked more like a plucked chicken than a bird of prey, and he quickly scurried from the arena.

With a thud, the badger slumped down and stared out at the spectators, his eyes sad and tired. Sighing, his sides heaving, he lay his head on the ground, and the force field around them faded. Ratatosk edged near to the badger's face and pressed his muzzle to the god's.

"Don't yer go giving up on me." Buzz lip-read Ratatosk's words. "Open yer eyes."

But the badger's eyes remained closed. And Buzz wasn't sure they'd open again.

"I can't find them," a voice said from beside him. Buzz turned to see that Benjy was by his side again. The old man wrapped his cloak more tightly around himself. "I've looked everywhere, and I can see no sign of Sam or Amin—"

"You did this. All of you." Theo's voice, cracked with grief, drowned out Benjy's words as he hugged the badger and stared out at the audience. "You have allowed these gods to come to Crowmarsh and play games with us. No more. Wake up. It's time for you to wake up and see what is happening here."

Many in the audience were silent as they looked at Theo. Faces that had been full of fervour and bloodlust were becoming confused.

Berchta was on her feet. "Don't you dare listen to this boy. Listen to your gods. For if you don't, your fate will be the same as his." A ball of flame appeared at her fingertips, and she hurled it at Theo.

"No!" Buzz cried, even as the goddess's flaming ball was met by another orb of flame. Both balls extinguished with a hiss.

Berchta looked up.

Standing at the top of one of the stairways to the arena was Sam, with Amin on his shoulder. In his hand, Sam held the cyphon.

Berchta's mouth hung open. "What are you doing here? I sent you to the Jade Pavilion."

Sam smirked as he and Amin came to the bottom of the staircase and into the amphitheatre. "But the equinox is here. Doesn't the winner want to claim their prize?"

"I haven't decided on the winner yet." Berchta's fingers grazed her brooch. "And I won't be rushed." She tilted her chin. "Still, it probably makes it easier that you are here. It will focus the gods' minds, and we will cease with this buffoonery." She crooked a finger at him. "Come and sit by my side. I need to decide what to do with this boy, squirrel, and dead badger."

Theo flinched at her words, but Sam did not move a muscle.

Amin began to laugh. "It is you who will take orders from us, not the other way round," he wheezed.

Berchta peered disdainfully at Amin, almost as if she was only just noticing him. "What are you talking about, you little runt?" She sneered. "I'd actually managed to forget that I'd even left you festering in the Jade Pavilion. I really should have put you out of your misery after your better half abandoned you."

Amin's face twisted with fury. "You know nothing of misery . . . yet. It is time for you, all of you, to be eradicated." He snatched the bear claw from Sam's hand. "The cyphon calls you. Return to the beginning. It is your end."

Berchta's eyes went wide. "No, it cannot be." Her hand raised, as if to shield herself from the claw, she threw herself to the ground. There were screams as many of the gods scrambled from their seats. They climbed over one another to get away, a blur of hooves, tails, and scales. Those that could, took to the air. Buzz spotted Zelus carrying away a grateful-looking rainbow serpent.

The believers watched their gods flee, and those who still seemed to be under their spell were awoken. "What are we doing here?" Buzz heard Mrs. Garrison cry. "I have a delivery of hydrangeas due." She staggered out of the ruins. "And why on earth am I dressed like this? I look terrible in yellow."

Others followed her, and Buzz realised that although the people of Crowmarsh were looking around them as they left, they weren't really seeing; no one even seemed to notice the giant badger that lay in the middle of the arena.

"Buzz, stop gawping," Benjy said. "The time has come. You must finish planting those discs." He dropped the cloak on the floor and stepped into it. A moment later he appeared next to Sam.

"Hello, Amin," he said. "It's been a long time."

CHAPTER TWENTY-FIVE

AGE OF THE GODS

"You," Amin snarled. Buzz had never seen so much hatred etched onto someone's face.

Then it was a clash of bodies. Benjy grabbed at the cyphon. Amin refused to let it go. Sam was caught in the middle.

"Buzz, give 'em here." Ratatosk was by his side and reaching into the sack. "Yer need to go and get Theo. He won't leave Moritasgus, and it ain't safe for him in the middle of that arena."

Buzz looked down at the squirrel. "There're not many discs left, but you need to plant them. It's not easy. The ground is really hard."

Ratatosk held up a paw. "I'm a squirrel. Burying small, hard, round things is what I do. Now go get Theo."

"Sorry, Ratatosk," Buzz said. "Mari might need some help as well."

The squirrel nodded, and Buzz sprinted across the arena to

his friend. "You can't stay here, Theo."

"I'm not leaving him." Theo laid his head against the badger's soft pelt. "He saved me so many times. After you left, it was Moritasgus who saved me from that feathered dragon thing, and he tried to keep me safe from Berchta as well."

"He'd want you to stay safe," Buzz said gently. "Don't let his sacrifice be wasted."

"Let go!" Buzz heard Amin roar.

He turned and saw Benjy yank again at the cyphon. Amin's tentacles were wrapped tightly around it and he was wrenched off Sam's shoulder with a wet ripping sound. Sam dropped to the floor like a puppet who'd had their strings cut.

Mari ran to him and flung one of her arms around his shoulder. Half dragging him and half walking him, they got away from the battling Benjy and Amin. Behind her, Ratatosk continued to plant the last of her discs.

"Just listen," Benjy cried as he continued to wrestle with his other half. "The cyphon's magic won't work yet. But it will work. You must trust me."

"Trust," Amin snarled. "You abandoned me. You left me for dead."

As they continued to tussle for the claw, the sound of cold laughter filled the arena.

"I was a fool to think that was the real cyphon, Benjamin. You were just trying to disrupt the equinox. The way you always do." Berchta rubbed at her brooch. "But enough is enough."

Fire gathered at her fingertips, and then a jet of flame shot out at Benjy and Amin.

"Benjy, watch out!" Buzz cried.

Mari's great-uncle threw up his cloak, ready to disappear, but he was not fast enough. Flame lit up the cloak and engulfed him and Amin.

Mari and Sam rushed forwards, knocking Benjy and Amin to the ground and patting out the flames. Berchta looked on, a smile on her lips. Finally, the flames were extinguished, and Mari held up the cloak.

"Benjy's gone," she sobbed. "Amin, Benjy, and the cyphon. They're all gone."

Berchta dusted off her hands and looked around at them all. "Right, just you lot to tidy away now." She crooked her finger and Sam, Mari, and Ratatosk were plucked off the ground and dumped next to Buzz, Theo, and the very still badger.

Berchta strode towards them, staring down at them, her face strangely sad. "And now, time to destroy you all. What a waste. You could have been a great god, Sam. I wanted to change the world."

"Tell me what it would have been like," Sam begged.

And so Berchta did. She spoke of a world where mortals lived for their gods again. Where gods got to decide the fates of everyone and were the puppet masters. She went on and on, and Buzz realised that Sam must be trying to delay the goddess but they were still out of options.

"It would have been glorious," Berchta finished.

"It could still be." Sam scrambled to his feet. "It was Amin's idea to find the cyphon. I can see now that this was wrong. Give me another chance."

"I can't believe it," Mari said. "You're betraying us again."

Buzz couldn't say anything at all. Deep down he'd thought it was Amin turning Sam to the darkness. *But that isn't true,* he realised. Sam had abandoned them, and Amin wasn't there to drip poison in his ear. *How can he do this?* Buzz wondered, staring at his friend. Sam looked tired, maybe even a little weak, but it was most definitely him making this decision.

Berchta's eyes were uncertain. "Don't think I don't want to. With your potential, you could have led us into a renaissance once you'd learnt all there was to learn. It would have been the reign of the gods once more."

"It still could be. Let me prove my loyalty to you." Sam turned to look at Buzz and the others. "Let me destroy them." He smiled. "Let me blow them to smithereens."

CHAPTER TWENTY-SIX

THE RETURN

Ratatosk bared his teeth. “Yer a nasty piece of work, young man. Do yer know that?”

Sam ignored him.

Berchta’s eyes were pleased, but then her smooth forehead creased with suspicion.

Sam sighed. “You seem hesitant to give me an answer, Berchta. Are you worried that I’ll do a better job than you when it comes to eradicating them?” He looked down at his hands and wriggled his fingers experimentally. “You’re probably right. I’m a new god, after all.”

“Sam, you don’t mean this,” Buzz said. “It doesn’t matter what happened between us. We’re your friends.”

Sam did not even bother to look their way.

“I’ll do anything,” Buzz implored. “Give you anything. Just stop. Please.”

Sam finally looked at him and raised an eyebrow. "What, you'd even give me issue eight of *Captain Phantom*?"

"Yes," Buzz cried. "Anything."

Mari shook her head. "This is crazy. He's toying with you, Buzz, and I can't believe you guys are talking about comics at a time like this."

"Yes, stop teasing them, Sam," Berchta said. "It's mean." She grinned. "Let's put them out of their misery, and I'll do the honours, thank you very much." She looked thoughtful. "A fire bolt or an ice bolt."

"What's the most powerful?" Sam asked.

"They're about the same," Berchta said. "But an ice bolt is my favourite. You get to keep a souvenir." A surge of magic left her fingertips.

Everything slowed down. Buzz watched a flare of white fire come towards them. It was quite beautiful; it had tiny ice crystals in it. He saw Mari hold Ratatosk close. He saw Theo close his eyes and sink further against the dead badger, but Buzz couldn't close his eyes. Destruction was racing to meet him, and he couldn't pull his gaze away. Through the film of his tears he saw Sam turn his head from them and begin to edge backwards, as if he couldn't bear to see what was about to happen or even be close to it.

Then Buzz felt something. A surge of heat from behind him. He turned. It was Moritasgus.

The huge badger was standing on his feet, a golden light

pouring from his chest. It was a liquid gold, much more powerful than the light that had protected Theo from Huitzilopochtli's spear. The gold flowed over them, creating a dome just as Berchta's ice bolt hit.

Just like the spear, Berchta's bolt bounced off the force field and ricocheted straight back at the goddess.

It hit her. Before she could move an inch or even utter a cry, she was frozen solid.

Buzz took in a gulp of air. "Did that all just happen?" he asked. "How?"

"I don't care." Mari was hugging Ratatosk even more tightly. "We're still here and not a huge block of ice. That's the important thing."

"Help," the squirrel squeaked. "Get off me, will yer?" But Buzz thought Ratatosk looked quite happy in Mari's embrace.

"You're alive." Theo's arms were around Moritasgus.

"Thanks to that young man over there," the badger said in a deep voice.

"What young man?" Theo asked. They all followed the badger's gaze over to where Sam stood watching them a few metres away. He looked nervous.

"'Ave yer lost yer mind?" Ratatosk cried. "He's the one that betrayed us."

The badger shook his head. "I was as good as dead. Right on the threshold. I could even hear the Great Bear calling me, but then I felt that boy's hands on me. I heard his voice, and I felt his power as it flooded into me. He told me to protect you all but to wait for the right moment."

"He set her up," Buzz said. His eyes went wide. "Just like Captain Phantom did to Crusher Zero in issue eight." He ran over to Sam. "You even tried to tell me your plan."

"Yeah, I saw what happened earlier with that spear. Thought I might get it to work again." He looked down at his feet. "Sorry if I scared you, mate. Sorry for it all. I wasn't myself when Amin was on my shoulder, but once he was gone, I could see how stupid I'd been." He ran a hand through his hair, dislodging his jade circlet. "It just felt nice to have someone who would listen to me. Who thought I was good enough."

Buzz shook his head. "You were always good enough. It was me who messed up. Wanting magic and danger instead of appreciating what I already had."

"Trust me, mate, I get it," Sam confessed. "It felt amazing to be that powerful, but I feel much better now that I've given it all away."

"Your power's gone, then?" Mari asked as she and the others joined them.

"I've got what's left of it," the badger said cheerfully. "And that's not very much at all."

Sam shrugged. "I had to give him all of it to bring him back with enough juice for that force field." He held up a hand, and the badger gave him a high-five. "Nice work, by the way."

"Thanks," the badger said. "It was quite a shield." His face fell as he looked over Sam's shoulder. "I'll try my best to do it again, but there's not much power left."

Buzz followed the badger's gaze. Coming down the stairs of the arena was El Tunchi. Behind him were Buzz's mother, sister, and Mari's grandmother.

"Ooooooooookayyyyyy." Theo drew out the word. "I'm not gonna lie. I don't get this. Who's the green guy, and what is he doing with your families?"

Buzz's mouth went dry. "His name is El Tunchi, and he's come to take me away. And there's not a thing we can do to stop him."

"Buzz," El Tunchi said. "It is good to see you again."

Sam, Theo, Mari, and Ratatosk all stood in front of Buzz.

"Well, it's not good to see you." Mari glared.

"You're not taking him," Sam added.

"No way," Theo continued.

"No how," the squirrel finished.

El Tunchi opened his mouth to reply, but Tia put herself between him and Buzz's protectors. "Everyone just calm down," she said. "No one is taking Buzz – at least, if everything goes to plan. But thanks for looking out for my little brother."

"Tia, what are you doing here with him?" Buzz asked. "What are any of you doing here with him?"

His mother pushed past the others and gave Buzz a fierce hug. "I thought I told you not to leave the house."

"I'm sorry, Mum," he said. "I had to."

She smiled at him and hugged him again. "It doesn't matter now." She looked over at El Tunchi. "We've come to an arrangement."

Buzz felt his stomach twist into knots. He looked over at El Tunchi. The little green guy looked excited, bouncing on the spot and whistling merrily to himself. He kept on eagerly scanning the horizon.

"Or rather, my brother did," Mari's grandmother revealed.

"Uncle Benjy?" Mari questioned. "He's alive?"

"Oh yes, your great-uncle Benjamin is alive, and from what he describes, more together than he has been for a long time." Esther gathered Mari in for a hug. "I'll try to explain, but I'm not sure where to begin."

"Let me do it," Tia offered. "Once his cloak went up in flames, Benjy managed to transport himself one last time. He asked to go home. The cloak sent him to Esther's house."

"Thing is," Esther explained, "the fire that consumed Benjy and Amin was so hot, it fused them back together. And when my brother landed on my rug, he was whole once more." Esther sniffed. "He made quite a mess, and I'd only just finished tidying up after my little episode."

"Yes, it was all quite dramatic." Buzz's mum's eyes were very wide.

"You were there?" Buzz questioned.

"Yes, Tia and I had gone to Esther's house to try to find you. We knew that wherever you were, you were going to be with Mari."

"And we wanted to find you quickly because things were getting seriously freaky in Crowmarsh, and El Tunchi wanted his payment." Tia reached out and ruffled Buzz's hair. "We needed to keep you safe."

El Tunchi began to chuckle. "Obviously, I was following them. I was waiting to pounce once they'd found you. I hid in the shadows of Esther's house, and I heard Benjamin's story. Heard how Benjamin had lost the cyphon somewhere when he transported." He rubbed his hands together. "Then I offered them a new deal."

There was the sound of wood and stone. It was coming from the top of the arena.

Everyone looked up, and Buzz saw Uncle Benjy. No – Uncle Benjamin. Benjy was gone. Benjamin looked older but much happier. In one hand he held the cyphon, and in the other he held El Tunchi's staff. It reverberated on the stone of the staircase as he descended into the arena.

"He found the cyphon." Buzz's mother let out a sigh of relief.

"I told you he would," El Tunchi scolded. "My staff has never failed to find an object."

Buzz couldn't help but stare at his mother. She seemed to be taking all this talk of cyphons and magical staffs in her stride. *I should have told her and Tia about the Runes of Valhalla instead of keeping them secret,* Buzz realised. Instead of keeping his two worlds separate, he should have made them one.

Great-Uncle Benjamin smiled as he walked past the frozen

Berchta. "Looks like you've got things under control here." He held up the cyphon. "Now all we need to do is get the rest of those gods into this claw and find them a new home." He handed El Tunchi his staff.

"I can't wait," the little green man said. "An actual purpose. The first time in centuries."

Benjamin held out a hand to the rainforest spirit. "We will do it together, and the path will be long and dangerous. I look forward to it, friend."

El Tunchi smiled widely, showing all his sharp, pointy teeth.

Great-Uncle Benjamin looked over at Buzz and Mari. "It's time for you both to go home. I'll deal with the gods and gather them all up."

"But don't you want to come home with us as well?" Mari asked. "You've been gone for so long."

Benjamin looked over at his sister. "It was amazing to come home, but I understand now that I'd never really left it. Home has always been in my heart." He took his sister's hand. "I'll be back one day, once I've found a new home for the gods. It will give me time to learn to live with Amin once more. To accept that he is part of me."

Theo turned to Moritasgus. "Don't worry about this cyphon thing. You can stay right here with me. I've got a shed at the bottom of my garden. It's warm and dry and—"

"No, Theo." The badger shook his head. "My time in this realm has passed. I will go with the others and find this new home."

"But—" Theo began.

"Be happy for me."

Theo looked like he was trying to swallow down tears, but he nodded.

"And don't go getting yourself into any more trouble," the badger said. "You are far too brave for your own good."

"Brave," Tia scoffed. "Theo?"

The badger fixed her with a fierce gaze. "The bravest mortal I have ever known, and I have known many and lived many centuries."

"Right." Tia was looking at Theo in amazement, and Buzz noticed that Theo was blushing.

Buzz rubbed at his eyes. He was beyond tired. "Okay, let's go home."

El Tunchi coughed. "Aren't you forgetting something?" He threw a leather pouch up into the air, and Buzz caught it.

"The Runes of Valhalla," he said. "I'd almost forgotten."

"Yer keep them safe," Ratatosk said. "And don't leave it so long to come and visit me next time. Yer know where the World Tree is."

Mari tickled the squirrel under his chin. "We'll come soon, but first, I think we'll all be quite busy getting Crowmarsh back to normal."

"Mortals have a great ability to adapt, accept, and forget," the badger said. "Crowmarsh will be fine."

"You're right," Mari said almost to herself. "Mortals' greatest power is their ability to adapt. I was fighting against the fact that Hel was a part of me. But she is. I see that now. And I know that she will move on when the time is right for us to separate."

"Well, this is our time now." Uncle Benjamin held up the claw, and it began to vibrate.

"The cyphon calls you. Know, gods, that this is the end of your time here but the beginning of the rest of your lives."

EPILOGUE

Buzz, Mari, Sam, Theo, and Tia looked into the cauldron.

"I wish for a new chess set made in the style of One Dream," Tia said.

Buzz shook his head. "That's just creepy."

"Why?" Tia scooped a large box out of the cauldron eagerly. "I like One Dream, and I like chess. It's the perfect combination."

"I think it is a great idea, Tia."

"Thanks, Theo."

"I wish for a telescope," Mari said. "Like, a really good one that proper scientists use." She looked over the edge of the cauldron, and her eyes went wide. "Perhaps something a little smaller. I don't think they'll let me take that on the plane." She gave a coo of delight as she reached in and pulled out a long box.

Sam muttered something under his breath, and he then pulled out a figure of Dortmeld riding Captain Phantom's bike.

Buzz laughed. "I guess the cauldron is supposed to be full of inspiration and imagination."

"Okay, my turn," Theo said. "I'm gonna get myself some new footwear." He reached into the cauldron, and Buzz expected him to bring out some shiny white sneakers, but instead it was a sturdy pair of walking boots.

Theo shrugged. "I spent a lot of the time in the forest with Moritasgus. Some proper boots would have helped." He looked over at Buzz. "What are you going to wish for?"

Buzz looked around at his friends and sister. "I'm good, actually. Got everything I need."

"Good," a voice said from behind them. "Because it's time for Ceridwen's cauldron to go back."

Buzz turned to see his father standing in the doorway to their cellar with his arms crossed. "And it's not a toy. It's a very powerful and magical artefact."

"Where'd you say you got it from again?" Buzz asked. "I can never remember how to pronounce it."

"Tír na nÓg." Professor Buzzard looked forlornly at the cauldron. "If you knew the things I had to do to find it." He shook his head. "It would have been the perfect payment for El Tunchi."

"No offence, Dad, but I think our solution was better." Tia pursed her lips. "You did steal this, after all."

"I was desperate," Buzz's dad protested. "I thought my son was going to be taken away. And the creature I stole it from has been in a deep trance for a couple of thousand years learning the mysteries of the universe."

"But he could wake up at any moment, Professor Buzzard," Mari said. "We should have returned it already, really."

"You're right, but we had to wait for the World Tree to heal," Buzz's dad said. "I've spoken to Ratatosk, and he said Yggdrasil is all better. It will transport us, no problem."

Buzz looked at the people around him, and grinned. "Well, let's do this quickly. I've got a horse-riding lesson later, and then we've got to go and get the newest issue of *Captain Phantom*."

Sam grinned. "It's like I said. It's all about priorities."

TO BE CONTINUED . . .

ACKNOWLEDGEMENTS

This novel and also *The Unmorrow Curse* are the result of many hours of hard work, imagining and ultimately believing that I had something meaningful to offer to young readers.

But I could not have done it alone.

Initial thanks must go to my mother, Monica Richards, for instilling a deep love of reading in me and even patiently typing up my stories when I was little. I was a harsh taskmaster!

Thank you to every single English teacher I've had from infant school to university. You have all seen something in me and nurtured it. You taught me that stories are important. That they are powerful. Most importantly you gave me the confidence to write them.

Special thanks to those who have read drafts over the years and offered advice – you know who you are and I really appreciated it!

I need to say thank you to all those friends who said I could do it – even when I doubted myself, even when I felt like I was losing the race. Extra special thanks to my agents, Caroline

Walsh and Christabel Mckinley, for seeing something in my writing, and for being supportive of all the directions that my career has gone in.

Huge thanks to team UCLAN: Hazel, Charlotte, Becky and Nicki.

Lastly, I need to say thank you to my husband David Nasralla. Thank you for the great ideas. Thank you for challenging me to be better. Love that we are building a life together and I look forward to new adventures with you and our fabulous kids.

Thank you.

HAVE YOU READ BUZZ AND MARI'S FIRST ADVENTURE?

Part Fo

DEAD R

The electrifying serial continues...

In THE SLOBBERERS, Rory and Dawn were chased into the night by horrifying bone-sucking slobberers – only to be confronted by killer sheep and a bus trip from hell in BATTERING RAMS.

Home again in CROAKED, but not for long. Kamikaze frogs, kidnap, and a crazy snail all pointed to one thing: the quest for the truth had to continue.

But who is the boy in the tree? How come he's Rory's double? Is this the answer to the mystery? Or are there more secrets to uncover and solve?

And what other dangers lie ahead?

Read on. DEAD RINGER will tighten its grip.

MORRIS GLEITZMAN & PAUL JENNINGS

Wicked!

Part Four

DEAD RINGER

PUFFIN BOOKS

Puffin Books
Penguin Books Australia Ltd
487 Maroondah Highway, PO Box 257
Ringwood, Victoria 3134, Australia
Penguin Books Ltd
Harmondsworth, Middlesex, England
Viking Penguin, A Division of Penguin Books USA Inc.
375 Hudson Street, New York, New York 10014, USA
Penguin Books Canada Limited
10 Alcorn Avenue, Toronto, Ontario, Canada M4V 3B2
Penguin Books (N.Z.) Ltd
Cnr Rosedale and Airborne Roads, Albany, New Zealand

First published by Penguin Books Australia, 1997
10 9 8 7 6 5 4 3 2 1

Typeset in 10/15pt Cheltenham by Midland Typesetters, Maryborough, Victoria
Made and printed in Australia by Australian Print Group, Maryborough, Victoria

National Library of Australia
Cataloguing-in-Publication data:

Jennings, Paul, 1943- .
Wicked!
ISBN 014 038775 7 (pt 1)
ISBN 014 038776 5 (pt 2)
ISBN 014 038777 3 (pt 3)
ISBN 014 038778 1 (pt 4)

I. Gleitzman, Morris, 1953- .
II. Title.

A823.3

Series editor: Julie Watts
Series designer: George Dale
Cover and text illustrations: Dean Gorissen

DEAD RINGER

ONE

It was like looking into a mirror. The boy who stared at me through the tree branches had my eyes, and ears, and hair. Even my nose. There was a bit of fuzz on his top lip. And he was a bit taller and had a couple of pimples.

But apart from that, the boy was me. He blinked back – stunned – not believing what he was seeing.

I tell you this. I had been chased by slobberers. And I had looked into the jaws of a giant frog. I had seen Dawn's dead mother smile at me.

And had followed a snail compass halfway across the state. But all that was nothing compared to this.

I knew this boy. And he knew me. But how can you know someone you have never seen before? And why was my stomach jumping? Why were my hands clammy?

I felt like you do on Christmas morning when you get an unexpected present. It was like witnessing a birth. Weird. Really weird.

'Aagh, the snail's out. The snail's escaped.' Dawn's shrieking voice came up from below.

I couldn't see the ground from where I was. But I realised with a shock that the infected snail must have escaped when I dropped the box. The snail that was seeking my next of kin. That wanted to kill my father.

'It's heading up the tree,' came Gramps' shaky shout. 'It's infiltrating our defences. Get the beggar.'

The boy was puzzled. But I was scared. Was my dad up there somewhere? I had to protect him. I scrambled out in the branches. 'Dad, Dad, Dad,' I yelled. 'Where are you? Look out. Jump. Get out of the tree. The snail's coming.'

No one answered. There was no one else up there.

I peered down and saw it. Coming up the trunk at a great rate of knots. The fastest snail in the world. I searched wildly for something to hit it with. I tried to snap off a small branch but it wouldn't break. There was only one thing to do. I pulled out my apple-man and started swatting wildly at the snail.

It was a bad idea. The snail vanished. Where was it? Where was the rotten thing? Where had it gone? Oh, shoot. It was crawling around on the head of the apple-man. It was sticking its face and horrible eyes into my apple-man's nostrils. Without thinking I grabbed the apple-man by the legs and started bashing its head against a branch. I didn't give a thought to the apple-man. I just had to get rid of the infected snail. It was clinging on like crazy.

I held the apple-man as steady as I could and bent back my finger. Flick. *Whap*. The snail spun off into the air and fell towards the ground.

'Look out, Dawn,' I shouted. 'It's back down there somewhere.'

'Got him,' came Gramps' excited voice. 'Got the bludger.'

'Put it in the box,' I yelled. 'Put it in the box.'

Then I forgot about the snail and turned to the older version of myself.

He was holding something out at me. At first I couldn't make sense of it. How did he get that? He had my apple-man. In his shaking hand he held out my apple-man, almost pushing him into my face.

RORY

Something was wrong. Something was very wrong. I looked down at my own shaking hand. I was still holding my apple-man. His head was a bit dented and there were sort of lumps under his shirt that I hadn't noticed before. I could feel them with the tips of my fingers. But he was still my apple-man. So how could the boy have it?

The answer was simple. He had one too – just like mine.

'Where did you get that?' I said in a shaking voice.

He came closer and examined me carefully. 'Where did *you* get my face?' he said.

I tried to stop myself from fainting. From falling out of the tree. I tried desperately to fit all the pieces together. 'Concentrate,' I told myself. 'Work it out. Slowly, slowly. Bit at a time.'

The boy was a bit older than me – okay.

The boy looked just like me – right.

The boy had an apple-man – no doubt about that.

The snail was after someone related to me – Dawn had worked that out already.

My father wasn't up the tree – rats.

So the snail must be after the boy – that was the only answer.

So.

The boy must be related to me.

That's when it all clicked. The thought hit me like a train rushing out of a tunnel. Suddenly it all made sense.

'You,' I whispered to the boy. 'You ... You must be my ...' I could hardly get the word out. I seemed to choke on it. 'You're ... my ...'

'Brother,' he said softly. I could see tears forming in his eyes.

I had a brother. All these years he had been alive and I never knew. I was all mixed up inside. Why hadn't I been told?

I was confused. I was heartbroken that Dad wasn't there. But I had someone new. At that moment the world became a little more friendly. I didn't seem quite so alone.

My brother and I both started to sob. He reached out and grabbed my arm. He pulled me close. 'You're only a little squirt,' he said. 'But you're mine. A blood relative. I thought I was alone.'

A blood relative? That's right. The snail had been after him. Not Dad.

After a bit he managed to say, 'Your ... our ... my mother. And father. Are they still alive?'

I nodded. And hoped that I wasn't lying.

'What are they like?' he asked in a trembling voice.

I couldn't think what to say. 'Well,' I managed to get

out. 'That gap between your teeth. That comes from Dad. And those pointy ears. They come from Mum.'

'Mum?' he said. 'Dad?' He seemed to have trouble getting the words out. 'I had a mum,' he said. 'And a dad. They were both killed.'

'But . . .' I started to say.

'Wait,' he said. 'My real parents were only sixteen when I was born. I never met them. They gave me up for adoption. That's all I know about them. My new parents were wonderful. But they died in a car crash. And I ended up here. In the cottage homes.'

I didn't know what to say.

He looked so sad. 'Tell me about your parents,' he said. 'Because they are my parents too, you know.'

I knew what he said was true. But it still made me feel funny inside. Having a brother – a real brother – was good. But I wasn't sure that I wanted to share my parents . . . again.

I started to tell him my story. It came tumbling out. Full of stuff about Dad and Mum and our step-family.

Halfway through the story a voice came floating up from below. 'Rory. What are you doing up there?' yelled Dawn. 'Hatching an egg?'

'That's the one I told you about,' I said to my brother. 'That's my step-sister. Big bad Dawn. She's . . . She's . . . all right, I suppose.'

'Hang on to your britches,' I yelled at Dawn. 'I can't come down yet.'

There were more interruptions from below but Howard and I ignored them. We talked and talked and talked. Both learning what there was to know about the other. My new brother got upset when I told him about Mum being in hospital. And Dad being in danger of infection. I tried to explain about the germs but he didn't believe that part of it.

'That's bulldust,' he said. 'Are you weird or what?'

'Come down and see the snail,' I told him. 'It's after you. It wants to infect you. You'll see.'

'It'll be a long time, little brother,' he said, 'before I'm scared of a snail.'

We both climbed down the tree and jumped onto the grass.

'This is Dawn,' I said. 'My . . . your . . . our step-sister.' She was standing there with her mouth hanging open like one of those sideshow clowns.

'What?' said Dawn slowly. I could see that her mind was working overtime. She just couldn't figure it out. For once she didn't have a clue what was going on.

'This is my brother Howard,' I told her.

She was shocked. Totally gobsmacked. She just stood there looking from me to Howard and back again. She couldn't take it in. But there was one thing I noticed. Straight away.

She liked him.

'And this is Gramps,' I said.

Gramps had the engine running on the Morris Minor and the bonnet up. At first I thought that the car must have broken down. But it hadn't. Gramps was cooking something on the cylinder head of the engine. He grabbed the meal with his pliers and held it out towards my brother.

'Hello, Howard,' he said. 'Do you like escargots?'

Howard looked puzzled. Was he wondering why Gramps didn't seem surprised to see him? Or was he just trying to figure out if his new family really ate that sort of thing?

As if to answer his question, Gramps popped the hot snail into his mouth and began to munch. 'Delicious,' he said. 'Absolutely delicious.'

TWO

I was stunned. A step-brother I'd never heard of had just dropped out of a tree. I was gobsmacked. I was flabbergasted. But the shock hadn't affected me as badly as it had Gramps. He'd gone ga-ga.

'Gramps,' I screamed, 'spit that out at once.'

Gramps smacked his lips. 'Top tucker,' he said, swooshing the snail round in his mouth.

'Don't be a dope,' I yelled at him. 'Just because the infection wasn't after you before, doesn't mean it can't change its mind. Even microbes get angry when you eat them.'

I turned to Rory and Howard for support. Howard was staring at us all and slowly backing away. I could tell he thought we were mad. A gang of loonies. A few billion brain cells short of a step-family.

I turned back to Gramps, who was still chewing happily. 'Do you want to turn into a walking monster?' I shouted at him, scared.

Everyone was looking at me now. Gramps as if I was sadly misguided and Howard as if I was a mental case and Rory as if I was a thoughtless and hurtful step-sister.

Which I was.

Suddenly I realised it wasn't the microbes that were angry, it was me. Gramps was as bad as all the others. All the people I cared about ended up sick or hurt or dead. Dad in hospital with a damaged leg. Mum at the bottom of the river. When were people in this family going to start taking care of themselves?

Gramps swallowed the snail.

'Mmm-mmm,' he said, 'I could go another dozen of those.'

I held my breath and watched Gramps anxiously. Would the infection race through his body and turn his skin blotchy and make his memory even worse than it was now? I hoped desperately that Rory and I were right about the illness. That it only infected people who were related by blood. And that each new victim had to be related by blood to the person infected before them.

Gramps wasn't related to Eileen by blood, even though she'd squeezed a couple of his blackheads.

Gramps gave me a hug. 'It's okay, love,' he said. 'I used to eat snails by the barrow-load in France in the war. Scientists have proved that if you heat a snail above a hundred and six degrees Celsius, you kill any germs on it.' Gramps frowned. 'Or was that frogs' legs?'

I felt like shaking him, even though he was an old man and I loved him and his teeth weren't that secure.

But I didn't.

Because at that moment I realised how much danger we were in. A big group of kids had gathered round and were staring at us. Now that Gramps had finished his snack, they were staring at Rory.

'Gramps,' I whispered, 'we've got to get Rory out of here. Hospitals call the cops when people steal one of their patients. Rory's probably on the TV news. If he's recognised we'll be arrested.'

Gramps frowned. I hoped he was thinking about how we could get out of there without causing a disturbance. I know I was. Then Howard did something that saved us the trouble.

He touched Rory. Just put his fingertips gently on Rory's arm, the one that was purple and blotchy with the infection.

'Were you born like that?' he asked softly. His own skin looked pale and smooth next to Rory's.

Rory stared at Howard's arm. His eyes filled with

tears. Suddenly he turned and pushed through the circle of gawking kids and broke into a lopsided run down the road.

'Quick,' I yelled at Gramps.

We struggled through the kids. I helped Gramps get the bonnet of the car down. Just as I was about to leap in, I saw Howard standing nearby, watching.

I'd never seen so much sadness on one kid's face.

Even as I opened my mouth, I knew it was a mistake. I knew I'd regret it. I didn't want another step-brother. I didn't want another kid living at my place sticking jammy knives in the margarine. I didn't want to have to share Dad with anyone else.

But he just looked so sad.

'If you want to find out about your parents,' I said, 'hop in.'

I got into the car. Gramps revved the engine and started doing a forty-nine-point turn. The other kids were staring at us and gabbling excitedly and yelling things.

Howard was standing very still. He looked scared and confused.

Gramps finally got the car pointing the right way. Just before we shuddered off down the road, Howard clambered in.

It was incredible. He was almost identical to Rory.

Bigger, but a dead ringer. And he was holding an apple-man that was a dead ringer for Rory's apple-man.

'Welcome to the family,' I said.

'Thanks,' he said. He didn't sound too sure about it. 'You know,' he continued, 'people who suffer from crazy ideas about, say, killer snails and giant worms and steel sheep can get treatment. I can give Rory the name of a child psychiatrist.'

'I think,' I said, 'you'd better keep your head down.'

Howard ducked out of sight. I peered anxiously through the dusty windscreen. The street was empty. No sign of Rory.

I had a sick feeling in my stomach. What if he got lost? What if the infection wiped his memory and he forgot who he was and where he lived? The thought of Rory ill and lonely made my eyes prick.

'Perhaps he's gone for a milkshake,' said Gramps. 'Can you see any milk bars?'

'I don't think he wanted a milkshake, Gramps,' I muttered.

'A burger?' asked Gramps hopefully

I sighed. The infection might be vicious and unstoppable, but at least it didn't seem to have made Gramps any worse.

Then I saw Rory ahead in the distance. He was turning down a side road. By the time we got there he was out of sight again. We skidded round the corner with Gramps flailing at the wheel and complaining about the stress on his suspension. After a few minutes I saw Rory again, heading out of town into the scrub.

When we caught up with him, he was crouched by the road, gasping for breath and rubbing his bad leg.

I gasped too. He looked worse than ever. The purple blotches were starting to come down his other arm. They must have spread right across his chest.

I leaped out of the car and went over to him. I put my face close to his. 'I'm sorry I said that stuff about the infection turning Gramps into a monster,' I said quietly. 'You're not a monster, okay?'

Rory didn't look up. 'Why did the infection get me first?' he whispered miserably. His eyes flicked towards Howard. 'Why not him?'

Howard was standing watching us. 'If that's an allergy,' he said, 'I've seen something a bit like it before. Similar but not as bad. There's a kid in the home who's allergic to food colouring and offal.'

I turned to him. 'Keep quiet,' I said, 'and you might learn something.'

'Whoo,' said Howard, amused. 'You're pretty young to be a school principal. Does your dad work for the Department of Education?'

I ignored him. This was exactly what I'd always

feared having an older brother would be like.

The pits.

I turned back to Rory. Gramps was hugging him and promising him ridiculous numbers of milkshakes and burgers.

I took a deep breath. I didn't feel good about what I was going to say, but it had to be said.

'Rory,' I began, 'the snail wasn't going after your dad, it was going after your brother, right?'

'Give her a gold medal,' snorted Rory.

'Remember what we said,' I continued gently. 'We know your father's involved with the infection one way or the other. If he's not the next target, he must be the one who sent it in the first place.'

'*You* said, not we said,' hissed Rory angrily. '*You* were the one who said that.'

His face was starting to change. Whatever anger did to the infection, it was happening now. His face was shrivelling and twisting and distorting.

I glanced at Howard, whose own face was pretty distorted too. With amazement.

I pressed on. 'It *is* possible your dad's behind all this. Until we know for sure we've got to be careful, that's all. For your sake and your mum's sake and all our sakes.'

Rory's face was hardly recognisable.

I looked at Howard again. He was staring at Rory, stunned, and I could tell that all of a sudden giant worms and steel sheep didn't seem quite so dopey,

'You're just jealous,' spat Rory, glowering at me. 'You're just jealous that both my parents are still alive.'

I felt fury wrench my own face out of shape and I turned away before I did or said something I'd regret even more than bringing Howard along.

'My dad's not evil,' continued Rory. 'When we find him, you'll see.' Suddenly he was yelling at me. 'You'll see.'

I stared at him, my own step-brother who I wouldn't have recognised even if he had a name tag on. This stranger was the one person in the world who could help me find out the truth about my mum's death. I felt ill.

'Tomorrow,' Gramps was saying, furiously polishing his glasses and peering anxiously at Rory. 'We'll go and find your dad tomorrow.'

'No,' said Howard.

We all turned and stared at him. His eyes were shining and he looked different too. Kind of determined and almost grown-up in a bossy sort of way. I had to admit that the times I'd imagined having a big brother, he did have big brown eyes like Howard's.

'Tomorrow's too long to wait,' said Howard. 'I want to go and find my dad now.'

THREE

The approaching night had already begun to swallow the sun. Gramps, big bad Dawn, Howard and I scrambled into the Morris Minor. I sat next to Gramps. Dawn and Howard snuggled down in the back seat. We were so tired. A lot had happened in just one day.

There should have been a lot to say. But we just sat there wrapped in our own thoughts as Gramps drove us through the darkness. Each one of us was carrying a different sadness.

I wanted to find my father. I didn't believe that he had sent slobberers to get me. I thought the germs were after *him*. The snail had been going for Howard. Now that it was gone, Howard might be safe. But Dad could be in danger at this very moment.

I couldn't tell what Howard was thinking. He had just met me and found out that I was his brother. And I had told him that the mother he had never met was seriously ill in hospital. And his father was in peril. The poor kid. He must have been going through hell.

And Dawn. She wanted desperately to know what happened the day her mum died on the bus. I wished that I could remember. I would have told her if I could.

And Gramps. He just couldn't work out what was real and what wasn't. But his daughter had drowned in the bus. He must have wanted to know what happened to her as much as Dawn did.

Sometimes Gramps said a lot of silly things. And at other times, a lot of wise things. But mostly he just kept his thoughts to himself. I had the feeling that there was a lot more going on inside his head than he let on.

Finally Dawn spoke up. In a loud voice as usual. 'The snail was after Howard,' she said. 'It wasn't interested in Rory's dad at all.'

'Why not?' I said.

'Because he's not related to your mum.'

'They used to be married,' I yelped. 'In the good old days before step . . . families. You can't get much more related than that.'

Dawn shook her head in exasperation. 'Yes,' she

said. 'But Eileen is not a blood relative. People are not even allowed to marry a blood relative. Your father is not related to your mother by blood.'

She was right. I hated to admit it but she was right.

'So,' said Dawn. 'There's no sense in rushing off looking for your dad, thinking you've got to save him. He doesn't need saving.'

'But we still want to find him,' I said.

'Why?'

Howard answered the question for me. 'Because he *is* our dad,' he said quietly.

That shut Dawn up for a bit. But only for a bit.

'He sent both apple-men,' said Dawn, looking at Howard's where it sat between them. 'Karl knows something about this disease. The slobberer spelt out his name. But how are we going to work out where he is?'

'Good point,' said Gramps. 'Where's the compass?'

'You ate it,' I reminded him.

Gramps shook his head. 'I'm old and tired,' he said. 'I don't know what I'm doing half the time. I must have been bloomin' hungry to eat a compass. I wonder if the magnet will pass straight through.'

We all lapsed back into silence. Dawn didn't really want to find our dad. She just wanted to stay with me till I remembered what happened on the bus the night her mum died. That's the only reason she was interested in me.

Gramps suddenly put his foot on the brake and pulled over next to a small clump of trees. It was completely dark outside. Night noises filled the air. Crickets chirped. Gum leaves rustled gently in the trees above. Somewhere nearby a wallaby bounded through the bush.

'No point wasting petrol,' said Gramps. 'We haven't got much so we'd better decide where we are going.'

Suddenly a splatter of liquid splashed across the windscreen and bonnet. Gramps jumped out and looked up into the branches above. 'A possum,' he yelled. 'A rotten possum is piddling on us.' He started wiping at the bonnet with his sleeve. 'Terrible stuff,' he yelled. 'Really eats into the paintwork.'

We all started to laugh like mad. Suddenly, for just a few minutes, we were not step-kids or adopted kids or jealous kids. We were just three friends laughing at something funny in the night.

'Wait a minute,' said Dawn. She stopped laughing and stared at Howard's apple-man. 'Let's have a look at your apple-man, Rory.'

I switched on the yellow roof light and took out my ugly little doll.

Both apple-men had been loved to bits. They were

worn and flattened from being shoved inside our pockets.

'Mine came in the mail one day, years ago,' said Howard. 'The package was posted in the city.'

'So was mine,' I shouted. 'Maybe that's where Dad lives.'

Dawn examined the two shrivelled-up dolls closely. 'The clothes are home-made,' she said excitedly. 'There's no labels on them.'

She was right.

The stitching was crooked and loose. Not like the sort of thing done in a factory. Both apple-men had the same navy-blue jacket and pants. The clothes were exactly the same – except for one thing. Mine had the letters AMP sewn on to the pocket.

'AMP. That doesn't make sense,' I said.

Howard stared at his apple-man. It had the letters ACO sewn on to the pocket. He said it aloud and frowned. 'That doesn't mean anything either,' he said.

'Jeez,' said Dawn. 'You can tell you two are related. Can't you work anything out? Both uniforms were made from the same bit of material. Put the letters together.'

'ACOAMP,' I said. 'That doesn't mean anything, smartypants.'

Gramps was still outside picking something off the

bonnet of the Morris Minor. He finally stopped and got back into the driver's seat.

'Try it the other way around,' said Dawn.

'AMPACO,' said Howard. 'What's that?'

'An oil refinery,' said Gramps. 'That's where Karl used to work.'

'What?' we all screamed at once. 'Why didn't you tell us?'

'There was a reason,' said Gramps. 'I know there was a reason why I didn't mention it. But I can't remember what it was. Oh, yes. When they shut down . . .'

'Hey,' shouted Dawn. 'Look at your apple-man, Rory. It's changing.' Everyone stared.

'It looks the same to me,' said Howard.

'No,' said Dawn. 'It's grown fingers.'

I hugged my apple-man close to my chest. Dawn tried to grab him but I held on tight.

'They're funny fingers,' said Dawn. 'No fingernails. She touched one of the little fingers and then pulled her hand away. 'Yuck,' she said. 'They feel like, like . . . a bit of worm or something.'

I peered inside the apple-man's blue uniform. The fingers were actually shoots growing out of the apple itself. They ran down inside the sleeves and out of the cuffs.

'Did it always have fingers?' asked Howard.

'No,' said Dawn. 'We'd better get rid of it. Fast.'

I hugged my apple-man even tighter to my chest. Those little apple-dolls were all we had to remind us of our Dad. There was no way I was going to throw mine out.

'Why does he have to get rid of it?' said Howard in a strained voice.

'Could be a spy,' said Gramps. 'Spies are always shot when they're caught.'

'There could be more slobberers in it,' said Dawn.

'There aren't,' I yelled. 'They've all gone. The apple's just started to grow a bit. So what? I've seen potatoes do it too. It's just an apple with a few suckers.'

'Listen, kids,' said Howard. 'I really can't believe all this stuff about slobberers. I'm not throwing my apple-man out and I don't think Rory should have to either.'

Dawn started to punch the seat. 'You two,' she shouted. 'Are so . . . so . . .'

We all knew that she was trying not to swear.

Gramps tried to calm her down. He passed over a grubby piece of newspaper. 'These'll cheer you up,' he said. 'Anyone like a chocolate-coated almond?'

Dawn glared at Gramps' little offerings of peace. Then she grabbed one and shoved it in her mouth.

I looked at the paper carefully. 'No thanks,' I said politely.

RORY

Dawn screamed and jumped out of the car. She started spitting and coughing as if she was choking.

'You knew,' she screamed at me. 'You rotten fink. You knew.'

'What's up with her?' said Howard.

This time I did laugh. I laughed like crazy.

'Possums,' I said. 'They don't just do pee, you know.'

FOUR

We decided to camp for the night. It was my idea. I wanted to show Worm Boy that it took more than a mouthful of possum poo to stop my brain working.

'I reckon,' I said, 'we should sleep here instead of driving on and getting even more tired and skidding off the road and rolling the car and being killed.'

Nobody argued with that.

Rory showed that he still had a working brain too, which was a relief. The way he'd cacked himself over Gramps' chocolate almond mix-up, I'd started to worry that the infection and lack of sleep was turning his brain into that stuff they use for kitchen sponges.

Suddenly he went serious. 'I reckon,' he said. 'Howard should sleep in the car.'

Nobody argued with that either. Including Howard, even though he was the tallest so the car was going to be more uncomfortable for him than anyone else. We all knew leg cramps were better than sleeping under the stars and being exposed to possible attacks by relentless and vicious microbes.

As Rory and Gramps were getting out of the car, Howard cleared his throat. 'Thanks for bringing me along,' he said. 'I'd rather meet my real parents and risk snuffing it than be stuck in that home.'

Rory's eyes shone. He looked more like himself than he had for hours. 'In this family,' he said, 'we don't leave brothers behind.'

It was a nice thing to say, even though up until that afternoon it hadn't exactly been true.

'Tosh,' said Gramps to Howard. 'A healthy young bloke like you shouldn't be talking about death. You'll probably be getting married soon.'

Howard's cheeks went pink. 'I'm only fifteen,' he said.

It made me feel funny inside seeing Howard blush. Sort of warm.

Then I had an awful thought. Did they put fifteen year olds in jail? Kids who ran off from homes probably got into big trouble. I asked Howard what would happen if the police or social workers caught him.

'It wouldn't be pretty,' said Howard. 'I'd probably be history.'

'Don't worry, Howard,' I said, 'we'll look after you.' It felt strange saying that to an older kid, but Howard gave me a grateful smile.

'I'm starving,' said Rory to Gramps. 'It's okay for you and Dawn, you've eaten, but me and Howard haven't had anything.'

'Very funny,' I said.

'I did have a chocolate cake in the boot,' said Gramps thoughtfully. 'But that was a couple of years ago.' He had an idea. 'We could catch that possum and roast it.'

Rory said he wasn't that hungry after all.

'Oh well,' said Gramps, 'at least we've got some water.' We all perked up. 'In the car radiator,' he said. We all groaned.

Gramps promised us he hadn't bunged in any anti-rust chemicals, so we had a couple of mouthfuls each. It was better than nothing.

We built a camp fire. Then we dragged Gramps' old tarpaulin and blankets out of the boot and made up beds on the ground and one in the car.

'G'night,' said Howard with another grateful smile as we shut him in.

After shifting some rocks from under my blanket and staring into the camp fire for a bit and thinking about curried-egg sandwiches with chips, I tried to go to sleep.

DAWN

Even though I was exhausted, it wasn't easy. The blanket smelled of car oil and the hot rusty water had only taken away about one-quarter of the taste of the possum poo.

Plus I was worried about Gramps. What if the snail was stronger than Gramps' digestive juices? What if it was swimming around inside him spreading the disease? An old person might not be able to survive an infection like that.

The bush was alive with strange noises. I listened fearfully. Then I told myself to calm down. The slobberers and the sheep and the frogs were all dead. The only way another creature could get infected and come after us was if the hospital people didn't keep Eileen in quarantine properly.

I hoped the sheets of plastic across the hospital corridor didn't have as many holes in them as Gramps' blanket.

Thinking about Eileen made me think of Dad. Was he still in hospital with his bung leg? Or was he out in the night somewhere, worried and angry, searching for us with the police and state emergency service? I rolled over, scraped my pelvis on a rock I'd missed and wished remote bush camping spots had phone boxes.

Then things got worse. Thinking about Dad made me think of Mum. I had a silent cry. I often thought about her at night, wondering if she really had been the wonderful loving Mum I remembered, or whether she'd just been faking it and had actually been a miserable suicidal drinker like some people said.

I could hear Gramps snoring softly on one side of me. On the other Rory's shape was still and silent.

'Rory,' I whispered, 'are you asleep?'

'I would be,' he hissed, 'if you weren't yakking.'

'I was just wondering,' I said, 'if you'll be seeing any visions of Mum tonight.'

'How do I know?' he replied crossly. 'I'm not a telly. These things aren't scheduled. I can't look at a listing in the paper and see "9.30: Rory's infection gives him more hallucinations and he discovers why Dawn's mum crashed the school bus and died." '

'Sorry,' I said. Even though I felt very disappointed, I felt a bit guilty as well. It was amazing how quickly you could forget that another person was suffering an awful infection when you weren't.

I must have gone to sleep soon after that because the next thing I knew I'd snapped awake.

There was movement nearby. Twigs crunching.

I froze.

In the faint moonlight I could just make out two large figures. They were bigger than sheep. They were even bigger than slobberers.

A horrible thought hit me. What if the frogs weren't all dead? What if they'd come back for a second attack? Rory and Gramps had defeated one giant frog. Maybe this time the frogs had sent two.

Trembling, I groped around in the darkness for a weapon. A stick, Rory's smelly socks, anything. I'd have given all the curried-egg sandwiches in the world for my steel fence post.

Nothing.

Then one of the figures spoke. 'Sorry,' it muttered. 'When your bladder's as old as mine it needs a regular empty.'

'That's okay, Gramps,' mumbled the other figure. 'I could do with one too.'

My body went limp with relief as I watched Rory lead Gramps into the bushes for a pee.

Three seconds later I was tense again. What if Eileen had infected something else? What if the hospital had cockroaches? They could get in and out of Eileen's room even if the door was sealed with silicon grouting. I shuddered as I thought of giant cockroaches scuttling towards us through the bush, huge eyes bloodshot with hatred.

Or bedbugs. The hospital could have bedbugs, which would escape when the sheets were changed. I didn't even know what a bedbug looked like, but my blood still ran cold when I thought of one twenty metres tall with Howard in its mouth.

Or spiders. Or snakes. Or the hospital caretaker's cat.

Suddenly I realised the bush noises had got much louder. What was that? It sounded like something doing horrible things with its own saliva. I couldn't hear properly because my heartbeat was thudding in my ears. I peered frantically into the darkness. All I could see were the black shapes of trees.

Then I realised something else. Rory and Gramps hadn't come back. I opened my mouth to call to them, then closed it. Better keep quiet. I couldn't remember if cockroaches had ears or not.

Trembling, I stood up and fought off a powerful urge to go to the car and wake Howard. It wouldn't be fair, he was more at risk than any of us. Instead I started taking terrified steps in the direction Rory and Gramps had gone. Soon I was among the trees.

I heard the saliva sound again and remembered Rory's description of the giant frog's long slimy tongue.

'Oh no,' I sobbed under my breath, 'the frogs are back.'

Things rustled. Shrill noises rang out and I couldn't tell if they came from tiny throats or huge hungry ones. Wet things brushed against my face and I didn't know if they were dewy creepers or strings of frog saliva.

I panicked and ran. Struggling through tangled undergrowth and branches that clawed at me. Then I burst out of a clump of bushes and froze. Silhouetted against the moonlit sky were several massive shapes. I prayed they were trees. Almost fainting, I waited for the sound of a huge tongue moving at speed.

Suddenly something long and dark shot out in front of me. I stifled a scream.

'That's the Southern Cross,' said Gramps' voice. 'My favourite.'

It was an arm. Gramps' arm, pointing.

'Wow,' said Rory's voice.

I couldn't believe it. They were star-gazing. While I was losing years off my life with fear and stress, they were star-gazing.

Anger cleared my vision. I saw that the massive shapes were trees, not frogs. Trembling, I leant against one.

Stifling the scream had been hard, but it took even more effort to stifle the urge to strangle Rory. I didn't know what made me angrier, that he thought star-gazing was more important than finding out the truth about my mum's death, or that he was doing it with my Gramps.

I was about to inform him of the ancient belief that

stars are actually the souls of selfish and thoughtless step-brothers glowing with embarrassment. Then something happened which completely distracted me.

Frantic, fearful shouts came from the direction of the car.

'Howard,' I yelled. Rory and Gramps stared, startled to see me. Then we tore back to the car.

I pulled open the rear door. Howard was clutching his blanket around him, white-faced even in the yellow car light. He was sweaty and panting.

'My parents . . .' he sobbed. 'They're all dead.'

I held his hand. 'It was just a dream,' I said, hoping desperately I was right.

'Nightmare,' said Gramps. 'I often get 'em if I have a warm drink just before I go to bed.'

I told Rory and Gramps to go back to sleep. No point in us all being awake.

'Come on, Gramps,' said Rory sulkily, 'I think they want some privacy.'

Howard squeezed himself across the back seat and I sat in the front and talked to him. I told him about his mum and what a good person she was despite her temper and messy bathroom habits. Then I surprised myself and asked him if he had a girlfriend. He said there was a girl at the home he'd quite liked but he didn't think he'd ever see her again.

'What about you?' he asked sleepily. 'Have you got a boyfriend?'

I was glad it was dark and he couldn't see me blush. 'No,' I said, 'I haven't really had time.'

Howard didn't say anything, but I sensed he knew I wasn't telling him the whole story. So I told him the whole story. I don't know why. Stuff I'd never told anyone, not even Dad. How I was waiting desperately to grow out of being an ugly tomboy. How I feared that I was doomed to be one forever. How if what people said about Mum was true, I was probably being punished in some way for having an evil mother.

When I finally shut up I saw that Howard was asleep. I didn't mind. I hadn't meant to blab so much anyway.

With his eyes closed and his face scrunched up he looked almost as young as Rory. I wondered if we'd be able to save him from being infected. I hoped we would. He looked so hurt and he'd had such a tragic life that I wished I could make myself the target of the infection instead of him.

At least that would give me a better chance of finding out the truth about my mother's death.

FIVE

Camping out is all well and good. But when all you have is an old blanket on the ground and no pillow it's the pits.

The sound of kookaburras told me that dawn was approaching. I stood up and shivered and tried to shake the pain out of my stiff neck. Gramps was snoring softly and sleeping just as if he was at home in his own warm bed.

Mist crept through the gum trees and joined a long, soft cloud that floated just above the ground. Nearby my apple-man stood to attention and seemed to watch silently like a small, stiff sentry at the end of his night shift.

Peace. Absolute perfect peace. 'Wouldn't it be nice,' I thought to myself, 'if we could just stay here and live. Catch rabbits and listen to the birds. No germs. No slobberers. No worry.'

Then my heart felt heavy. No Mum – and no Dad either.

The peaceful thoughts drained away. We had to get going. We had to see this through. We had to move Howard to a safe place before some creature infected him. And we had to find Dad – if he was still alive. We had to discover what it was all about. I walked over to the Morris Minor and looked inside.

Dawn was sleeping softly. Her face seemed gentle and happy. She was even prettier when she was asleep than when she was awake.

A painful thought made me frown. I felt the germs stirring and coming to life inside me. My arm ached and throbbed. The world seemed a dark and unhappy place.

What was happening to me?

Jealousy. That's what. Dawn had spent the *whole* night in the car with Howard.

She had fallen asleep with one arm draped over the seat. Her hand was resting on Howard's knee. And I didn't like it. Not one little bit. She was *my* step-sister first. She should have been resting her hand on me. Not him. She probably thought he was more mature than me. I grew more and more angry.

'Hey, you two,' I yelled. 'Wake up. We have to get going.' I banged on the roof of the car so hard that it shook. Dawn and Howard sat up and stared around in fright.

'What is it?' yelled Howard.

'Time to go,' I said grumpily.

'Keep your shirt on,' said Dawn. 'It's only just got light. It's still early.'

I stared around the clearing and tried to control my jealous thoughts. After all, Howard was my brother. And who cared about Dawn anyway? She was just a bossy step-sister with a cute turned-up nose.

'What's for breakfast?' said Dawn, smiling at Howard.

'What about snails?' he said.

Dawn shook her head and laughed as if it was the funniest joke in the world.

'How about chocolate-coated almonds?' I asked.

'Very funny,' said Dawn.

No one laughed.

I walked away in embarrassment. My little apple-man was still standing to attention. But he was different.

His fingers had grown. In fact they were so long that they touched the ground.

'Hey,' I yelled.

'What?' said Dawn.

I opened my mouth to say something but nothing came out. I *couldn't* tell them. I couldn't bring myself to say the words. It was as if a battle was going on inside my head. I wanted to scream out and say, 'The apple-man's fingers are growing. The snail must have infected him when I was in the tree. The germs can infect plants too.'

But instead I said nothing.

I could almost feel the disease inside my head. Trying to take over my brain. Trying to make me do its will. Feeding on my jealousy and anger.

Terrible thoughts filled my head. Dawn and Howard were ganging up on me. All she wanted was for me to remember what happened to her mother on the bus. After that she would probably try to get rid of me. Dawn hated my apple-man. If I told her about his fingers she would make me destroy him so she could be alone with Howard. And she didn't like my dad. She didn't care that he could get infected.

Dad gave me that apple-man. He was my friend. Standing there in his blue refinery uniform. So what if he *was* growing fingers? It was probably going to help us.

That's the way my mind was working. The stupid thoughts rushing around inside my head seemed perfectly normal.

So I didn't say anything. I just watched as the index finger on the apple-man's right hand grew out like a moving piece of rope.

I said nothing as it slowly and steadily wormed across the ground towards the sleeping figure of Gramps.

Closer, closer, closer.

Still I kept quiet. Still the words of warning that I wanted to shout would not form in my mouth.

The finger – no, it wasn't a finger. It was a sucker. Or a creeper. Something like that. Whatever it was it had almost reached Gramps. It wormed its way up to the little cup that he had put his false teeth into. It climbed up the cup and crept inside. It was drinking the water.

Gramps snored. Dawn and Howard looked at each other with big smiles. They hadn't seen it.

I struggled. Oh, I really struggled with the terrible germs that were fighting a battle for my mind.

The root crept towards Gramps. Was it going to put its terrible finger into his ear? Or his mouth? Was it going to drink him?

I tried to say something but I couldn't. The words just wouldn't come out. In the end I managed to point. 'Aagh,' was all I could get out. A sort of strangled cry. 'Aagh.'

Dawn and Howard stared. And stared. And stared. Not at the apple-man. But at me. What was wrong? Suddenly I realised. My face must be twisted and ugly. Changing with the black thoughts that were swirling inside my skull.

I forced my feet forward. I staggered towards Gramps

like a drunken man. 'Aagh,' I gurgled. 'Aagh . . .'

Suddenly Gramps sat up. He reached into his pocket and took out the little silver pocket knife that he used to peel apples and pears. He flicked open the blade and with one swift slash, cut off the end of the creeping root.

'Gotcha,' he shouted. 'A Finnigan doesn't sleep on guard duty. I've been watching you for a while.'

Dawn screamed as the cut root started to whip and curl around like a worm that had been chopped in half.

'Into the car,' yelled Gramps.

I threw a look at the apple-man. Some of his other fingers had reached the ground by now. They disappeared into the soil. They were sucking up moisture. One of the fingers of the other hand was writhing its way towards the car. Faster and faster.

Dawn grabbed Gramps by the shoulder and started to pull him towards the car. But he broke away and hurried back to the cup. 'I'm not going anywhere without my teeth,' he yelled. He grabbed his teeth and shoved them into his wrinkled mouth. Then he tottered to the car and fell into the driver's seat.

I just stood there watching it all. I wanted to help Dawn and Howard and Gramps. And I also wanted to help my apple-man tear them to pieces. Oh, terrible, horrible thoughts. What could I do?

Think. Think peace. Think beauty. Think love.

I stared at the whispering trees and the morning's blanket of mist. I heard the happy call of the waking kookaburras. I thought of my mother's smile as she read me a story in bed. I thought of Dawn and her funny laugh and her soft hands.

Then I turned my back on my old companion the apple-man and ran to the car and jumped inside with my friends. It was a huge wrench but panic drove the sadness from me.

'Go,' I screamed to Gramps. 'Go, go, go.'

Gramps started the engine and put the car into gear. He let out the clutch and the back wheels spun.

'Faster,' yelled Dawn. 'Faster.'

Faster? Didn't Dawn know anything? It wouldn't be hard to go faster. We weren't moving at all.

I threw a glance out of the back window. Thick smoke filled the air. A sharp smell of burning rubber stung my nostrils.

'What's up? said Howard. 'Is the engine on fire?'

'No,' I screamed. 'The wheels are spinning. The tyres are burning. Stop, Gramps. Stop.'

It was just as if the back of the car had been tied to a tree with a rope. Except the rope wasn't a rope. It was a finger. A root. A horrible curling creeper sent out by the apple-man. It was wrapped around the back bumper.

RORY

There was no way that the Morris Minor was going anywhere.

Howard was in the front with Gramps. And I was in the back with Dawn. I could feel that my face was going back to normal. What was happening? Was it because I'd done the right thing and sacrificed my apple-man? Was that like having calm thoughts?

I took Dawn's hand and gave it a squeeze but she didn't seem to notice. Maybe she was just too occupied with the plant tendril that was hanging on to the back bumper.

'This car's got holes in it,' she shrieked.

'Like this one,' said Howard calmly. He sure was a cool customer. He was pointing at a green tendril snaking its way through a rusty gap in the door. He took Dawn's mother's shoe and started hitting at the horrible root. No panic. Just calm action. The tendril took no notice. It kept on coming. A bit like a cobra rearing its head out of a basket when a snake charmer plays his flute.

'Give me that,' yelled Dawn.

She grabbed the shoe and shoved it at the tendril. Straight away the writhing finger started to retreat. It squirmed back out of the hole as if it had been stung.

My mouth just fell open. In Dawn's hand the shoe seemed to have a power all of its own.

The shoe had scared the tendril. But my apple-man was busy in other directions. One long shoot was wriggling down into the ground. Plants need water. And it wanted some. Badly.

'Right,' said Gramps. 'We're getting out of here.'

He put the car into reverse and backed up towards the place where my apple-man was growing. The tendril that had attached itself to the car fell slack. Gramps shoved the Morris into first gear and let her rip.

'Racing start,' I screamed.

The Morris Minor leapt foward like a Ferrari off the starting line.

'Way to go,' I yelled as the Morris rocketed forward in a shower of stones and smoke.

The tendril suddenly tightened as the car took up the slack.

Twang. The bumper bar was ripped straight off the car. It bounced up into the air with the tendril still grabbing on to it.

We sped on to the road and raced away like a bat out of hell. Gramps grinned. 'Yahoo,' he shouted.

But he was too early. I looked back in disbelief. There was only one word to say and I said it.

'Shoot.'

Out of the back window I could see the tendril

following. It was growing in fast-time. Streaking along behind us like a skinny piece of living rope.

'Faster,' I yelled. 'Faster.'

The car rocked and bumped and lurched along the road. The landscape was growing lonelier. And drier. All night we had camped without one car passing. I hoped and prayed that another car would come. But I knew it was unlikely. We were in this on our own. On the edge of the desert.

The speedo was showing fifty-five miles an hour. Gramps read my thoughts. 'About ninety kilometres an hour,' he said. 'We can't keep this up.'

He was right. The tendril was coming up fast behind, growing and stretching at enormous speed. 'It's catching us,' I shouted.

The tendril suddenly started tapping at the back window like the finger of death beckoning. It sent a shiver down my spine. Dawn screamed.

'It's after me, isn't it?' said Howard.

I didn't have time to answer. The tendril suddenly curled down and grabbed the Morris' towbar.

The car stopped with a bang, just as if it had hit a brick wall.

SIX

The jolt was so violent that my head snapped forward and my chin banged onto my chest. Then my head flew back and smacked against the rear parcel shelf.

My brains turned to curried egg.

Something was holding me tight around the middle and for a moment I thought it was Mum's strong arms. Thanks, Mum, I thought. Without you I'd have gone over those front seats and through the windscreen.

My eyes cleared. I looked down. It was only the seat belt. Same difference, but. Mum had made Gramps put those seat belts in.

'What did we hit?' mumbled Gramps.

'Nothing,' said Rory. 'The root grabbed the towbar.'

'Flamin' towbar,' growled Gramps. 'I should have listened

to Louise. She told me it was a dopey idea putting a towbar on a Morris Minor.'

'Start the engine,' said Rory. 'Quick.'

'No point,' said Howard. 'Even if we can snap the root again, it's faster than us.'

'He's right,' said Gramps.

From under the car came a scratching, slithering sound. The root was wriggling around the chassis, looking for a way in. I gripped Mum's shoe but it was no good. There were too many ways in for one shoe.

'Block up all the holes,' I yelled.

We tore off our windcheaters and socks and clambered over each other, stuffing them into rust holes and the gaps around the clutch and brake and accelerator pedals.

Then we held our breaths and listened.

Scratch, scratch.

Slither, slither.

Suddenly the root shot across the windscreen. Halfway up it stopped, pulled back from the glass and swivelled from side to side, white hairy tip pointing towards us like a blind snake sensing the movements of its lunch.

I tried not to tremble.

'Flamin' mongrel,' muttered Gramps. 'If I had my

rotary mulcher in here, you'd be history.'

The root ignored him. It slithered across the bonnet and into the front of the engine.

'Oh no,' said Rory. 'It's going to try and come in through the dash.'

We stuffed more socks into the air vents. I'd been wearing the same pair for two days and two nights, so I hoped the infection had given the root a strong sense of smell.

Then we heard another sound. The squeak of metal turning against metal.

'What's it doing?' breathed Howard.

I had a horrible vision of the root slowly undoing all the nuts and bolts until the car fell to pieces and we were left sitting in the middle of a pile of spare parts.

But it wasn't doing that. 'It's unscrewing the radiator cap,' said Gramps.

The squeak was replaced by a slurping sound, like liquid being sucked thirstily up a straw.

'It's drinking the water in the radiator,' said Rory.

Gramps rummaged under his seat. He pulled out a metal tyre lever.

'No mongrel drinks my radiator water,' he yelled, opening his door.

'Gramps, don't,' I shouted. I pointed out the window at the flat dusty plain all around us. 'There's hardly anything growing out there. That means no water. Once the root's finished the radiator it'll want to drink you.'

To a thirsty root Gramps would have looked like one of those dried goatskin water bags from Greece only more wrinkly.

I pulled Gramps' door shut and locked it.

The slurping sound stopped.

'What now?' said Rory.

'I think I should go out there,' said Howard quietly.

We stared at him.

'It's here because it wants to infect me,' he went on. 'I really appreciate you protecting me, but let's get it over with and then perhaps the root'll leave us alone and we can go and find Dad.'

'No,' said Rory.

'Why not?' said Howard.

I opened my mouth to give Howard a couple of million reasons, but Rory got in first.

'Because,' he said quietly, 'there might not be a cure.'

He looked so scared and lost when he said that, and so brave, that I wanted to put my arms around him. I didn't. Kids got really embarrassed if you hugged them in front of their older brothers.

'You and Mum are infected,' said Howard. 'If there's

no cure, I don't want to be left . . .' He couldn't finish the sentence. His voice choked and his eyes filled with tears.

Rory leant over and hugged him. 'Dad'll have a cure,' he said. 'He's got to.'

I had a strong urge to ask Rory how Karl would have a cure if he was just the next innocent victim, but I didn't.

Rory stopped hugging Howard. 'You're not going out there,' he said fiercely.

'Okay,' said Howard.

'You're a brave lad for volunteering,' said Gramps. 'When we get out of this I'm going to recommend you for a medal and a job in the bank.'

Howard gave a little smile. I could tell he was starting to like his new step-grandfather.

Then I saw a movement outside the car. A thin hairy root tendril was wriggling through the dust towards Howard's door. We heard it scrabbling its way up the duco. We waited for it to appear at Howard's window. It didn't.

'Where's it gone?' said Howard after a couple of minutes.

I was trying to see it through my window but I couldn't.

'Perhaps it's given up,' I said.

No such luck. A faint rattling sound came from inside Howard's door. What was it doing? We strained our ears.

Suddenly I noticed something that sent a chill through my guts. The handle on the inside of Howard's door was vibrating slightly. Howard had decided not to open his door, so the root was going to open it for him.

'It's inside the lock,' I yelled. 'It's trying to pick it.'

Anger surged through me. How dare that slimy, sneaky apple-man root threaten a kid who was prepared to sacrifice himself for us?

I grabbed Mum's shoe and pressed it against the inside of the door as close as I could to the lock.

'Cop that,' I hissed.

'Hear hear,' said Gramps. 'I wish I had my spray gun.'

But this time the shoe didn't have any effect on the root at all. I didn't understand it. The rattling continued. Then Howard's door unlocked with a snap. I threw myself forward and pushed the handle into the locked position and held it there. Howard put his hands on mine and we pushed till our knuckles were white and we were dripping with sweat.

Rory and Gramps leaned over the other side of Howard and pressed their hands against ours. We stayed that way for what seemed like hours. It was hot and cramped and painful and every second I expected the root to burst in through the base of the handle and rip the skin off our hands.

But something made me stay there. Something apart from fear and desperation and the fact that Howard and Rory and Gramps were pressing so hard I couldn't have got my hands off the handle even if I'd wanted to.

Crouched there shoulder to shoulder with my two step-brothers I felt something unexpected. I felt like I was in a family. It was a good feeling and I didn't want to lose it.

The root had other ideas.

Suddenly it changed tactics. We saw it shoot up the outside of Howard's window. It slithered across the roof, shot down the outside of Gramps' window and scrabbled under the floor before climbing up my window.

We fell back into our seats and watched in horror as the root wound itself round and round the car. It didn't stop until it had wrapped itself around us about twenty times.

'Why's it doing that?' whispered Rory.

I didn't know.

I didn't want to imagine.

SEVEN

My apple-man had started off okay. But germ-carrying slobberers had grown in him. And now he had become infected himself. He had put down roots and turned into a wicked plant. It wanted to get Howard. And it would kill anyone who tried to stop it.

My apple-man had been my friend for so long.

Now it was our enemy. My heart was aching at the thought. Dad's gift was trying to kill us. I couldn't bear to think about it. But I had to.

One thing I had was a good imagination. I could let my mind wander and take me into all sorts of places. And I could see what that crawling, writhing finger was capable of.

If I tried to protect Howard the tendril could wrap itself around my neck and squeeze until my eyeballs bugged out. It could choke off my windpipe so that I couldn't breathe.

It could get Gramps and drag him out of the car by his legs. It could send little suckers into every hole in his body. I shuddered at the thought.

Then it would go for Dawn. She was strong. She was tough. She would put up a good fight. But in the end it would get her. Wrap itself around her lovely hair. And pull her down into the earth. Suck her into a rabbit burrow. Bury her forever.

It was strong was that tendril. As strong as steel rope. And it was growing stronger by the minute. Little apple leaves were sprouting along its length. Taking in energy from the sun. Giving it strength. And it was putting down more roots. Suckers pushed down into the ground looking for moisture. It was building itself up for the final attack.

On Howard.

What would it do to him? It would leave him alive. To infect another plant or animal. Which could then infect Dad.

First it would put a tiny sucker into Howard's mouth. And infect him. Or drop a little seed into his ear. Then roots would grow. Eating into his brain. Tracking through his veins and nerves. Feeding on the anger and fear inside him. Spreading the germs into every cell.

Just like the infection was doing to me.

I stared outside at the bleak landscape. Nothing. Not

a person to help. The sun beat down fiercely on the Morris Minor. Heating it up. Heating us up. We had no water. No food. Nothing to look forward to. Except death.

Death in the form of a vine that was slowly tightening its grip on our metal prison.

An hour ticked by. And another. We couldn't get out. And we couldn't stay.

'We need water,' said Howard. 'Or we'll die of thirst. I'm going to get out and fight the rotten thing. It's only a plant.'

'No,' I said in a dry, rasping voice. 'Look.'

Something was moving on the horizon. Far in the distance I could see smooth shapes moving. Yes, yes, yes. Help was coming. Just in time. I strained my eyes, trying to see.

'Look,' I said. 'Dune buggies.'

'Panzers,' said Gramps.

'No,' said Dawn. 'They're not machines. And they're not people either.'

'Oh no, not frogs,' I croaked. 'Please don't let it be frogs.'

The brown shapes grew larger. Running on four legs. Not frogs. They looked like running rocks. Smooth animals. Moving towards us at a fast pace. About ten of them.

'Pigs,' yelled Howard. 'Feral pigs.'

We slumped down into the seat. If only it had been dune buggies. Pigs were no use.

Or were they?

The pigs trotted furiously in a straight line towards us. What did they want?

The tendril, that's what. The pigs started scratching and chewing at the plant and its roots. They worried at the earth with their slimy snouts and dripping green teeth. They dug and pawed with their claws. They began munching and chewing. Ripping and tearing. There wasn't much food in this dry country. The pigs were starving hungry.

'Hooray,' shouted Gramps. 'Reinforcements.'

We all smiled and cheered. And patted each other on the back. The feral pigs were attacking the terrible tendril.

But the plant was not so easily defeated. A thin, whip-like sucker shot out and wrapped itself around the biggest pig's tail. The plant lifted the whole pig up by the tail and started swinging it in a circle. Faster and faster like a propeller on a plane. The pig squealed and grunted in terror. It was nothing but a blur. Its squeal became a high-pitched whine.

The other pigs suffered the same fate. Suckers grabbed them all by the tail and swung the terrified animals around in the air at a furious speed.

Suddenly the plant let go. The pigs arced up into the air. Higher and higher as if they had been shot out of the barrel of a cannon.

Then they began to fall. Down, down, down. Twisting and turning. Squeaking in terror. Each pig hit the ground with a soft, sickening thud. One or two of the poor creatures twitched and then lay still. The others didn't even move.

They were all dead meat.

Like we would be if we didn't do something.

The vine began to squeeze the car. It creaked and groaned under the strain. The roof began to buckle and collapse. We all ducked our heads and slid down in the seats.

There was no one to help. We were on our own. My whole body was wracked with fearful shaking. My head felt like it was filled with a million bees. I hated this plant. I hated the germs.

I was only a kid. I didn't want to die in the desert.

'Let's get out of here,' I shrieked.

My head seemed to spin and twirl. The floor underneath me bumped and shook. I felt the wheels turning. I heard the engine groaning. The exhaust backfired loudly. I looked along the row of seats and stared at all the kids from school. Laughing and joking and shoving each other.

I winced as the gears crunched and groaned. Morris Minors didn't have synchro on first gear.

Neither did 1975 Leyland buses.

EIGHT

Rory's eyes opened wide. He sat up staring. For a second I thought he'd seen something on the back of Gramps' neck. A root tip wriggling out of Gramps' collar or something.

My heart thumped.

But Gramps' neck was okay. Rory's eyes weren't even focussed on Gramps.

'Waylan,' he shouted excitedly.

I didn't understand. The only Waylan we knew was Waylan Hicks who used to be in our class in first year. I peered through the windscreen into the heat haze. Had Rory seen Waylan Hicks coming towards us across the scorched plain with a really big pair of gardening shears?

It seemed unlikely, though when you're suffocating in a car surrounded by dead pigs and an evil tree root, anything's possible.

'Waylan,' yelled Rory. 'Sit over here.'

My heart went from sheep-dip pump to fence-post excavator. Suddenly I realised what was happening. The thing I'd been praying for since yesterday.

Gramps and Howard had turned round and were looking at Rory anxiously.

I put my finger to my lips. 'He's back on the bus,' I whispered.

Suddenly I didn't care about the root or the pigs or the heat. I wanted to grab Rory and beg him to tell me everything he was seeing and hearing of my mother's last hour of life. But I didn't. Even though I'd never actually seen a person having an hallucination before, something told me I should keep quiet.

I waited, sweat pouring off me, for Rory to give more clues.

Rory started swaying from side to side in his seat as if he was being driven along a bumpy road. That made sense. The road out of town to Rory's old place was bumpy all right.

Suddenly he gave a jolt and stopped swaying. 'See ya, Lochie,' he shouted. 'See ya, Ellen.'

Kids I hadn't thought of for years suddenly tumbled into my memory. Lochie Dunbar who moved to Adelaide. Ellen McIntyre whose mum made her change schools after the accident because she reckoned our school bus was too dangerous. Which was a slander on Mum.

I blinked back tears.

A thought hit me. I glanced anxiously at the root wrapped around the car to see if Rory's shouting was affecting it. Enraging it and making it more determined to get us.

It wasn't moving. Its strands were still stretched tightly across the windows. Except they didn't seem to be quite as tight as before.

I didn't look for long because Rory was swaying again. Then he stopped with another jolt. 'Bye, Kylie,' he yelled.

Gramps and Howard were staring at him, open-mouthed. 'He thinks he's on the bus,' Gramps whispered to Howard. 'With Alan Fosdyke and Des Kyle. The German bus we nicked from Rommel.'

I didn't try and explain to Howard. There wasn't time. My brain was working feverishly.

Rory's place had been the last drop-off on Mum's afternoon school-bus run. He used to live way out of town, over the river. The drop-off before that had been . . . had been . . .

'See ya, George,' called Rory.

Of course. George Dale.

Rory started swaying again. George must have just

got off. That meant the bus was on the last leg of its journey. The ten-minute drive from the Dales' place to Rory's place across the bridge. With Rory the last person on the bus.

Except for Mum at the wheel.

I felt dizzy with heat and thirst and excitement. In ten minutes I'd know the truth. The truth I'd been waiting five years for.

Then something happened that almost made me faint.

Rory spoke again. 'Pretty good, thanks, Mrs Enright,' he said. 'Though my dad's a bit sick.'

Mrs Enright. That was Mum. Rory was speaking to Mum.

I heard myself give a cry. I couldn't stop it and I couldn't stop the tears filling my eyes.

Mum was alive.

In Rory's terrible, sick, wonderful vision Mum was alive.

I wanted to be there so much. Just to throw my arms round her. Just to say goodbye and tell her I'd always love her.

No. More than that. To try and save her.

Something was slithering. A scratching, sliding noise next to my ear. 'The root,' yelled Howard. 'Look at the root.'

I tore my eyes off Rory. The strands of root were sliding down the window and hanging loosely off the car. I didn't care. I turned back to Rory. Who was looking at me.

'I'm parched,' he croaked.

I saw instantly he wasn't on the bus any more. 'No,' I screamed. 'Go back. Please.'

His lips were cracked and dry. 'I need a drink,' he whispered.

I bent forward and started rummaging on the floor of the car, desperately hoping that Gramps had left an old soft-drink bottle there with some dregs in it. Or a plastic bag with a damp window-wiping cloth inside. Anything to moisten Rory's mouth so he could go back on the bus and tell me about Mum.

Nothing.

Just the metal tyre lever and Gramps' little pocket knife and one of the curried-egg sandwiches from wedding.

No fluid of any description. I was losing Mum for the sake of a mouthful of liquid.

Suddenly a rage bigger than anything I'd ever felt exploded inside me. I nearly crammed the sandwich into Rory's mouth, even though it was two days old and the bread was hard and dry and it was super-hot because Mrs Conti didn't understand the strength of curry powder. I just managed to stop myself.

It wasn't Rory's fault that his dad had sent him a slobberer-riddled, infection-spreading apple-man. And it wasn't Rory's fault that thirst had interrupted his vision.

It was the root's fault. The stinking apple-man root that had drunk all our water.

I grabbed Gramps' pocket knife and wound down my window and started slashing at the poxy root.

'No,' yelled Howard.

'Put the window up,' croaked Rory.

'Scumbag,' I screamed at the root. I hacked and sawed wildly. The root was like steel cable and the little knife wouldn't go through. But I did manage to scrape off some of the brown hairy skin. The wound I made was wet and purple. The root quivered angrily.

'Suck on this,' I yelled. I scooped the lumpy curried egg out of the sandwich and rubbed it into the purple wound. The root flailed against the side of the car as it tried to uncoil itself.

I grabbed the tyre lever and forced my door open and squeezed out.

'No,' yelled Howard and Rory and Gramps.

Too late. I was on my face in the dust. I scrambled up and turned round and started pounding the root with the tyre lever. I was pounding Gramps' car too, but I didn't care.

'You're compost,' I screamed at the root.

I could feel it crunching under my blows. The last couple of loops slithered from around the car.

'That's it,' I yelled. 'Rack off.'

Instead of snaking away across the dusty plain, the root reared high above me. I gripped my weapon. 'You want more, mulch-breath?' I screamed.

It wanted much more.

Before my eyes it grew twice as thick, from a finger to a hairy, knobbly hosepipe. Then in a blur it cracked itself like a giant whip.

The noise it made was painful. But not as painful as when it flew at me and flayed me across my back. And even that searing white-hot pain wasn't as bad as the agony and despair and fear I felt when it coiled around and around my body like a rough-skinned steel snake and started to squeeze.

To be continued...

The electrifying six-part serial continues next month...

'There was an explosion of flame and a loud whoosh. A blue and yellow fireball hurtled away from us along the road. We stood and watched it, open-mouthed, until it disappeared over the horizon.

' "Unreal," yelled Howard.'

But what IS real is the terror and danger lurking beyond the horizon, and the sickness that's threatening them all.

Will they get out of the bush alive?

Will Howard be the next victim?

Can they find Rory and Howard's dad in time?

Time is running out...

ThE AUtHoRs

Morris Gleitzman & Paul Jennings are Australia's most popular writers for children. They are also very good friends.

Now, for the first time, they are writing together. Twice as weird, twice as funny, twice as spooky, twice as mind-blowing. If you loved their books before, you'll love Wicked! twice as much.

There's never been anything like it.

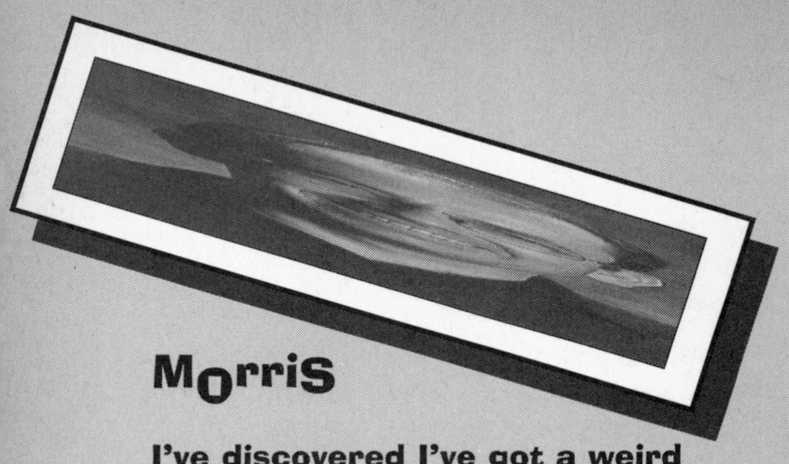

MorriS

I've discovered I've got a weird habit. When I'm working on a story, I tend to eat the same stuff as I'm writing about.

While I was writing Worry Warts, which is about a boy who lives in a fish and chip shop, I ate heaps of fish and chips.

And while I was working on Sticky Beak, which is about a girl whose dad has an orchard, I ate loads of apples.

Now I'm writing a story about slobbering worms and exploding frogs and killer snails.

I've sort of lost my appetite.

PAul

My father used to drive a Morris Minor. He was mad about cars. I caught the bug from him and now I have a little collection of historic cars.

Once when I went to the snow my grandkids' sandwiches were cold so I heated them up on the cylinder head of the engine.

Rory mentions three cars in this book. He knows a bit about cars. He would like a Ferrari.

So would I.

About Dean Gorissen

That's me, the illustrator.

From an early age I was taught that a little love goes a long way. I was also taught that a picture is worth a thousand words, but Paul and Morris might not agree with that.

I don't have a Ferrari (or a Morris Minor), but once I rode an elephant. It wasn't very comfortable. Now when I go for a joy-ride, I ride a motorbike instead.

Here's what one Wicked! kid, Bill, thinks of THE SLOBBERERS...

'The slobberers are the best "creature-enemy" bad dudes I've ever read about.'

Here's what another Wicked! kid, Ben, said about BATTERING RAMS...

'I love it! One of the funniest books invented. The first time I heard the word "slobberers" I jumped out of bed and asked my dad to come down to my bedroom, because I was so scared.'

MORRIS GLEITZMAN & PAUL JENNINGS

Wicked!

PART TWO

Here's what Ben's sister, Rebecca, who is also a Wicked! kid, thinks of CROAKED...

'I didn't think you could get much better than Paul Jennings or Morris Gleitzman on their own. Together, WHAM! THEY'RE DANGEROUS!! Family disputes, double trouble and the greatest ending ever.'